DOHVA - THE LAND WITHIN

Dohva - The Land Within

Sophie Haeder

First Printing, 2024

ISBN Paperback 978-3-911451-01-7
ISBN Hardcover 978-3-911451-02-4
ISBN eBook 978-3-911451-00-0

www.sophiehaeder.com
@sophiehaeder on Instagram

Only birth can conquer death—the birth,
not the old thing again, but something new.
If death closes in, there is nothing we can do,
except be crucified—and resurrected;
dismembered totally, and then reborn.

From *The Hero With a Thousand Faces*
by Joseph Campbell

Prologue

M agnus' eyes widened as the serene skies above Dohva shattered with a deafening roar. Multiple rock masses bigger than Lake Methar tore through the fabric of reality and crashed into the land. The impact was cataclysmic, sending waves of dust and sand into the air, and made the earth vibrate beneath his feet. He was thrown flat on the ground and hurled to the new-cut edge of this flying continent.

Digging his fingers into the ground, he held on for dear life as scattered masses of stone hit the ground again just a few hundred feet away. He wished he could cover his pointed ears, topped with golden metal ornaments, to shield them from the echo of the impact, but he dared not let go. In stunned disbelief, he watched the madness unfold. A chasm was being torn into the land, and on the other side must be the city of Gahaal, or what was left of it. In the other direction, he could vaguely make out the edge of the mainland, so he figured that the land he was lying on had been cut off completely, a leftover crumb of a slice of bread. The mainland of the flying continent of Dohva was drifting away, and he knew what that meant. There was no magical force holding up the small piece of land he lay on any more.

A moment later, there was a stunned silence. He rose and brushed the dust from his cream and gray robes and turban. Everything around him was obscured by a fog of kicked-up dirt and sand. Carefully, he walked toward where the ancient castle of Parhat, dedicated to Umbradil, father of justice, was carved into the rock of the mountain. He could make out the shapes of at least a hundred people as the dust settled. They all ran around the newly formed island like a hive of frightened ants as it slowly tilted. A sickening sensation washed over him as gravity shifted beneath his feet.

With a newfound urgency in his movements, he pushed through the crowd toward the entrance of the castle of Parhat in search of his companion. The island began to tilt rapidly to its south-eastern side, threatening to topple over and send its inhabitants to their doom.

He found Nirella in the crowd near the entrance and pulled her with him. "We must act quickly to stabilize this land. There's not much time left. You know our plan, we must stick to it at all costs," Magnus explained in a breathless voice.

"Yes, follow me. We must run through the castle, down into the heart of the mountain." Nirella's long white braided hair cascaded down her back to her leather slippers as she ran. Her green tunic shimmered in the daylight.

"My friend, I want you to know that it has been an honor to learn from your people. Truly, I mean that. I know I'm not always the most pleasant company, so I'm very grateful to have had the opportunity to gain such great knowledge," Magnus said as he ran through the open castle gates and down a long stone corridor.

"Ah, don't be like that, Magnus. You know very well that we like you and that you are more than welcome here," Nirella replied with a dismissive wave of her hand.

Half-running and half-sliding, they made their way through the next set of wooden gates into a massive stone chamber dimly lit by six floating orbs of magical light. They walked past the huge table in the center of the chamber and down the next hall. Now narrower and with even less light, their path led them deeper into the mountain that encased most of the castle. Finally, they reached a spiral staircase that led to a cave in the center of the mountain. Until now, the cave had been a wine cellar, ideal for keeping the expensive liquid from the rolling hills north of the city of Onja at a constant temperature throughout the year. All the barrels had rolled to the south-eastern side, leaving a large empty space in the center, into which a single cone of light shone through the thick stone of the mountain.

"Perfect, as if the multiverse has seen our intent," Magnus exclaimed, leading the way to one of the barrels. "We need four of those metal rings from the barrels fused into one long one. Do you think you can patch them together?"

"Oh, yes, I think that can be done. Some tools would be helpful though." Nirella started to search one side of the cave, and Magnus brushed a hand over his sharply trimmed goatee and looked around the other side in search of something that could help them in their attempt.

"Ha! This might do." He held up a flat-ended screwdriver with a triumphant twist of his hand, like he was performing a spell with a wand.

They hastily removed the metal from the wood by bending each slab of metal outward. Then Nirella called the Fire Element to her palms to weld the metal together. It was a slow process, but it was what had to be done. The plan was set and they had to follow it to stabilize this newly formed island and any others that were doomed to fall into the infinite depths below if they failed.

Finally, they placed the newly forged metal around the cone of light on the ground, a ring about twenty feet in diameter.

"Okay, let's get started right away." Magnus stared at their accomplishment.

"Do you need any other components?"

"No, but I need you to stay away from the metal ring. I must call upon all four elements and unite them." He gently pushed her towards a safe place at the back end of this cave. He had spent over a decade in Dohva, and he could feel its ancient power coursing through his veins like a drug, much like the strange fog they smoked back in Undarath. It was intoxicating, revealing a staggering reservoir of power he hadn't known existed within him. Channeling all four elements into one person was a very dangerous undertaking in its own right, something that had never been done before, and that alone could kill him. But deep down, he knew he could not stop, and that delving further into his soul would consume him completely as he sought more knowledge, more power, and more magical abilities. He felt the urge to become the most formidable figure in the multiverse, but it was an insatiable desire. Despite this realization, he remained resolute in his chosen path. *I hope I've made the right choice,* he thought to himself.

"Do not interrupt the ritual. Do you understand? Even if it may look dire for me." Magnus ordered with an intense stare.

"Yes, of course." Nirella nodded, looking frightened and determined at the same time.

"Agthar-Etar-Estem-Emedel!" Magnus shouted, looking up at the hole in the ceiling, and the floor tilted a little more beneath their feet, the air itself vibrating as his voice echoed throughout the cave. Louder and louder he sang his magical phrase.

Suddenly, a beam shot down the hole into the center of the metal ring, pulsing and glowing. It began to fill the ring with waves of elemental force, Water, Fire, Earth and Air mixing in a dangerous dance. A ball of raw elemental power emerged from the ring and filled the space inside the ring, tied to a flowing stream that led through the opening in the roof. As Magnus stopped chanting, they saw some of the barrels roll back to the other side of the cellar.

"The island has stabilized! It worked!" Nirella paused and looked at Magnus. "You know what has to come next?" Her eyes glittered, her eyebrows knitted together in a worried furrow.

"Yes, I understand. It must be done. Thank you again, Nirella. Until we meet again." With a somewhat mad smile, Magnus stepped into the orb and his body dissolved.

Nirella had to shield her eyes from it as it glowed in unbearable brightness. "Farewell, Magnus, my friend. Your sacrifice will not be forgotten," she said and turned to head for the stairs.

By the time she reached the outside, the crowd that had gathered up the hill at the edge of this newly carved island were all staring up. Nirella followed their gaze and stood in awe. Out of all their desperation, they had woven a tapestry of elemental magic to protect their home from certain destruction. They had managed to draw upon the very essence of the elements, creating a barrier that encircled all of Dohva, lifting the shattered landmasses back into the air, where they floated as islands in the sky.

Nirella stood there, rejoicing in her new creation. Flickering lights from the elemental sphere bathed her homeland in a mix of colors.

1

Avala

Avala wished for a storm, an angry, growling mass that would answer her call. But here she was again, standing guard at the southern port, bored, not a cloud in sight. In the distance, she could see the vague outline of the opposite island, Parhat, named after its massive mountain and the castle that was carved into it and built around its front. Everything was tinted with a bluish hue, but Avala could still make out the sizzling tether that ran from the mountaintop all the way up to the sphere that surrounded all of Dohva.

What are they doing inside that mountain? For centuries we have celebrated this festival every year. Ten people are chosen to be enlightened by the power of the elements, their souls finally free to rest and not be reborn.

"What's on your mind?" Garon glanced at her from the side.

"I'm just keeping an eye out for a storm. This festival gives me the creeps every year. Maybe if there was a storm, they would simply skip it this time." Avala stared up at the sky as if it could hear her plea.

"Don't be silly. It's the most important time of the year, and the most exciting as well. Finally, something's happening again. And also, this is why we're here, to calm the sky." Garon nudged her shoulder with his.

"Hmm... I don't know. I wish we could learn more about the lore of our land. I'm just... curious, I guess." Avala's eyebrows knitted together in an anxious ridge. Something felt different today, a tingling at the back of her neck that made her hair stand up and her hands clammy.

Garon took a step towards her and kissed her on the forehead, a noble gesture and rare, as he did not often show affection during their working hours. She looked deep into his light brown eyes, which always reminded her of the wasteland around Lhudar, like sand and warm stone. A soft smile curled around his mouth, and she could feel his love for her. His kind heart had fallen for hers the day they had moved into the Stormguard barracks. They had met during the tour for the newly arrived recruits. Even though she had not planned to get attached in this way, Garon had really grown on her.

"How about you go and visit Mereth, and I'll finish up here on my own?" Garon suggested.

"I would love that, thank you. I haven't been able to visit her all week," Avala replied with a huge grin on her face.

"Please, go on then. I'll see you later," Garon said, smiling back at her.

Avala looked around, seeing no one in sight, and leaned over to kiss him before she left.

The beautiful city of Gahaal was decorated with festoons that showed the symbols of the four elements they served. The golden roofs were a bulbous, rounded shape that tapered smoothly to a point at the top, resembling the shape of an onion. The white stone buildings shimmered, reflecting the glimmer of the elemental sphere. It was a cloudless day. The city bustled with energy; everyone seemed to be in high spirits, in a hurry to get everything ready for the Festival of Enlightenment. The smell of freshly baked goods combined with the scent of roasted meats filled the streets and even reached the port gate. A mild breeze was pouring through the city. It was a nice day, warm, sunny, and joyful. So why was she in such a bad mood today, thoughtful and filled with melancholy?

She descended the stone steps, passing the Temple of Air, where workers were already setting up the stage for the upcoming celebration. Continuing onward through the first ring, then the second, and further down, she left the Air

Ward behind. Each ward corresponded to an element, creating a staircase leading down from the peak of the island. The Air Ward lay at the top, followed by Water, Earth, and finally Fire at the bottom. In the center of each ward stood a temple dedicated to its respective element. It was a considerable descent from the Air Ward down to the Earth Ward where Mereth lived. Avala had been a resident here since joining the Stormguard many years ago, and though she knew a few shortcuts, navigating the vast city still took time, which was why she hadn't managed to visit Mereth during the last few days.

Avala finally arrived at the bottom left corner of Gahaal—she had always thought it looked exactly like a piece of layered cake, where the layers slid down towards the pointy end of the piece. Now she approached a beautiful building with a colorful array of flowers adorning its front. Climbing three steps to reach the red door, she entered without knocking. "Mereth! Are you here?" Avala called out as she stepped into the living room.

"Stop yelling, I'm in the kitchen," came the reply from the back.

Avala made her way through the room and turned left into the open doorway leading to the kitchen, where a delightful aroma greeted her. "What's cooking?" Avala inquired, her mouth watering.

"Just a tomato stew with eggs and herbs, and some freshly baked bread by the oven." Mereth nodded toward the still-steaming loaf.

"Looks like I arrived just in time," Avala remarked, reaching for the bread.

Mereth playfully swatted her hand away. "Oh, no, you'll wait like the others. By the way, could you go upstairs and fetch Kumar and Leam, please?"

"Sure." Avala hugged her friend from behind. Mereth returned the hug, leaning her head against Avala's.

"It's nice that you're here today. There's something I want to tell you, but let's wait until after lunch," Mereth said, turning her attention back to the stove.

Avala ascended the stairs to Leam's room, where he and his father Kumar were busy building a fort out of wooden blocks. It was a humble home, but it was entirely theirs. They had managed to create this wonderful life together, and their love permeated every room.

"Hey, you two, Mereth has lunch ready downstairs," Avala announced upon entering the room.

"Avala!" Leam exclaimed, rushing toward her. "It's been too long. I've missed you."

"I've missed you too, little one," Avala replied, planting a kiss on his curly head.

They descended together to find Mereth already seated at the table, staring out the window. Avala knew that look all too well; something was bothering her. Perhaps that was why Mereth wanted to talk to her. She should have come earlier. If Avala lived here with them, it would be easier to stay close, to know what was on Mereth's mind today. But this was not her home, not her life to live, not her family, not really.

As they joined her, Mereth turned her attention back to them. "Please, eat. It's wonderful to have all my loved ones gathered together at one table again," Mereth said, reaching for the bread.

They enjoyed their meal, sharing laughter and conversation. As they cleared the table, Mereth turned to Avala. "Would you come for a walk with me?"

"Of course. You mentioned there was something you wanted to tell me." Avala's curiosity was piqued.

Mereth nodded and headed for the front door. They walked in silence for a few minutes, enjoying each other's company, before Mereth finally spoke. Her eyes glistened slightly and her mouth curved into a comforting smile. The wind blew through her long, pale, curly hair. She was so beautiful.

"What I need to tell you is..." Mereth paused, reaching out to grasp Avala's hand. "The High Monks have chosen me as one of the Ten."

She waited for a response, but Avala couldn't seem to find the right words.

Why would they choose her? She is only in her fifth life, there are others much older than she is. They can't do this to her. She has a child, a husband, and friends who depend on her. It must be a mistake.

"Avala, are you all right? I know the thought is overwhelming, but it is an honor to be picked. I talked to Kumar, and he will take good care of our little boy. It is time for me to go." Mereth's smile faded.

"I know you're trying to be convincing, but how could you be ready? Leam is only five, he needs his mother. Mereth, are you sure this is what you want?" Avala couldn't hide the anger that was rising up in her.

"It's not like I can say no. I'm trying to see the good in it, Avala," Mereth said, now nearly sobbing, anger and fear in her eyes.

"So you are not sure it's the right thing, then? What if you talk with the High Monk again, ask him if you could step down? Surely there must be someone who really wants this honor. Someone sick of these endless lives," Avala said, a rush of emotion clouding her voice.

"If I ask him, and he says no... I'll be devastated. I can accept it now, but if I fight and lose..." Mereth glanced towards the towering beam of elemental force that extended behind the city, reaching towards the sphere in the sky. A colorful beam of inevitable doom.

"Mer, please, you have to try. Not just because of Leam, or Kumar, but because of me. What am I going to do without you? You are my family. I don't have anyone else." Tears filled Avala's eyes. She tried to push them back, taking a deep breath.

"Okay, I'll talk to him."

It was getting late, nearly sunset, nearly time for the main event of the festival. Avala was sitting at a table of cheering comrades. The old tavern the Happy Mug was right next to the Stormguard barracks and had always been their go-to place. It was a big tavern; there was a dance floor in the middle, surrounded by long wooden tables, the ceilings adorned with huge chandeliers hanging above each of them. Now jugs of wine and beer stood amid festive foods on the tables—braised lamb, roasted piglet and glazed figs.

Everyone was dressed in the same well-made uniform of the Elemental Stormguard, gray robes of silk with silver and blue stitching of clouds and swirls of wind. The wide trousers were puffy and had a tight seam at the hem. Avala looked down at herself, suddenly feeling like she was looking at a stranger. Today, everything seemed wrong.

Someone gave her a little nudge in the ribs. "Why are you looking so gloomy today? I thought visiting Mereth would cheer you up?"

Avala looked up and saw Garon, with his square clean-shaven jawline, smiling at her.

"Mereth is one of the Chosen Ten. It just doesn't feel right," she said, looking for a sign of understanding in Garon's face.

"I know you two are very close, but this is the way it's supposed to be, Avala. It's the same every year. Why does it bother you so much this time?"

Avala's grim expression must have given him a hint that he'd said something wrong.

"That's not how I meant it. I know why it bothers you, and that's perfectly normal, but this moment will come for every one of us, for some sooner than later." Garon tried to touch her cheek. She flinched, and his hand just stopped in midair. Avala wasn't in the mood for his joy and his affection, not now.

They had been courting for some years now, not really a couple, but not really only friends, either. It was an awkward in-between limbo, and Avala didn't want to address their relationship, afraid of what he would want from her and what would come next. She wasn't ready to settle down, or marry, or have kids. Avala didn't know if she would ever be ready for that. Once she had almost become a mother, but the elements had decided it wasn't right for her...

"I know, but this is Mereth, she is all I have. I can't just let her be sacrificed. It will be the end. I'll never see her again. And what about her son, don't you think he deserves to grow up with a mother?" *Please show me some understanding,* she thought desperately, but in the back of her mind she knew what his point of view was; they had discussed it over and over again, but somehow they never seemed to find any common ground. His strong sense of fairness and rules and the urge to be a role model made him fixated on the idea that this was the only way it should be. She could understand his ambitions, but wasn't a leader supposed to be willing to look at things from all sides and decide on the best course of action, even if it wasn't the way it had always been done?

"Avala, it is an honor, and it is peace after the many lives she has lived. This is the way it goes, and there's nothing you can do about it." Garon looked worried now, maybe a bit annoyed. His speech was a little slow and somewhat off. Maybe he had just had too much to drink. But how could he be so cold about it? He knew how much Mereth meant to her. She had thought he would be the one to understand.

Avala stood up, not knowing why or where to go. "What if there is a way to change it?" Tears filled her eyes. She tried to blink them away, and swallowed hard. A million thoughts moved through her mind like a dark and monstrous shape, trying to impersonate the most terrifying version of a reality that could exist. A reality without Mereth. *How could they do this? What kind of cruel leadership would sacrifice its own people, and for what? No, they can't take her away from me.*

Avala left without waiting for an answer. In the corner of her eye, she saw Garon stand up. "Wait!" was the last she heard before the door closed behind her.

Avala strolled thoughtlessly through the city. For a long time, she walked up and down the various districts of Gahaal. The celebration of the Festival of Enlightenment would take place in the Air Ward. But her feet carried her farther and farther down, from alley to alley, as she watched the children with their festive ribbons tied tightly to wooden sticks. Today was a day of rest for everyone in the city, a day of celebration and tradition. A flag hung from every window, an array of different shapes and colors, some painted with ornaments or patterns, some blank. But all were moved slightly by the wind. The music around her faded and she could hear the whispers of the Air Element, the static of lightning hiding somewhere in the sphere above. Avala shook her head and walked on, letting her feet take her wherever they wanted to go.

Hundreds of people had already gathered around the stage and started clapping and cheering by the time she finally circled back to the southern port. Avala must have been wandering around the city for at least an hour if they were already starting the ceremony. She stared at the island of Parhat before her. A high stone arch surrounded the pier where the beautiful griffons waited for their departure to Parhat.

The four High Monks of the Elemental Orders stood on the stage in their ankle-length colorful silk robes, red for Fire, blue for Water, green for Earth, and gray for Air, with white belts around their waists. They would soon announce the chosen ones before taking them to Parhat. Somewhere deep inside the mountain, they would be sacrificed and become one with the elements. No one but the High Monks had ever seen it.

One of the High Monks held up a hand, and the crowd fell silent.

"The time has come! Please join us in celebrating the Chosen Ten of this year's Festival of Enlightenment," said the High Monk of Fire. He was an elf, like her, his almost waist-long brown and gray hair pulled back into a tight bun at the back of his head. He had no beard; no one in the order was allowed to wear a beard. His forehead was tattooed with the traditional markings of the Flamingforce. Waves of red ink, starting between his eyes, curved into a V across his forehead.

He began to list the names of the chosen ones. None sounded familiar to Avala except Mereth, second on the list. Avala looked at her, looking for a sign that Mereth had spoken to the High Monks. Mereth scanned the crowd and Avala waved to get her attention. As their eyes locked, Mereth gave her a sad smile and just shook her head.

Everything around them seemed to slow down. The cheering was distant, as if Avala was far away. Her eyes were fixed on Mereth. Avala began to panic, the fear rolling over her like a heavy wave, pushing her under a dark surface, unable to breathe or see what was around her.

Suddenly, a flood of memories washed over her and she saw her mother. It was her first life, her first years on this plane. Mereth had looked so different then, her straight hair a hazel brown, her face as white as a porcelain doll's, her figure small and thin. She had hugged Avala and kissed her on the forehead.

"I will always be with you, my little sunshine. And if I die, I will find you again," her mother had said with the warmest of smiles.

Mereth's name then had been Zaraa. Over the centuries she had had many names, many faces, but they'd managed to find each other in every life. But this was to be Mereth's last day. Avala tried to think about what life would be like without her, but she could not imagine it. Her mother and closest friend would be gone forever, but the emotions that would come with that felt too far away to grasp. Perhaps her mind was protecting her from such pain until it became reality. If her mind had a voice, it would say: *Not now, wait, let the moment come.*

When she snapped back to reality, the High Monk was still giving his speech. "... for it is the greatest honor of our people to be chosen to be enlightened, to reach the highest level of being, to become one with the elements. You will now make your way to the griffons and embark on your final journey." He waved his hand at the ten people standing on the stage, some of them looking proud, others apprehensive. Mereth's eyes remained fixed on her, tears making them glisten.

Avala tried to make her way through the dense crowd, longing for a hug or a kiss goodbye, but her progress was slow. Meanwhile, Mereth and the others descended from the stage and made their way to the pier, where the griffons awaited them. Avala pushed her way forward, shoving and maneuvering past people, her focus solely on reaching Mereth. Finally, she reached the front row and found Mereth's soft, warm hand as she walked.

"I love you," Avala whispered to her mother, tears streaming down her face.

"I love you too, my sweet girl," Mereth replied, releasing her hand and continuing up the jetty.

A moment later, they were in the air. Avala stood at the edge of the harbor, looking up at the blue sky. She tried to shield her eyes from the glow of the elemental sphere to get a better view of her. There she was. Mereth turned her head and waved, blowing a kiss in the direction of the port.

Avala sank to her knees. She felt her heart breaking. Slowly, the griffons moved up and away, until they were just small black specks on the horizon. The people behind her, ready to see the spectacle of souls rising to the sphere of elemental power that surrounded them, began to make their way back to the center of the Air Ward of Gahaal.

Someone tugged at her sleeve. There he was, his small face at her level while she was still kneeling on the ground. Leam looked just like Mereth, with light shaggy hair, tanned skin, and piercing green eyes. He would surely steal any girl's heart when he grew up. He had tears in his eyes. Leam wrapped his small arms around her neck.

"Is she really gone, Avala?" he said, sobbing, holding on to her tightly. Avala just stroked his back. What was she supposed to tell him? He was so young, how could he understand what this meant?

"Leam, we should go see the lights. You loved it last year, remember? And it will be even more special tonight," a warm, familiar male voice said right next to them. It was Kumar, Mereth's husband for the past three lives. They had promised each other to be together until the end of time—well, or until someone was sacrificed. Still, they shared a special bond, almost as strong as Mereth's and Avala's own. Avala had always been a bit jealous of their perfect relationship, that unbreakable bond between them, something she had never really found in another person.

Kumar's skin was red around his brown eyes. Tears were slowly running down his cheeks. He brushed them away. "Come on, you as well, Avala. She would want us to watch. And it is also a proper farewell." Another tear ran down his face. He picked up Leam and pulled Avala to her feet. Silently, they wandered back to the center of the Air Ward, where the celebrations were still in full swing. The white stone buildings of Gahaal were now gray with the fast-approaching night. People laughed and chatted and drank at the many stalls set up around the Temple of Air.

A band was playing on a stage in front of the temple. Avala, Kumar and Leam found their way to a free table with a good view of the mountain.

It felt like hours passed before the stream of elemental energy atop the mountain of Parhat began to glow and shimmer in the now-dark night sky. The band, three stout-looking halfling girls, began to play a slower tune. They played violin, piano and drums. The sound was a bit melancholic, maybe even sad, but as the light grew brighter and brighter, they picked up the pace and it became a festive, rhythmic beat. It was just a melody without anyone singing to it. Somehow it fit the moment perfectly. The glow grew and rose into the night sky until the whole sphere was glowing and it was almost as bright as day. It was mesmerizing, beautiful, magical, and terrifying.

Avala had never thought of it this way, but they were stuck inside this elemental wall. All life depended on its energy somehow. They had never really learned how that had happened. Had it been like this since the beginning of time? Or had there been a completely different world before?

Kumar sat next to her with Leam on his lap. He was curled up in his father's arms, staring at the lights in the sky. Deep sobs rose in rhythmic waves from his small body. Kumar's face had taken on a grim look, as if he was doing everything he could to keep from breaking down in the midst of all these people. Avala put her hand on his and squeezed it a little.

"She is enlightened now. Maybe one day we will be where she is," she said.

2

Sineth

As usual, Sineth was busy around the village, attending to tasks that others seemed to overlook. The rope of the bridge leading to the central pillar of their ramshackle swamp village had come loose again, and Sineth was the only one who cared enough to fix it. After that, he endured an hour-long debate between Bethdor and Una about who should be the village's main blacksmith. *As if we don't have more important things to discuss,* Sineth mused, only half-listening to the escalating fervor of their argument.

"Stop that. Una has been our blacksmith for a decade. She has earned her place here. And I don't see why we can't have two blacksmiths. We would all benefit from some new gear. Una could certainly use some help with that, don't you think?" Sineth interjected, trying to ease the tension.

"Yes, but he insists on being better than me, and I can't stand his bragging about things he knows nothing about," Una shouted. Bethdor turned bright red with anger and let out a low growl.

"This woman is driving me nuts," he shot back, at a level with Una's big, half-giant chest.

They made a strange sight, the two of them. Bethdor was a clean-shaven dwarf with a chest-length orange beard, tattoos covering his bare skull, and muscular arms. Una was twice his size, with red hair cascading down her back in a thick braid, her stern and weathered face softening to sweetness when she laughed. Una had really grown on Sineth, but Bethdor, not so much. But as one of the leaders of this strange tribe, Sineth couldn't afford to play favorites, even though Una was practically one of the elders as well.

"Okay, enough of this childish nonsense. Just pull yourself together and get back to work, both of you. Bethdor, I suggest you find a new location for your workshop, somewhere at the other end of the village. That way you can both work in peace and I won't have to listen to the same gripes every week." Sineth gave them both a stern look. They exchanged a last glance before nodding in agreement.

After that, Sineth finally made his way back to his hut. A nice cup of tea would ease his nerves.

He leaned his arms on the railing in front of his little home. Above, in front of, and beside him were a multitude of other platforms with huts built around stone spires connected by wooden bridges. Beneath him was the muddy brown-green water of the swamp. It was amazing what they had accomplished in the past few years. The Dread Pool Marshes could easily be the least hospitable place in all of Madin, and yet they had managed to make it their home.

Sineth took a deep breath of the cold air. It always smelled like mud and wet wood here. He looked down at his weathered, dirty hands. When he snapped his fingers, a single orange flame appeared. Sineth played with the flame a little, making it bigger and smaller, and then made it disappear again. He found himself smiling. Maybe there was a chance that they could really make a difference. If they gathered enough people, gained more allies.

The fog still hung heavy between the towers of their village and the swamp below. It never really lifted, and in the early morning hours it was hard to make out many details. Sineth grabbed the cup of hot tea from the old wooden table beside him and took a sip. A herbal, lemony scent filled his nose. This was an excellent tea. Maybe someone had brought it from Karaz; it was definitely not from Madin. At least, he had never had tea like this in all his years, or lives, in Madin. Or maybe he just couldn't remember. It was hard to tell.

"Sineth!" someone shouted from the right. "Sineth, there is a man here who wants to speak with you."

Sineth moved toward the sound of the voice, trying to make out the shape of the person through the thick fog. *Not again. I just started drinking my tea.* Sineth exhaled with a sigh. A moment later a figure emerged from the mist.

"Ah, Quinn, it's you. It's hard to see anything right now. Who is this man?" Sineth said to the little halfling boy in front of him. Quinn looked like he had cut his hair recently, probably by himself. His normally shaggy, shoulder-length mop was now cut close to his head. Only a few small curls remained.

"He said he wanted to trade information. He said he was from the Dark Kingdom." Quinn almost whispered the end of the sentence, cupping his hand over his mouth to shield it from unwelcome ears. "Also, he's green, very tall, and has tusks." Quinn looked very proud of himself for remembering that fact.

Sineth laid a hand on his shoulder. "Okay, so he's an orc? That definitely adds up with his information about being from the Dark Kingdom. Did he say what kind of information he's here to trade?" An uneasy feeling crept up his spine. He had never met one of their kind before. There was a lot of talk about the Dark Kingdom. Especially about their queen.

"No, but I think he'll tell you. He wanted to talk to our leader, and you are the closest thing we have to a leader, so..." Quinn waved his hand dismissively and began walking across the creaking bridge to the next platform. Sineth followed, still clutching the cup of tea.

After passing Una's blacksmith workshop, the two reached the largest spire in the center of the village. Rounding the spire, they entered the main hall. People were eating their breakfast, murmuring about the huge orc standing in the far corner of the room.

As they approached, Sineth took in the orc's appearance and demeanor. He was impressively tall, easily over seven feet. It was hard to tell at the moment, though, because he was hunched over, as the hall wasn't built for his size. He looked grim and very unhappy to be here among all these people. His face also showed signs of hunger and self-control. A huge beast that tried to fulfill his duty, but would rather tear into anyone near him.

Sineth bowed slightly. "My name is Sineth. Quinn here told me that you want to exchange information with the Resistance. I am one of the founders, so maybe I can help you with that." He smiled politely at the orc.

"I am Gorth, and I come by order of the Dark Queen. Is there a place where we can talk in private? Perhaps outside this cave." Gorth looked up at the ceiling with a grunt and then back at Sineth.

"Of course, please come with me." Sineth led him out of the room and back to his hut. The bridge buckled under the weight of the orc's form. For a moment, Sineth thought it might give way, but they both made it safely to the other side.

Sineth placed two chairs outside the hut and offered one to Gorth, though he feared it might break beneath this creature.

Gorth sat down, the chair creaking loudly but not breaking. With a small sigh, Sineth sat down beside him. "Would you like some tea or something stronger?"

"Strong is good, keeps the cold from creeping into your bones." Gorth looked down at the water below.

"You don't like water?" *I guess even the biggest monsters are afraid of something.*

"I came here to tell you that our queen is planning a revolution. She heard about your little rebellion and sent me to ask if you'd like to join forces." Gorth's voice was deep and harsh. His breath was a disgusting mixture of rotting flesh and a hint of the whiskey Sineth had poured for him. He sounded more intelligent than Sineth had thought their kind was.

Never underestimate anyone, Sineth had always told himself. "Okay, so you gave me the information about a possible revolution. What information does the Dark Queen Venja want from us in return?" he replied as politely as possible.

"You are a bunch of misfits from all over Madin. You must have a lot of information about the cities, their people and their defenses. In exchange, she offers you a place in our ranks. Protection, and the revolution you want, but can't win alone." Gorth stared at Sineth with his black eyes. Most people would probably wet themselves in the presence of that staring, snarling hulk of a beast. Perhaps Sineth had seen too much of his own inner monster to be afraid of another.

"That sounds good to me. We have no problem with betraying this damn country, but I need to talk to the rest of our group before I can make a decision. Do we have a time limit to respond to your queen's offer?" Sineth asked.

Gorth placed a piece of parchment on the table. "This is a map to the nearest entrance to our kingdom. If you decide to join us, come to us and we will discuss the next steps for you and the Resistance, and the plans for Queen Venja's revolution. But be aware, if you trick or betray us, we know where your stinking swamp village is. We are many, and there will be nothing left of you." Gorth stood and took the bottle of whiskey.

"Nice to meet you, Gorth, and my regards to your queen!" Sineth called after him as Gorth walked away.

"Sure," Gorth growled and disappeared into the mist.

"Do you think it is a good idea to get into bed with these people? They are monsters, thieves and murderers. Creatures of the dark. They only follow their own rules. What will they do to us if we can't give them the information they seek?" said Hartaba, an old gnomish woman with short white hair, a big nose, and wrinkles all over her weathered face. "Sineth, my friend, this is not wise. I know there aren't many of us, and it may be years before we can make a move on our own, but it will be for our cause and ours alone. Who knows what this Venja is up to."

Sineth loved this woman like a mother, but if she had her way, they would stay hidden in the marsh forever. Hartaba was not a risk-taker, but a caretaker. *If it had not been for her, what would have become of me?* And he thought back to the day he had met Hartaba.

After Molna was killed, Sineth had left his studies in Lhudar and gone as far away from all that madness as he could. After weeks, he had ended up in Fyre, a small trading village where the West Road and the Edge Pass met. Alone and more broken than ever, he sat down by the river. The air was fresh and clear, no comparison to the dust-filled shithole of Lhudar from which he had escaped. As the evening drew to a close, Sineth had no idea where to go next or what to do with his life from here on out.

After a while, Sineth pulled a fishing rod out of his oversized backpack and threw the bobber into the ripples of the fast-moving river to catch a meal. He stared aimlessly into the distance. It looked like the lush green tall grass beyond the river went on forever. The wind pushed it around so that it looked like waves itself.

"Calming, isn't it?" a voice said beside him.

Sineth almost jumped. Normally he could hear a mouse scurrying towards him, but he had not heard this woman coming.

Sineth did not want company, for he was tired of pretending to be okay. But this woman did not leave. "Can I help you?"

"Oh, my dear, may I help *you?*" she asked him back, her head tilted to one side.

Then Sineth looked at her. She wore a gray hood over a long woolen dress, muddy at the edges. Her hands were deep in the wide sleeves. Hartaba did not look as old as her voice suggested, though her eyes looked wise beyond her years.

"I don't think there is anything or anyone that can help me. But thank you for asking," Sineth said with his usual charm and a confident smile.

She did not leave. Hartaba just stared at him expectantly, not at all satisfied with his answer, waiting for him to say something. Like a mother waiting for her child to admit a cheeky lie.

Hartaba had seen through him, then and every day after. There was no pain he had managed to hide, no fear that had escaped her watchful eyes. It was annoying, but he was still so grateful for her.

"I don't want to risk anyone's life or put you in danger, but this is a unique opportunity to get things going. I mean, if Venja is not with Madin, she's with us. Sure, she'll have her own agenda, and she's definitely not to be trusted completely, but could we at least give her a chance to explain her plans?" Sineth said with a pleading smile.

"I don't like it either. It's too risky and that big green guy gives me the creeps. I don't want to imagine what the rest of her people look like," Una grumbled, crossing her arms in front of her chest. She had been one of the first people to join the Resistance and had been instrumental in building this village and making it the place they all called home.

Sineth looked at all their faces, scanning their features for some sign of approval. About twenty people made up the leading council of the Resistance. Now, for once, they all seemed to be in agreement.

"What if I go alone? I'll go to this entrance to the Dark Kingdom and offer the information I have and my help in carrying out Venja's plans in exchange for their help, should we need it in the future. After all, she could be a strong ally. On the other hand, if we don't side with them, we'll be their enemies as well. I don't think that's wise." Sineth looked around the room. Some muttering began, and they discussed his offer among themselves.

It was noon by now. Some light shone through the open doorways of the large stone cave. Everyone was sitting on wooden benches that they had pulled up in a circle. There had never been much etiquette among the people of the Resistance. *Gorth was right, we are a bunch of misfits, outlaws and thieves,* Sineth thought to himself. But they were also innocent people who had been wronged by the High Monks and their rule to the point of no return. Take Una, for example; all she had ever wanted was to open a blacksmith shop in Riptar, but the Elementals—members of the four Elemental Orders—insisted that only the Fire Elementals should take up this craft. It had taken her some time to stop hating Sineth just because of his magical powers. *I mean, how can it be that only elves are imbued with elemental power? Why are powers not available to everyone? And if they aren't, shouldn't only the Ele-mentals be sacrificed for their wicked ritual?* He had wondered about these things over and over again. But he had never come to a satisfactory conclusion.

After a few long minutes, Hartaba raised her short arms in the air to calm the rest of the group. "You may go and seek out what you are looking for, Sineth, but we do not wish to fight their war. If you choose to be with them, you can. There's no bad blood. You're always welcome to return. If they wish to help us, that would be too kind, but I doubt it. They have been isolated in their Dark Kingdom for as long as anyone can remember. They don't care about people outside their own. But please, try to talk to this queen if you must." She slowly rose from the bench, picking up her stick that had been lying next to her.

"Thank you, Hartaba. I will try my best to secure the help and friendship Venja promised," Sineth said while everyone was already standing up or talking again. Did he really believe in it? A friendship or even an understanding with a people no one had ever seen before? Creatures of unknown race and temper, with a queen who was said to be cruel and powerful beyond imagination? Sineth had to try, he needed to try, for there was no way they could ever challenge the Elementals alone. Only a few of the Resistance members possessed magical abilities, and even then none that could stand against the power they would have to face.

"Do you have everything you need?" Quinn asked as Sineth packed his bag with food and water.

"I think so. This isn't my first adventure." Sineth gave him a little wink.

"Are you going to come back to us? This village won't be the same without you. Besides, I will miss you," Quinn said with a sad shrug.

Sineth gave his short hair a little rub and pulled him into a hug. "I'll miss you too, little one. Take care of the others for me, okay? Especially the old leaders, they need a little recklessness in their lives."

He shouldered his bag and took one last look around the village. *I never thought I would be sorry to leave this place.*

3

Garon

The light shone through the high, rounded window of
Garon's room in the Stormguard barracks, hitting his
face and waking him with a searing pain in his head. The
brightness hurt his eyes. *What time is it?* Garon tried to
squeeze his eyes even tighter and pulled his blanket over his
head. As he relaxed a little, he caught a whiff of his own foul
breath, a combination of alcohol and garlic. He recoiled and
jumped out of bed, grabbing the bucket of water next to the

small washstand to empty his stomach of last night's endeavors.

Garon sat down on the ground, his knees drawn up, the bucket between his legs. He felt terrible. He should have stopped after the sixth beer, but Pentho had been in a fantastic mood and had persuaded him to drink liquor that was ignited before being swallowed in one big gulp. At some point they'd ordered food and drunk even more. The rest was a blur. How had he even managed to find his way home? Still, it had been a great night. They had had such a good time, playing cards, listening to a band, dancing and joking. The only thing that could have made it even better would have been if Avala had joined them.

Garon looked out the window, the daylight illuminating his face. He didn't see her very often these days. Avala mostly kept to herself or went off to try to talk to the monks about the ritual. Frankly, she was acting a little weird. Perhaps because of Mereth's death? But it had been almost two months. Sure, she and Mereth had been very close, but she had known this day might eventually come. *It's probably going to happen to all of us; that's the way it's supposed to be.* Garon wished he could talk some sense into her, but she was as stubborn as she was pretty. *Maybe I should ask her to have dinner with me and talk. Try to get her to let it all out, and then hopefully we can move on.* Avala had been so close to him before the Festival of Enlightenment; it felt like she had finally let down her guard and given them a real chance. But now she was more distant than ever.

Garon heard a knock at the door and, without waiting for an answer, Ignar, one of his best friends, entered the room. Ignar was the picture of health, showing no signs of the previous night. *What an ass.* Why was it always Garon who ended up with a hangover?

"Hey, man, you look terrible," Ignar said with a grin on his face. His auburn hair was combed into a quiff, his freckled face clean-shaven and beaming.

"Why do you look so picture-perfect? And what have you done to your face? It looks like you dipped it in goose fat."

"Mock me all you want, you stinking fool, but you better get up; your shift starts in half an hour." Ignar gave him a small kick in the side, then offered Garon a hand to help him up.

Garon got up carefully, afraid he would get sick again. The whole room tilted. As a child, he had accompanied his father to Lake Methar. Sometimes, when the wind churned the water and created huge waves around their small fishing boat, he had felt the same dizziness, as if the world around them suddenly felt wrong. Garon would raise his arms to calm the wind, surely the only reason his father had taken him out so often. He had sucked at fishing. Right now, though, his condition couldn't be cured by his magic.

"Well, I guess I should hurry then. Have you seen Avala?" Garon asked while he put on some fresh clothes.

"Funny you should ask. She's actually waiting for you downstairs." Ignar looked at Garon curiously, his voice carrying a judgmental tone. Ignar didn't like Avala very much, never had. He said she was only interested in herself and no one else. But Garon couldn't disagree more. Ignar just didn't know her like he did, and hadn't bothered to try.

"Really? Has she told you what she wants?" Garon asked.

"What is it with you two? I don't get it. Are you a couple, or friends, or just comrades? Isn't this uncertainty nerve-wracking?" Ignar asked, crossing his arms over his chest.

"I would say we are all of those things, but I'm not sure what her answer would be. That's why I want to talk to her." Garon pushed his way past Ignar and out the door into the stairwell.

The Stormguard barracks were bustling; everyone seemed to be awake and in a hurry, doing something or just chatting in the corridors. The barracks was a beautifully built longhouse, three stories high, topped with small towers and a large one in the middle, all ending in golden onion-domed roofs, like most of the buildings in Gahaal. In the center was a large staircase that split in half, the left side leading to the women's quarters, the right side to the men's quarters, which made up the first and second floors of the building. On the ground floor were the common rooms for all the Stormguards of the Elemental Order.

There, in a large leather chair in the main hall, sat Avala, her long black hair cascading down her back like silk. She looked into the fire that was roaring in the hearth at the far end of the room.

"Don't forget, Garon, you have about twenty minutes before your shift starts at the southern port, okay?" Ignar said to Garon, who was staring at Avala's back.

"Sure, I'll make it quick." Garon winked at Ignar and made his way down the stairs to meet Avala. "Hello, you look beautiful today," he said with a gentle smile. "Ignar told me you were waiting for me?"

"Yes, I have a favor to ask of you," Avala said, standing up. They were only inches apart. Garon could not remember the last time they had been so close. She smelled good, sweet and fresh, like clean clothes and some kind of flowery perfume. He could easily lean forward and kiss her. Without him being aware of it, his hand wandered into her hair and his lips touched hers. She didn't flinch or pull away; she embraced him. She kissed him back, her hands on his back.

When they stopped and looked at each other, she smiled at him. How he'd missed her smile; it could make you do the most ridiculous things.

"I'd like to switch shifts with you. The High Monks have finally granted me an audience to discuss the Festival of Enlightenment. The meeting is tomorrow evening, and I've been assigned the whole night. I could do your shift now and you could do mine tomorrow?" Avala said, still smiling her irresistible smile.

"Sure, no problem. I'm just a bit confused. We haven't seen each other much since the festival, so I guess I feel a little used. You're practically seducing me into doing you this favor. Not that I don't like it, but I'd like this attention every day." Garon gave her a cocky half grin.

Avala kissed him again. "I know I've been a little distracted these past few weeks. Mereth's death has been a lot for me. It just raises so many questions, and it feels so unfair." Garon looked at her worriedly, so Avala continued. "I know how you feel, and maybe that's why I've been so distant. It's just hard for me to accept that this was the way she had to go, I guess." Her eyes began to shine and fill with tears.

"I may not understand you, but I'm still here for you. At least I want to be. I know sometimes you feel like she is or was your only friend, but there's me, and you have a lot of people here in the Guard who would like to be your friends if you would only let them be," he whispered in her ear as he gave her a tight hug.

"I know, thank you." Avala wiped the tears from her cheeks.

"What do you want to talk to the High Monks about? You know they won't tell you all their secrets." Garon smiled, trying to make it sound like a joke to lighten the mood.

"We'll see," she muttered.

Garon looked around the room. People were staring at them. *It must look like a breakup in the middle of the common room to them.* It made him angry. He was supposed to be the one without drama, the person people could look up to, not some schoolboy chasing a girl who didn't want to be chased.

"Avala, what are you doing? Don't do anything stupid." Garon looked at her worriedly. *She just can't let go, can she?*

Why is she always running headlong into walls? Life could be so easy if she would just let go and let life happen to her. They could be a couple, maybe even get married and have kids, but something inside him told him that wasn't going to happen. Garon tried, he really tried, to feel for her—Avala's emotional trauma, her ups and downs and all the chaos in between. But what about him? His feelings, his goals, his dreams? Avala never considered that. *Honestly, Ignar is right, she is selfish.*

He took a step back and looked at her. "Okay, I guess you should go then. My shift starts in a few minutes; you'll be late."

Avala gave him one last kiss on the cheek, soft and quick, like the brush of a feather, and left without another word.

He was sitting in the common room, drinking a glass of whiskey, when Pentho stepped in front of him, a jovial grin on his face. "Well, you look like shit. Shouldn't you be standing around the southern port today?"

"You sound like Ignar. Leave me alone, Pentho, I'm not in the mood for your mockery," Garon said dismissively.

"Friend, what's the matter with you? You're not the typical day-drinker. Playing the irresponsible, gleeful prick is my job. You're supposed to be the golden boy who will lead us all." Pentho tapped him on the shoulder.

Garon didn't react; he just stared into the fireplace at the end of the room, wondering what Avala was thinking when she looked into it. Usually, looking into the flames eased his mood—the play of colors, rising and falling in the hearth. But not today.

"Seriously, what's wrong with you?" Pentho leaned directly in front of Garon's face, his hands on the sides of the chair, blocking the view of the fireplace behind him. He looked worried.

The three of them had been friends for decades, ever since they had started training to become Stormguards. Two goofballs and him, the driven one. It had been a perfect symbiosis. Garon had kept Ignar and Pentho in check, and they had pushed him out of his comfortable routine. But now it felt like the tables had turned.

"I'm fine, it's just stupid girl drama. Nothing to be sad or angry about anyway." Garon stood up, shoving Pentho aside.

Pentho looked as fresh and healthy as ever. For the sake of the elements, they should both tell him their secret hangover remedy. Garon really didn't know how they did it. No matter how hard the night had been, no matter how much they drank, they always looked perfectly fine the next day. It was annoying. Besides, there hadn't been a day since he'd met Pentho when Pentho had been in a bad mood. Always the cheerful one, always with a joke on his mind, his short black hair perfectly styled, his robes fresh and without a single wrinkle.

"Let me help you. Is this about Avala again? That girl will be your ruin, my friend. How about a nice hot bath and maybe some tea?" Pentho said in a jovial voice.

Garon stopped and looked at him. "Sure, why not."

"Perfect, and if that doesn't help, there's always the Wild Blossom to distract you from your little friend," Pentho said with a wink.

"Pentho, I am not going to a brothel. Avala is just being weird again," Garon said with more force than he intended. Some other Stormguards around them stopped and stared at them for a second. Garon looked down, a little embarrassed. He really wasn't himself today.

Pentho leaned over and whispered to him, "Hasn't she always been weird?"

Garon gave him a surrendering glance. "Maybe."

As he followed Pentho down the hall to the bathroom, they anticipated the luxury of a huge hot tub, a communal amenity for all to enjoy. The Fire Elementals had constructed a vessel in the basement that held an ever-flowing fire. The fire heated the boiler, and from there the hot water was carried to the bath and to a few lucky high-ranking officers who had the privilege of having their own bathtubs in their rooms. A hot bath was a welcome relief for tired muscles after a long shift, especially after the cold of night duty. Just as he turned the corner into the corridor, he bumped into someone.

"Oh, Garon, I didn't see you there. How are you, my boy? It's been a while since I've seen you in combat training," Fandeth Elmor said warmly, squeezing Garon's shoulder.

"Commander Elmor, yes, sir, I've had a few hectic weeks. Some of my comrades came down with the flu and I volunteered to cover their shifts along with mine," Garon replied.

"Always showing discipline and kindness. But don't forget yourself, Garon. You still want to follow in my footsteps, don't you?" Elmor looked intently into Garon's eyes as if searching for the answer within.

"Of course, sir. It's my dream to become commander one day. You're such an inspiration to me. I'll be at the training next week, I promise," Garon assured him.

"Very good, my lad. Then off you go and enjoy your well-deserved time off." Elmor nodded, a warm smile of approval on his weathered face, in the direction of the bathroom entrance.

"Thank you, sir." With a slight bow Garon turned to join Pentho, who was waiting at the entrance to the bath.

"Well, well, the old man really seems to like you, huh?" Pentho remarked, nodding in the direction Garon had come from.

"He's been a mentor of sorts over the past year. I think he appreciates my ambition and supports my goal of becoming a leader," Garon explained, trying to make it sound less important to him than it was. In fact, he was counting on Elmor's approval. Someone who could speak well would make it easier to convince the Elementals to choose him as the next commander of the Stormguard. He was still quite young to be a superior—there were others with much more experience—but with Elmor's help, that might not matter so much.

"I knew you'd be bossing us around at some point the first time I saw you. You just have that attitude. A bossy attitude," Pentho teased with a grin.

"Oh, shut up," Garon retorted with a laugh before entering the bath.

4

Avala

The day after she had switched shifts with Garon, Avala sat in a long rectangular hall with wooden benches on either side. This hall, like most of the castle in Parhat, had been carved into the mountain. The ceiling had been sculpted into four arcs, showing each element in intricate detail.

For a long time, she leaned against the wall, staring at the carving of the element of Air—her element, at least for this life. Avala remembered the exact moment she had first felt her power. It had been at the School of Remembrance, when she was about twenty years old, which seemed ridiculously young now that she thought about it.

This was Avala's first life as an elf; time worked differently when your expected lifespan was six hundred and fifty years or more. Still, somehow it felt like only a few years ago, even though it had actually been one hundred and twelve years since that girl at school had teased her about her pointy ears. Avala had pushed her away and she'd flown fifteen feet across the room, crashing into a bookshelf. That was the moment Avala had known that this life would be completely different from the last ones she had lived. It was full of new wonders, but it also meant being one of the few and serving in the Elemental Order for the rest of her adult life.

After this incident, she had been transferred to the Stormguard School in Gahaal. She'd also learned about the other schools of elemental power: the Earthbinders in Himalus, the Flamingforce in Lhudar, and the Order of Cascade in Riptar. It was a strange feeling to have been part of this society for so many lifetimes and to be learning about these powers for the first time, even though they were such a large part of Madin's culture. But what still amazed her most to this day was her own power, the way she could calm the wind and make it bend to her will, create something as small as a breeze or as strong and powerful as a tornado. Even lightning bent to her will and followed her call when it threatened the city. There were still so many questions in her mind about her magical abilities and this world they lived in.

Avala looked at the closed double doors to her right; they led to the High Monks' Council Hall. Hopefully these doors would open soon and she could ask all these questions at once. Maybe it would give her closure. Somehow she felt in desperate need of answers to make sense of everything that had happened. Or maybe she was looking for answers that not even the Elementals could give her, like how she could silence those voices inside her for once, or how she could be at ease with herself. The memory of the discussion with Garon flashed through her mind again. *How can he possibly understand what's going on inside me when I can't even figure it out myself?*

Her elven ears picked up a commotion from the other side of the hall, right at the entrance to the castle. Shouting and screaming and the clash of metal on metal echoed through the massive gate that led outside. She drew her short sword and ran towards the sound; it was further away now. Carefully, she opened the gate and peered through.

Night had already fallen upon Madin. Cold air poured in, carrying a hint of iron. The door felt heavy against her arm, and she had trouble pushing it open; something was blocking it. Avala looked down to see what it might be. One of the castle guards was leaning dead against the door, his lifeless eyes staring back at her. His entire front was covered in blood, running down into a puddle. His throat was torn, almost ripped out. She felt sick; the smell of blood was overwhelming.

Suddenly, Avala's horrified gaze went up the hill, where a very strange high-pitched sound filled the silence of the evening. There was a fight going on between a couple of small dark-clothed figures and two larger figures in the grab of the Elemental Order, but it was hard to make out any details, as it was almost pitch black and everything was covered in a thick mist. The ever-changing colors of the elemental sphere gave off an ominous glow. In a flurry of thoughts, she remembered that she had switched shifts with Garon. She let go of the door and the body slumped to the ground. Avala jumped over it and ran, sword in hand, up the road through the damp air.

Up on the hill by the port, Garon fought a small hooded creature wielding two daggers, blood dripping from them. The other normal-sized figure was a woman wearing the robes of the Flamingforce. She clasped her hands together; as she moved them apart, a ball of fire floated between her hands. With a quick motion, she pushed the ball toward another of these small creatures that had appeared from the side. It burned and screamed, then ran over the edge of the island and disappeared into the void below.

Avala just stood there, frightened and lost. *What's going on here?* She couldn't make sense of it. She had never seen creatures like this before. Why were they here and why were they attacking?

"Do something, Avala, help us!" Garon shouted from the side.

The next of these creatures came at her, and she began to run her hand over her blade, increasing its power with her magic before driving it into the hooded figure in front of her. With a scream, it flew through the air, leaving a spray of blood in its wake. It landed at the edge of the island. Avala ran after it, kicked its body to the ground and plunged her sword into its torso. The hood was pushed back a bit and she saw a small green face with jagged teeth and two yellow eyes, but the life behind it was already gone.

Avala heard a loud squeaking and flapping sound from above; she stumbled back and fell over one of the bodies. In the air was a huge reddish-brown scaled creature with two massive wings and a long tail. On it was a green figure, larger than any human or elf she had ever seen, with tusks protruding from its mouth. Its body was covered in plate armor, depicting a single white crown on its chest. But the crown looked strange; two of its prongs were higher than the others and slightly curved inward. They reminded her of the horns of a goat.

A moment later, the woman next to her was stabbed by one of the smaller ones and fell face first into the dirt. Avala ran over to help her, but her body was limp. Garon was fighting off two of the creatures when a large claw came from behind him and lifted him off his feet. Avala saw him lose his grip on his sword.

"Ahhhhh! Avala, pull me down. Help me!" Garon screamed, his back pierced by the sharp end of the claw. The small green-faced creatures hopped onto the wings of the scaled monster, and they lifted higher into the air.

Avala pushed herself up and ran to the edge. Too slow, too late. They were way up there, and her magic was useless. She couldn't just summon lightning or create a tornado—if the creature fell, Garon would too. She tried to create a wind that would push them back to the island, but they were already too far away. She could hear Garon's screams, muffled in the air.

She stood there in shock, looking down at the five small bodies and the woman in the Flamingforce robes. For a moment there was absolute silence, only her own heavy breathing. Then she heard the crackling of fire and smelled the stench of burning flesh. The small bodies began to ignite and burn, filling the night air with smoke. She stumbled back a few steps. What kind of twisted magic was this? What was she going to do?

The High Monks! She had completely forgotten about them and her meeting with them. They could help her, help Garon. She ran back to the castle, stepping over the dead guard again. Her footsteps echoed down the long stone hall. Avala opened one of the huge double doors.

The room was lit by a large crystal chandelier in the center of the hexagonal chamber. The source of the light was clearly magical, for it was brighter than any candlelight she had ever seen. Her eyes fell on the table in the center of the room and she froze.

On the table, the High Monk of Fire lay in a pool of his own blood, greenish foam dripping from his mouth. Avala looked around the room; it was covered in crimson blood. On the floor and in various corners of the room, she saw the other High Monks, all covered in blood, stab wounds all over their bodies, and the same foam dripping from their mouths. The air was moist and smelled of death. She stumbled backward, outside, turned around and ran back through the hall as fast as her feet would take her, feeling sick to her bones.

She stepped into the night air and took a deep breath. In the distance, she saw the familiar sight of three griffons arriving on Parhat Island. Two guards on each of the griffons. They must have noticed the commotion.

"Thank the elements they are here." Avala ran up the hill towards them. One by one they jumped off the backs of the griffons.

"What happened here? We were on patrol and heard the screams and saw the smoke." It was another member of the Flamingforce, wearing the same bright orange robes as the dead woman and the bloody High Monk in the chamber.

"I, I don't know," was the only thing Avala could say. Her head felt empty, and in the same second she vomited on the ground.

"Check the High Monks!" the man shouted to some of the others. "We saw our dead comrade. Did you see what happened?" His eyes were piercing and cold, his voice full of anger.

Avala was on her knees. *She was killed by a small creature with daggers*, she thought, but nothing came out of her mouth. It sounded ridiculous; she had never seen one of these monsters before. Avala had heard stories of them. Creatures of the dark, hiding in the shadows, but she had never believed that they were real.

"Jahn, the monks are dead! They were killed. It looks like a slaughterhouse in there," one of the Elemental Guards shouted as he ran out of the hall.

Suddenly, they all looked at her. "Her sword's bloody and she's the only one here," one of them said to the others.

Avala looked down and saw that she was still holding her short sword in her right hand.

"Stormguard, get up. We will take you back to Gahaal and you will be put on trial in the morning." Jahn waved his hand for the others to take her away.

"No!" she shouted. "I didn't do this, you must believe me. I was waiting for my audience with the High Monks when a fight broke out and I tried to help, but Garon..." She trailed off.

"That may or may not be true, but you will be tried. You are the only one here, and there are no signs of other intruders."

"But there are bodies at the port, some small creatures we fought."

"There are no bodies at the port, woman." Jahn looked as if he questioned her sanity. There was no point in arguing with him. He was reputed to be the most law-abiding, straightforward person in their ranks. They began to lead her to the griffons.

If they take me and I am blamed for the murder of the High Monks, I am as good as dead. I have to move quickly if I want to help Garon or even get an idea of where they went. I must do this. He needs my help, Avala thought desperately as she was placed on the griffon in front of Jahn. As they lifted off the ground, she put her hands together and focused on the energy of the air. Avala could feel it pulsing through her veins, that familiar energy that brought her to life, filling her body with power.

With a quick twist and a shove of her hands, she forced all the energy out of her body and pushed Jahn off the griffon; he lost his footing and fell twenty feet to the ground.

Quickly she took the reins and began to race into the night, toward the direction she had seen the scaled beast fly.

For a second, she allowed herself to look back; she saw Jahn trying to lift himself off the ground with some difficulty. His jaw was clenched and the corners of his mouth curled up in a sneer of pain. A respected man, humiliated by a woman. She heard him shout into the night: "Get her, get the traitor!"

All the nights before, she had been thinking about this moment. How to talk to the High Monks. Every word she would say to them, rehearsing her questions. But she could never have imagined this—a scenario, a world without the guidance and rules of the High Monks. What would this world look like? Or would they simply name new ones and move on?

The only thing that mattered to her right now was to get Garon back. She owed him that much—to fight for him as he had fought for her for so long.

5

Sineth

Sineth walked up a narrow path, gravel sliding down with each step. He looked down at his feet, following the stones as they fell to the treetops below. He was exhausted, but there had been no good place to set up camp for the last few hours of his trek.

He followed the path up a steep incline, holding onto the ground with his hands to balance his weight. His heavy bag pulled him back, but he managed to push himself up to an almost level plateau between two mountain peaks. Sineth had finally made it to the top.

He just stood there for a few minutes, catching his breath and looking around. The view from up here was amazing. The colors of the elemental sphere cut through the darkness, tinting everything in a magical light. To one side, he could make out the edge of the mainland and the distant islands of Karaz in the dark; to the other, he could see the glowing sky reflected in the surface of Lake Methar. Then he started searching for a place to sleep.

The night air was cold and smelled of the freshness that comes just before rain. Sineth scanned the mountaintops around the platform for a cave or a small overhang that could give him some cover during his night's rest. It should be about three hours after sunset, but the days were short this time of year. Sineth found a small cave entrance; he had to crouch down to get inside. Hopefully it wasn't inhabited by a mountain lion, or a bear, or worse things that lived this high up in the Kuana Mountains.

After setting down his pack and spreading out his bedroll, he continued to scan the area for signs of a mountain bear lurking in the shadows. Exhaustion washed over him like a tidal wave, making his body feel as heavy as a boulder pressed into the ground.

His mind drifted to distant places as he dreamed of walking through the dense, fog-covered forests of Enthaat, finally reaching the calm shores of Lake Illtorm. There he removed his muddy boots and heavy woolen socks and let his feet sink into the cold, crystal-clear water. The warmth of the light on his face brought him a sense of peace.

Suddenly, a strident squeal shattered the serenity. Sineth looked up to see a dark shadow against the colorful sky, shielding his eyes to identify the source of the sound. But when he blinked and refocused, darkness enveloped him once more.

It took him a moment to realize that he was back in the cave, shivering from the cold air. Sineth pulled his thick sheepskin blanket over his ears as another shrill scream jolted him out of his comfort. In an instant, he sprang from his makeshift bed, hastily pulled on his boots, and made his way to the entrance of the cave.

Once outside, he looked up at the night sky, trying to fig- ure out where the sound was coming from. A second later, three large birdlike creatures flew toward him. He ran back to the cave entrance and ducked inside, staring at the grow- ing dark shapes in the sky.

Lights shot through the air, flames and lightning striking the shape closest to him. A pervading, high-pitched scream came from the figure, and then it grew larger and larger as it fell from the sky. With a loud thud and a crack that sounded like bones breaking, the creature crashed to the platform in front of him.

It was a griffon. He recognized the well-made saddle of brown leather, embroidered with the crest of Madin—a cir- cle that formed the shapes of the four elements in gray, orange, green, and blue. Sineth saw a leg draped over the saddle, the familiar sight of a Stormguard's gray robes.

Why are they hunting one of their own? he thought to himself. *But if they are chasing this person, if still alive, they could be helpful to my cause, or have new information that could be useful.*

"Fuck it." He ran out and grabbed the body, dragged it back into the cave and hid in the far corner.

For a moment there was complete silence, just his own steady breathing and, to his surprise, the very faint breathing of the body in his arms. Then he heard the flapping of huge wings and voices murmuring outside.

"Where is she?" a male voice asked.

"Maybe she was hit and fell before the griffon crashed?" a female voice said.

"Yes, maybe, but let's have a look around. I doubt she's alive anyway, but Jahn will not be amused if we come back empty-handed," the male said.

For a while there was silence again and Sineth hoped they had left. He looked down at the body, trying to make out the features of the face in the darkness of the cave. It was hard to see anything in here.

"Hey, I found something! There's a hole in the stone. Maybe she dragged herself in here," the woman said.

Oh, no, they can't find me. If they take me back to Madin, I'll be tried as a deserter. That's not going to happen. Think, Sineth, think of something, anything. His mind raced. Why had he taken the body? It was such an unnecessary risk. He could have just left it, stayed hidden, and no one would have searched this cave.

It was that itch again, the itch of opportunity just within reach. He couldn't help it, he had to seize it with both hands.

He fumbled in his pockets for the small black stone someone had traded him a few weeks ago. Hopefully the merchant hadn't cheated him. Sineth took the stone between his hands and squeezed it as hard as he could. "Braghdah," he whispered. A cloud of black smoke rose from the stone, and in a second the cave was a shadowy expanse. It had been dark before, but the glow of the elemental sphere had added a few shades of gray to the darkness. Now it was just black—no reflections, no light, no shadow, just black.

It worked, Sineth thought. He had always been a fan of magic—not the elemental kind they used in Madin, but the concept of creating something that didn't exist before. Changing odds, crossing places in seconds, maybe even changing time. There were no limits, if you were brave and smart enough.

He heard the male voice again. "Did you check it out?"

"No, I waited for you. What if she attacks me? You saw what she did to the High Monks. She's a monster," the woman said.

"I'm still not convinced that it was her. Perhaps her story was true? She's still one of us. Let's see if she's in here and then we'll fly back to Jahn."

"It's very dark in here. I can't see anything. Wait, I'll conjure some fire," the female voice said. "Strange, I can't see the flame in here. This place creeps me out."

"Then let's go, we've done as much as we can," the male voice said.

After that, Sineth only heard the scratching of their feet on the stone, then the flapping of wings again, and then silence.

How long can this darkness last? Sineth thought. He might as well rest now and decide what to do in the morning. At least no creature would dare to enter this darkness, so they would be safe for now.

He awoke as the light of day filled the cave. The smell of fresh snow hit his nose and he shivered for a moment. Before falling asleep, he had pulled his blanket over the woman to protect her from the cold. Now, however, he felt as stiff and cold as an ice sculpture himself. Sineth looked down at the body of the woman he had saved. Her head rested in his lap. She was still sleeping.

Now that he had a better look at her, he saw the burn marks on her right arm hanging out from under the blanket, the side of her back, and the lower part of her cheek. Some of her hair had been burned off as well. Still, she looked beautiful. She had very pale, almost marble-like skin and thick, long black hair that shone in the light. She wore the mark of the Stormguard on her forehead, swirls of glittering gray representing the Air Element.

What am I going to do with you? I can't take you to the Dark Kingdom, and I don't have the right supplies to treat such burns, but I can't just leave you here either. He let out a long sigh. He would take her back to the village, treat her wounds and find out what had happened to the High Monks. The other Madin soldiers had talked about what she had done to them. *What did you do to them?* he wondered. She did not look like a monster at all.

After he had eaten his ration for the day and relieved himself in the snow outside the cave, he tied her to his back, his backpack in front of him. This wouldn't be easy to track down, but hopefully it would be worth the trouble.

6

Kima

*O*h, *no, I'm going to be late again. I shouldn't have spent half the night sketching. Bon will be very angry.* Kima searched the room for her glasses and bag, pushing away layers of paper. *This is the one for the mechanical hand I drew. Good, now I have something positive to say when I get to work.* "Hey, Bon, I'm late again, but look what I found—the sketch you've been asking me for all week." *Maybe it's not so positive? We'll see, but where is my bag?*

As Kima frantically searched the room, her little bird Lady Zua sat down on her desk and cocked her head to the side. "I know, Zua, I know. I really should clean up this mess," she said.

Lady Zua was by far the coolest thing she had ever created, a little mechanical bird the size of a lime, made of shiny bronze metal with shimmering white opal stones for eyes. But it wasn't just a bird; it also allowed her to spy from the sky. With her goggles, she could see through Lady Zua's eyes. It was a great invention; even Bon had been impressed and asked her if she planned to sell it. But so much effort and time had gone into it, and she loved the cute little bird. Now she had a pet, and it wouldn't die if she forgot to feed it.

After fifteen minutes of searching, Kima finally found her things and headed out into the streets of Jazat. It wasn't far to Bon's shop, but the streets were crowded today. She pushed her way through the crowd. Kima looked up at the sky; it was filled with dark gray clouds. It looked like it was going to rain soon, or with any luck, there would be snow. The air was cold; she could see her breath. It looked a little like the smoke that came out of almost every house, rising into the winter sky in gray waves that smelled of burnt wood and coal.

Oh, how I love this city. The airships glided gracefully from island to island, their sleek forms cutting through the sky. Below, metal servant golems accompanied their owners, their movements precise and purposeful. In the bustling city, golems stood as vigilant guards, their metallic forms a testament to advanced craftsmanship. Towering buildings featured high glass windows, some tinted or mirrored to hide their interiors from prying eyes. Near the Magisters' Palace, the splendor was heightened, with well-cut hedges and intricate designs adorning every surface, creating a scene of unparalleled beauty.

She was lost in daydreaming again. The clock on the nearby red brick building chimed, reminding her how late she really was today. With an "excuse me" here and an "excuse me" there, she pushed her way through the crowd, moving as fast as she could.

A few minutes later, Kima stormed into Bon's Brilliant Bits, almost stumbling as she reached the huge dark wood counter. It was a large and beautifully designed shop. Everything had its place, and the most spectacular gadgets were displayed in glass cases around the room—enchanted robes, swords and armor, but also little things like a cute mechanical bee that had the ability to heal, or rings and bracelets with all sorts of magical properties.

Bon, her elderly gnome boss, sat in his little red leather chair. He was more like a grandfather, sweet and helpful, but also strict and lecturing. That was how Kima thought a grandfather should be, not that she would know. The floral smell of rose candles and hot metal hung in the air. Bon loved his scented candles; he said they made every day at work a walk in the park. And Kima guessed he meant it literally, because all the scented candles smelled of flowers, grass, pine, or sometimes honey. But he was right; it made for a cozy atmosphere.

"Well, look who finally decided to bless me with her presence," Bon said, not even looking up from a piece of parchment he was writing on. He was hunched over it, his monocle in one eye, his puffy white hair sticking out in all directions. There was something wrong with his beard, though.

"I'm so sorry, Bon. I just lost track of time a little. I was working on a new thing I wanted to try out. And I found the sketch of the mechanical hand," Kima said with so much excitement that even she was surprised. "Did you cut your beard? It looks different, but, you know, good different." Bon still stared at the parchment. "Are you that angry? I'm very, very sorry!" She shifted nervously from one leg to the other. Lady Zua flew over to Bon and sat down next to his hand, looking like the cutest thing ever. He smiled a little and looked at Kima.

"Hmm, that's fine. Please try to be on time, okay? You know I can't be angry with you for long. I cut it—the beard, I mean. It was stuck in a box that I'd enchanted so that it would only open if you said the password. I sat there for an hour trying to remember the word, but it just slipped my mind. It was written on a piece of paper on my desk, but I only remembered that after I cut off my beard. Well, it's more practical to wear it short anyway." He paused for a moment and stroked his beard, which now ended in the middle of his chest. He looked from Kima to Lady Zua. "Are you sure you don't want to sell it? It could fetch you a nice pile of gold," he said with a gentle smile as Zua hopped onto his hand.

"I can make another one if anyone asks." Kima tried to catch a glimpse of what he was drawing, stretching a little higher on her toes. "What are you drawing, a new creation?"

He put Lady Zua back on his desk. "No, no, this is some paperwork from the Magisters. It's about what I want to do with the shop when I die." He smiled, but he looked a little sad.

"Bon, you're not going to die. I mean, not in the next few years." Kima tried to look as positive as she could. He just stared at the papers and looked older than ever. "How old are you, Bon? Gnomes can get very old, can't they?"

He jumped down from his chair and walked around the large table. He was only a little taller than Kima, which was nice because most people were much taller than a little halfling girl. He put his weathered hand on her cheek. "Well, we can get very old. But my dear Kima, I am very, *very* old. I have lived this life for a long time, about two hundred and sixty-two years, I think. It's almost over, but that doesn't mean I'm gone. I will be reborn and live a new life. The question is, do I want to do the same profession again, or do I want to do something different? That's what the Magisters want to know. Should I sell the shop when I leave this body, or should they keep it for me until I am old enough to come back and work in it?" Bon gave her a little pat on the cheek, then turned and jumped back into his chair.

"So what have you decided?" Kima didn't like to talk about death; it always made her shiver. All that talk about re-birth—it just seemed strange to her that one could come back after their death. But this was her first life, so maybe it was normal that she didn't understand it.

"I'll sell the shop and see where this new life takes me. I could always open a new shop with my new name," he said with a big, joyful grin. When he grinned like that, he looked almost a hundred years younger.

Kima couldn't help but grin back. "I imagine it's refreshing to do something completely different after such a long time." Then it hit her. "But Bon, what am I going to do?" She didn't want to lose her job. Kima loved it here, and the last thing she wanted to do was go back to her parents' house. Besides, who else would put up with her weirdness and lack of discipline and time management? *I'm screwed,* Kima thought.

"Don't worry, my dear. I'm sure the new owner of this establishment will need employees. Why wouldn't they want you? You have a brilliant mind." He looked at Lady Zua again. "Now get to work. It is already past ten. If you don't start now, we might as well go out for lunch." He folded the parchment and sealed it with melted wax, pressing his ring into it.

Kima looked at him, suppressing the wave of sadness that washed over her. Then she went to the back of the shop and started working on the flying foldable boat she had invented.

7

Garon

Searing pain pulsed through his body, as if life had been drained from him. Every inch of his body felt scorching hot and icy cold at the same time. Garon tried to open his eyes, but they stuck together as if something had congealed and dried over them. It was difficult to force them open.

On the rocky ground in front of him he saw two huge black boots standing in dim light. It was almost as dark as it had been when his eyes had been closed. He tasted the salty, iron tang of blood as he swallowed. His mouth was dry, his tongue sticky.

Garon attempted to straighten up, but he couldn't get his limbs to move. He could feel the rough scraping of rope around his wrists. He was tied to a chair.

How had he ended up here? This shouldn't have happened to him. Never in his life had he been arrested or involved with shady characters. So how had it come to this? Why were they holding him and why hadn't they just killed him? Garon hated the feeling of powerlessness, not knowing what to expect or what they might do to him.

As he slowly lifted his head to inspect his surroundings, he stared into the large, square face of a giant orc. The orc grinned at him with yellow teeth and a horrible wave of foul breath.

"You are awake, little one," the orc hissed in his face. "She will be very happy about this, oh, yes, she will."

The hulking orc disappeared into the darkness. Garon couldn't see much, as the only source of light was a torch hanging on the wall next to him. It looked like he was in some kind of cave or alcove. Or maybe it was just night. But it sure smelled like a cave, filled with the stench of piss and rotting flesh.

Slowly, he began to remember bits and pieces of the battle at the port of Parhat. Garon had fought these small, shadowy, cloaked creatures, and then there had been this huge dragon-like monster in the air. After that, his memory was fuzzy; he only remembered the pain of something tearing through his back and then blackness.

This was not friendly territory; he had never seen an orc before. He had read stories about them; he knew that there were clans of them somewhere deep in the mountains, and there were rumors among the Elemental Guards that there was some kind of dark kingdom below the mountain range. Garon didn't know a single person who had ever been there.

Just as he was thinking about how to get free of the bonds around his wrists, he looked down to see that his legs were bound as well. But if he could just free his hands, it would be easy to get rid of the rope around his legs.

He tried to wiggle his hands and loosen the knot a bit. What wouldn't he give to have the power of the Fire Element? He could have just ignited the rope and walked away. But he needed to be able to move his hands to cast a spell, and even if he could, the only option would be a bolt of lightning, and that would surely send a horde of those green giants after him. It felt like the bindings were already loosening a bit, but he also felt the rope heating up from the movement and burning into his wrists. Garon stopped to let the rope cool down a bit.

A moment later, the huge green figure of the orc emerged from the shadows. "Little one, I have some questions for you," the orc said in his deep, rough, rumbling voice.

Behind the orc, four small green figures appeared, each with huge ears and a jumble of pointed teeth that reminded him of needles. One carried a pot, another a staff with a skull on top.

"Is the potion ready?" the orc asked.

"Yes, the queen herself prepared it," hissed one of the tiny green creatures.

"Good, let us begin." The orc grabbed Garon's sweaty blond hair and pulled his head up.

"We want to know how you defend your islands. What are the things you do, what's the magic you use?" he asked Garon, moving uncomfortably close, waves of his horrid breath hitting Garon's nose and making him gag.

Garon held his gaze and refused to speak.

"You should think about talking, little one. We have lots of tricks, and I'll be happy to try them all on you." They all chuckled, the orc with a deep, dark rumble and the little creatures with shrill squeaks. Their laughter echoed through the cave, making it seem as if there were a hundred more of them hiding in the shadows.

I'm trained for this; they won't break me, no matter what tricks they have. I won't let Madin down, and if I make it back, I'll be the next commander of the Stormguard. This is my chance to prove myself. I'll make it out, Garon thought determinedly and began to wiggle his wrists again. *Just focus on yourself. Find that pocket in your mind and stay there.*

"Okay, good. You don't want to talk. Let's start, Ugdar," the orc said, nodding to the creature with the staff.

Garon would have spat in their faces, but there was no moisture left in his mouth.

"It's my pleasure," Ugdar said with a little chuckle as he stomped his staff on the ground, releasing a cloud of darkness. His eyes turned black, and with a twist of his fingers, the creature pushed the cloud toward Garon.

At first, nothing happened. Garon tried to hold his breath as the cloud surrounded his head. All the faces were gone; there was only a kind of vacuum, like a mist, cold and wet.

After a while, he felt his body struggling to breathe again. His torso shook, and then he couldn't stop himself, he inhaled.

Garon's mind began to open and pain rushed in. He felt as if all his bad memories were crashing down on him at once, but not only memories—he felt the pain of every injury he had ever had.

The impact of a wooden sword against his chest reverberated through his body during combat training, knocking the air out of his lungs.

"Come on, you can do better than this, boy!" Elmor urged, holding out a hand to help him up.

Garon spat out dirt and wiped the remaining grit from his face. "Again." He had not been born a fighter; it had taken him time to adapt to physical combat, to master the art of parrying, dodging, and striking with precision. Magic had always been his preferred fighting skill. Fandeth Elmor had never been soft on him; he wanted Garon to improve, always emphasizing that one learned more from failure than from success. Every blow was an opportunity to grow, to address one's weaknesses.

Bang. Another blow landed squarely in his stomach, causing him to double over and fall to his knees, followed by another swing of the wooden sword that flattened Garon to the ground. "Again," Garon muttered.

"No, you've had enough for today. Get up and have a beer with your friends. You'll feel better tomorrow." Elmor pulled him to his feet. Garon tried to emulate him: strong, firm, yet kind and wise.

Another memory washed over him—the sting that had pierced his heart the moment he saw his dead mother. She lay on the bedroom floor, a pool of blood seeping from her mouth. Despite their efforts over the past few months to ease her illness, it had persisted. They had tried every available medication, but to no avail; her condition had only worsened with each passing day. Garon brushed her hair away from her cold face and planted a kiss on her forehead as he cradled her body in his arms. "You will be reborn, Mother, in a new, healthy body, with a new life waiting for you. I wish you peace," he murmured against her hair, savoring her scent for the last time—rose, her favorite soap.

And there it was again—Avala's face, smiling at him, then laughing and disappearing into the darkness. She was toying with him, a cruel joke to pass the time. Garon longed for unconditional love, to feel complete and safe. He longed for children and a home filled with joy and laughter, just like his mother's home had been. This life should have been brimming with everything, full of experiences, but he felt that dream slipping away into unreachable depths with each passing day.

Suddenly he felt like he was drowning, like liquid was being forced down his throat. He began to scream and push against his restraints, writhing and shaking, raging with pain and the very real near-death panic that was rising within him. His voice sounded muffled, strange, unlike himself, and somehow inhuman. And then it stopped; the cloud was gone, and Garon found himself staring back into the face of the hulking orc.

"How was that, as a little show of the tricks we can play?" Ugdar's voice was jovial.

"I... I'm not going to tell you anything," Garon managed to say, his voice sounding strange, rough and deeper.

He felt his bonds hanging loosely around his wrists. This was his chance to escape. Would he be able to find a way to safety in the darkness? It didn't matter; this might be his only chance to escape. Carefully he slipped out of the rope around his wrists. Garon tried to think of a way to free his legs. He had to act fast and then run like he had never run before in his life.

With a quick movement he pulled his hands in front of him, clasped them together and pushed them forward. A strong blast of wind came from his palms and the little creatures flew back into the darkness beyond the light of the torch. The orc landed a few feet from him. Garon rubbed his fingers together, lightning sparking between them. He pulled them apart, and with a snap of his fingers in the air, he launched lightning at the enemies in front of him. On the ground, the orc screamed in pain. Garon heard squeaks and screams in the darkness. This was his moment.

Rapidly, Garon fumbled with the bonds around his legs. Just as the orc tried to get up, the rope fell to the ground. Garon called for lightning to help him once more, and then he ran. He ran as fast as he could, stumbling through the darkness. He climbed up rocks, getting higher and higher, trying to find some kind of light. But there was none. It was strange that he could see enough to run and climb at all. It was pitch black in here; the only light was the small yellow spot of the torch below him.

He stumbled up the sloping cave floor, pausing now and then to listen to his surroundings. They were still following him; he could hear their screams below. Could they see him? It didn't matter; he had to get out of here. This was their domain, and he couldn't stand against them here. How many of them could live here? How big was this Dark Kingdom?

There was a rumble to his right and he stopped, listening into the darkness. Garon couldn't make out anything—it could be an animal or an enemy—but he could hear his own blood rushing in his ears. He began to climb again, step by step, as fast as he could, heading for what he hoped was an exit. Suddenly, his foot lost grip and he slipped back down a few feet. Every bone in his body ached, and the rock scratched his bruised skin. But it didn't matter; he just had to keep going. Otherwise, he might as well let himself fall into the pit below and die, because that was what would await him if those creatures caught him again.

Exhausted and more crawling than climbing, he reached some sort of building. He must have been climbing for a long time, but there was still no sign of the sky or a breath of fresh air. Garon heard voices below him: screams, rumbling and scratching on stone. They were coming closer, and he could barely muster the strength to move forward.

Suddenly a hand grabbed his arm and pulled him into a doorway.

"Shhh, don't scream. They will hear you," a woman's voice whispered. Garon could barely make out her face, just two piercing white eyes in the dark. "Come with me, I have a place where you can hide. They won't find you here." She pulled him with her.

They went up a spiral staircase into a circular chamber. Garon could make out the outlines of a desk, a bed, book-shelves, and a cabinet. The woman lit some candles.

Garon looked around and down the stairs. It seemed that this structure was made of solid stone. No bricks or wooden planks, just carved stone. The woman was leaning against the table. Her skin was dark, almost as black as the night itself, as was her hair. Only her teeth and eyes pierced the darkness of her body. She wore a black silk dress that fell loosely over her shoulders. A huge drop-shaped white crystal adorned her cleavage, embedded in a silver swirl, suspended from two chains on each side. This woman was the most beautiful human he had ever seen. Or was she even human?

Garon studied her features more closely—her slim figure and elegant face, the full lips and big eyes, and... pointed ears. Not human, but elf, like himself.

"You look terrible. Would you like something to drink and something to eat?" she said with a warm smile, scanning him from head to toe. His clothes were torn to shreds, his arms were covered in bruises and scratches, and his chest still showed signs of the wound where the monster had pierced him. He couldn't imagine how bad his face must look, and his throat felt like it had been scrubbed with steel wool.

"Water, please. Who are you, if I may ask?" Garon walked over to the desk and looked, paranoid, over his shoulder. Somehow he expected a horde of creatures to run up the stairs at any moment. Was this a trap?

"I'm Valeria, and you?" She poured some water into a wine glass and handed it to Garon.

He eagerly drank it all at once, not thinking that it might be poisoned or that he had felt like drowning just a short time ago. "I am Garon. Why did you help me? Not that I'm not grateful, but it was just a little too convenient."

"I happen to live here. These creatures are a torment to everyone. I just wanted to help. Why are you here in the dark?" Valeria stepped closer to him and stroked his bruised face.

"Why do you live here?" Garon said, trying to keep his guard up. *Don't trust her, don't trust anyone, don't let her trick you. If it feels like a trap, it probably is a trap,* he reminded himself.

"Because of my eyes. I'm almost blind in the light, and it hurts. So I decided to just stay in the dark. Only the neighbors aren't very nice." Valeria winked at him and squeezed his hand a little.

A warmth washed over Garon, a feeling of security that allowed him to let go of his tensions and worries. He felt safe.

"Well, I answered your question, now you should answer mine. Why are you here, Garon?" She walked back to the table and leaned against it, a mischievous twinkle in her eyes.

"I was captured and tortured by these creatures. They want information about Madin and its defenses." *Why are you telling her this?*

"They were really hard on you. You don't look very healthy." Valeria looked him straight in the eyes, her tall figure standing proudly. "Come, I can help you," she said with a smile, taking his hand and leading him to the bed.

She's so beautiful, so nice, why would she hurt me? Garon thought as he let himself be pulled towards the bed.

Valeria pulled a rat out of a metal box and held it. The little thing squeaked and wriggled in her hand, trying to free itself from her grasp. Then she touched his chest and he felt new energy flow into his body. The wounds around his wrists closed as the rat went limp in her hand.

"How did you do that?" Garon asked, staring at the dead rat.

"Magic. Don't you have magic where you come from?"

Garon didn't know what was going on. He should be worried, he should be on guard, but he felt fine. Everything was just fine.

"Yes, we have magic, but a different kind," Garon said with an easy smile. He felt drawn to her. This mysterious woman left more questions than answers, but he didn't care at the moment.

Garon touched her shoulder, then her hair, diving into it and holding the back of her head as he moved closer, tilting his head to the side. Their lips almost touched. He waited for Valeria to decide what to do next. She smelled sweet and floral, her eyes glowing with excitement as she pressed her lips to his.

Garon felt a pulsating rush, an overflowing passion as the length of his body touched her soft silk robes. This unbridled desire was nothing he had ever felt in this life, or anything he could remember from the past. He began to tear at her dress, pulling it down as he kissed her neck and cleavage.

Valeria smiled and let out a little giggle. She freed Garon from his torn Stormguard robes, apparently without realizing their meaning.

Why didn't she ask me why I was kidnapped? Shouldn't she be more curious about my being here? Garon wondered.

She rolled on top of him, pulled her dress over her head and threw it to the ground.

She is so beautiful. Her skin looks like silk, smooth and flawless. I just want to have her, take her as mine, Garon thought, giving in to his desires.

"Touch me. Here and here," Valeria instructed him, placing one hand on her breast and the other between her legs.

He did as he was told, caressing and rubbing her gently.

"Own me," she whispered, leaning close to him as she grabbed his hard cock and pushed it inside her.

What's going on, how did this happen? were Garon's last thoughts before he lost himself in a cloud of passion, their bodies tossing and turning, wild and without hesitation.

8

Avala

The last few days had been a blur. Avala remembered being carried, the bouncing of a person moving through the woods beneath her. Sometimes she could open her eyes and see the bearded cheek of a man with dark hair. His eyes were blue like Lake Methar, almost aquamarine. He breathed heavily, and his breath came out in white puffs of smoke in the winter air. When he looked back at her, smiling, he said something, but she couldn't hear it as she disappeared into the darkness.

So many memories flooded her mind, memories from this life mixed with those from past lives, all equal in truth and intensity. This strange feeling that she was not one person, but many, had always felt terribly overwhelming to her. Hearing these different voices in her head, laughing and arguing, living and overtaking her consciousness, it felt as if her mind was not her own.

Once she had decided to go to Himalus, to the Temple of the Whispering Tree, high in the mountains of Kuana. She wanted to seek out the monks there, who were believed to follow a deity, a goddess of sorts, who held the reins of nature and life itself. Although Avala did not believe in gods, she had hoped that with enough help, meditation, and self-control she would be able to silence the voices and memories once and for all. But no matter how hard she tried to gain control over her mind, the voices always crept back in, showing her long-past days in the woods, playing with sticks, playing hide and seek.

These were the good ones, the ones that made her smile and think of wonderful times. But not all of her memories were happy and uplifting. Some were dark as night and so cruel that she had to fight back the tears that would well up in the middle of the day, even when she was eating her lunch, laughter and joy all around her. At times she wondered if she was the only person who had so much trouble with her memories. There was the School of Remembrance in Madin where the children learned to manage their thoughts and memories at an early age, so that when the flood of memories from past lives came like a tidal wave, they would be able to ride it and not get drowned. Avala had been there, too, several times over the course of her lives, but somehow she had never really managed to control it all.

Avala awoke to the sound of voices shouting at each other.

"Why did you bring a Stormguard into the village, are you insane?" a harsh female voice said.

"That's not what we agreed on," another female voice said.

"I know, but they hunted her down and shot her out of the sky. I don't think she's with them anymore. And..." The male voice began to whisper, and Avala couldn't hear the rest.

She tried to push herself into a sitting position. Pain shot through her arms and she felt a sting in her chest. Her body felt sore and stiff, somewhat unfamiliar, as if someone had attached new limbs to it that didn't quite fit yet.

"Hello? Where am I?" Avala asked, inspecting her body with a careful touch. Her fingers brushed over the rough linen dress. Someone had changed her clothes. Feeling for bruises on her head, she could feel the soft skin of her bare scalp in places, and tears welled up.

"You're in safe territory now," a man said.

Avala looked around the room. It was made of wood and stone, it had only a few pieces of furniture, and it was filled with people. Directly in front of her was a familiar face, the man with the black beard and the astonishing blue eyes.

There was a long scar on the right side of his face, from his forehead to his chin, missing his eye by a hair.

He knelt in front of her and touched her legs. "Hi, I'm Sineth."

The moment he touched her and she looked into his blue eyes, something stirred in the back of her mind. It felt like a memory trying to push its way through the crowded space in her brain. Familiar, yet distant, like a shadow or a reflection of something. It unsettled her. She pulled her knees up and tugged her dress tightly over them.

"I am Avala. You carried me down from the mountain?" She knew she should be grateful, but she wasn't sure if she had traded prison for a far worse alternative.

"Yes, I did, and Quinn here healed you. We will not harm you, I promise," Sineth said with a smile, pointing to a small halfling boy on the left side of the room.

"How long? How long have I been unconscious or asleep?" Avala asked.

"About four days," Sineth said.

Oh, no, what about Garon? "I have to go, I have to find someone. A friend. He was captured by some draconic creature." Avala was now standing on the edge of the bed, ready to bolt. Her body rebelled against the fast movement.

Sineth pushed her back onto the bed. "Easy, you've been badly injured and you just woke up. You can't just go out there and chase some dragon."

"It wasn't a dragon. At least I don't think so... it looked different than the pictures in the books. Smaller, grayish-red

skin and no arms. The upper claws were part of the wings."
Avala looked through the open doorway into the misty sky
outside, memories of Garon being pierced by the creature's
claws coming back to her, his eyes wide from the sudden
pain. "The creature's scream was terrifying. We fought as
best we could, but in the end they took Garon. I don't know
why."

There was a pause. Everyone in the room stared at her.

*They think I'm crazy. Why shouldn't they? No one has ever
seen anything like this. It's a fairy tale.* And it was not the first
time people had looked at her that way.

"Thank you for saving me. But I really need to find my
friend. These creatures are up to something. They killed the
High Monks! I doubt they'll just drop him somewhere and
let him go. I have to help him, please," Avala begged as she
leaned forward.

"They killed the High Monks?" said the tall, bulky woman
in the back. Her voice was deep and curious.

"Yes, I saw it. There was blood everywhere. They slaugh-
tered them in the counseling hall of the castle of Parhat,"
Avala replied.

"And why were you in the castle? You are one of the Stormguard, you should have been at the port," said an older
gnomish woman.

"I, I just wanted to see what was going on. I heard strange
noises and screams." Avala didn't trust these people with her
thoughts about the Ritual of Enlightenment or her concerns
about the now-dead High Monks.

"That was your first lie. Or it was a kind of lie. Why would you lie about this?" The gnome woman pushed past the others to get a better look at Avala, a wrinkled old lady, leaning heavily on a walking stick.

How could she know that? Am I such a bad liar?

"I don't know what to say to that," Avala replied, a little startled. "What do you know about the Stormguard? And where am I?"

"Well, you could tell us the truth. My name is Hartaba. Child, we mean you no harm. We are a group of people who want to live free, without the restrictions and rules of the Elementals, without sacrifices and service to the cause. If this is what you seek, we can help you. If you're still with the Elementals, if you want to go back, we will blindfold you and lead you out of our village and you can find your way back to Gahaal. It's up to you," Hartaba said, her voice harsh and high. Avala smelled the distinct scent of herbs on her as she came closer. The woman's eyes pierced her like lightning bolts, searching, trying to figure out what to make of her.

Avala took a long breath. *I cannot find Garon alone and I cannot go back. I am against the sacrifices, or at least I want to know what is going on. Maybe they know something. They certainly have powers I have never heard of. Healing fatal wounds, reading people's minds like leaves in a teacup... And to be honest, what choice do I have? I'm not good at navigating through nature; if they just let me go somewhere in the wilderness, I'm not sure I'll make it anywhere. So I might as well trust them and take my chances.*

"I was waiting in the hall for a meeting with the High Monks. Then I heard loud noises from outside. Everything happened so fast; I was fighting in the harbor with two other Elemental Guards. One died and the other, Garon, was captured. So I ran back to the castle for help, but everyone inside was dead. I tried to explain it to the guards who came later from Gahaal, but the bodies of those little creatures that attacked us were gone. They burned after we killed them, but there was no ash on the ground, nothing left of them. The guards said I would be tried the next day, so I panicked and fled. I'm sure Sineth has told you the rest by now." Avala leaned back against the wall, tears filling her eyes.

It's just too much—all the blood, the bodies, and then Mereth's face as she waved and disappeared into the clouds. A few weeks ago, everything was fine. My only problem was Garon's intention for us to become a real couple and settle down. It seems ridiculously far away now. Like a dream, like some of my muddled memories from past lives.

"The description of these creatures—small, green, cloaked, moving like shadows—I've seen them before. They are part of Venja's army of shadow soldiers." Sineth looked as if he was far away, deep in thought.

"Who is Venja?" Avala replied, wiping away the tears from her cheeks.

"She is the Queen of the Dark. Her kingdom is a legend. Some say it fills only the inside of the mountains, others swear it extends under the entire continent of Dohva. Venja's beauty is said to be breathtaking and is only surpassed by her cruelty and lust for power." Sineth stared into her face. "I was on my way to the entrance of this very kingdom when I found you. I'm planning to start my second journey there in a few days. You could come with me and maybe you'll find your friend down there."

"Why would you go to such a place? And if this Venja has Garon, she probably won't just let him go." Avala hadn't had time to think about the details of Garon's rescue, but now it seemed impossible. *What did I think I would find at the end of this path? Garon tied to a tree, with a rope I could just cut and run away with him? No guards, no fight? Ridiculous.*

"I have some business to discuss with her, though things might have changed if she was the one to murder the High Monks." Sineth paused. "We need to be smart about this, maybe exchange some information to get Garon back. Think about what you can offer her. What price are you willing to pay to free him?" He smiled at her, a sad and pensive smile. "You should get some rest; we can talk more later." Sineth stood up and led the others out of the room. They whispered among themselves as they left Avala in this cold and damp room.

A dark kingdom, a beautiful queen, and an army of those little creatures, and maybe worse. How can we go in there and come out with Garon, or come out at all?

9

Sineth

He pushed the others out of the chamber that he had pre-pared for Avala. They were all excited about the death of the High Monks.

"This is a good thing. Maybe we can change some things before they're old enough to remember what happened," Hartaba pointed out.

"It could be the beginning of a new chapter, but only if Madin is open to change. Many of the Elementals are still alive, and they will soon choose a new group of leaders," Una replied.

"I like that girl, Avala. She seems nice." Quinn moved next to him. "She's very pretty too. I saw the way you looked at her. Not just now, but when you asked me to heal her. You like her," Quinn teased, knocking his elbow into Sineth's leg.

"Stop it, Quinn, this is not the time to talk about girls." Sineth hissed in pain; Quinn had hit a nerve. "I'm not sure we can completely trust Avala. I want to, but we still don't know what her intentions are. And if it really was Venja who killed the High Monks, I'm not sure we're still of any use to her. Do you think she would invade Madin?" He looked at Hartaba.

"My boy, there's always a chance that the Dark Queen would try that. But as far as I know, there's a good reason why she does not leave the darkness." Hartaba stopped and looked at him. "She can't see in the light."

"If that is true, why would she go to such lengths to kill the High Monks?" Sineth asked.

"I don't know. Either they threatened to destroy her kingdom, or she found a way to see in the light." Hartaba looked off into the distance; heavy fog billowed through the spires of their unique home. "But what do we gain? Perhaps we have a chance to talk to the people of Madin, to reason with them about the way we want to live our lives? But I doubt they would listen. Some might, but not many, I'm afraid."

Hartaba looked sad and tired. She had fought for this much longer than he had, and it showed. When he had met

Hartaba, she had been a wise old lady, but now it seemed as if her spirit, her spark, was fading away. It was sad to see.

After he had first met Hartaba, they had sat down on the grass and stared at the distant edge of the island. They had talked for hours about politics and the Elementals, and then they had come up with this crazy idea. What if they created their own society? A way to live life on their own terms? They had been so excited and passionate about their new-found purpose. And he had made a new friend.

Now Hartaba felt more like his grandmother—the one who cooked the best meals and gave the best advice, the one you could never be angry with for long. But she had become too comfortable with the life they had made for themselves. He needed her to be excited; they were so close to their goal. A part of him wanted to shake her, wake her up, give her new hope. But wouldn't that just be empty words? No, he had to believe that there was a chance for them, a chance to finally make a difference. To bring about the change they had hoped for.

"Do you still want to go to the meeting with Venja?" Una asked.

"Yes, maybe I can get some information about her plans. It would help us decide what to do next." Sineth tried to sound as confident as possible without showing his own doubts.

"And you will take this woman with you?"

"It might be a good idea to gain her trust. I have a feeling she knows a lot about the people of Madin. She could be an asset if we decide to convince people to share our vision for this land," Sineth said from the door of his hut. "Let's just think about it and decide tomorrow."

"Well, there is certainly a lot to think about," Hartaba muttered as she and the others walked across the bridge toward the center of their small village.

Sineth was restless, pacing around this small cabin-like chamber he had called home for over two decades. *This could be our chance to make a difference. We have waited so long for an opportunity. This is no time to hesitate.* He thought of Molna and the day they'd taken him away. "It is an honor," they had said. "Molna, you will be remembered as a saint. You have done a great deed for our community, and now it is time to be one with the elements." *A bunch of crappy words for the truth behind them. Killing people for some kind of fanatical religious cause. First they make us work for them, and then they tell us the highest reward is death.* "It's an honor." How he hated that phrase.

He had seen so many of his friends fight and die for honor, it made him sick. Molna had just been the latest and most painful loss. He had been Sineth's mentor, the one who had taken him in after his parents died. Sineth had been eight years old and human when it happened; this was his first life as an elf. If his parents had come back as humans, they would probably already be dead again. Time was a strange thing. For a human, life was as short as the blink of an eye. Now that he was an elf, life seemed endless. What could he accomplish in all this time? Would he look back one day and think of the short and uneventful life he'd had? Or would it be a life full of success and wonderful memories? He hoped for the latter.

Sineth's thoughts trailed off. *This woman Avala, there's something so familiar about her. As if I've known her since the beginning of time. I don't recognize her face or her voice, it's just the way she speaks and behaves, the expression in her eyes. The way she cried... But why would her crying be so familiar? It just doesn't make sense. Maybe it's some kind of mind trick she can do? To create some kind of emotional bond so that she won't be hurt or cast out by us?*

Think, Sineth, think... How would she benefit from this?

Sineth sat down on his bed. He should get some sleep; hopefully he could leave sooner rather than later. Make his way back up the mountain range to find the entrance to the Dark Kingdom. If Avala decided to join him, he could try to find out on the way. Ask her some questions. Maybe he would find out where this strange familiarity came from.

10

Kima

A cold wind blew over the Hill of Rebirth, just a half hour's walk north of Jazat. Kima pulled her cloak tighter. Two of the singers tried to catch their music sheets as the wind carried them away, and the fresh smell of snow was in the air.

There are a lot of people here, at least a hundred. I didn't know Bon knew so many people. It seems he was always a very nice guy, and after such a long life, you build up a lot of friendships over the years. At least he did. I miss him already. Kima walked through the rows of seated guests, looking for a good place to watch the ceremony.

The musicians got hold of their notes and began to play a quiet melody, almost like a child's lullaby.

"Dear guests, friends and family of Bon, welcome to the Celebration of Soul Ascension!" The speaker, a female elf, stood at the top of the hill next to a stone arch. Her long, silver-blonde hair was tossed about by the wind, shimmering in the faint light that pierced the thickly clouded sky.

What is it about these elves that every one of them has this strange elegance and beauty? I've never met one who was ugly or clumsy. Everything about this woman is perfect—her hair, her marble-like skin, and her night-blue robe with fur-trimmed edges. There's not a speck of dirt on her, while I look like a mess after walking all the way up that hill, Kima mused.

The elf continued her speech. "I am Edora, and I will lead today's celebration in honor of Bon Gunthard, a fine gnome craftsman and dear friend to many..." Then she went on and on about Bon's accomplishments in his long, well-lived life. About the deeds he had done for the Magisters, about every object he had created that was now a key part of their society.

I mean, clocks and flying ships are pretty cool, and there's no doubt that I love a good creation, but is that really all there is to life? To achieve something? To make a name for yourself? Everyone tries so hard to accomplish something worthy of a well-lived life, but while they're trying so hard, they forget to live. They forget that in the end the most meaningful thing to do is to live life to the fullest, to enjoy every day. Isn't it accomplishment enough just to sit in the garden and close your eyes and enjoy every ray of sun-shine, every breeze, and every bird that sings a sweet song? To be fully in the moment, to be still. In the end, I think it's wrong to put achievement above everything else. Because you may be thought of by strangers after you pass from this life, but you'll look back and feel the terrible loss of so many moments that just passed by with-out you even noticing the beauty of it, Kima reflected.

So the meaning of life is really to be in the present, because it's only going to be there for a moment, and then it's gone. Like Bon. Dear, sweet old Bon, who worked so hard and never com-plained. It's only been a few weeks since Bon told me he was going to sell his shop. Somehow he must have known that his time had come. Could she be like Bon? An entrepreneur, a master of her craft? Kima doubted it. She was too clumsy, lost in her own thoughts most of the time. A creator, yes, but a sales-woman, one who could run a successful shop? No.

After Edora finished her endless eulogy about Bon's life, she stepped into the arch behind her. In the center of the arch stood a stone altar with a lidded ceramic pot on top.

"Here are the remains of Bon, his physical form turned to ash, but his soul lives on somewhere in the elemental sky, waiting for his new life to begin. We're here today to bid farewell to this life and to celebrate the beginning of the new life's journey that lies before him. May his soul find its way back safely. Let us honor Bon and remember him for a mo-ment in silence." Edora closed her eyes and bowed her head.

Kima did the same. Fond memories flashed before her closed eyes. His laughter ringing in her ears, mocking her when she was frustrated with herself. Bon's hand on her shoulder, comforting her. His wise words, teaching her the arts of enchantment, always with a smile on his face. Filling her head with the best that magic had to offer. He never pressured or lectured her like her parents did. Bon's patience seemed endless. All the time she had spent in the crafting room of his shop, listening to him whistle or hum a cheerful tune, had made her life so much easier, reminding her that each day was a blessing, something special, not just a series of hours to pass. Bon really meant the world to her... and now she had to do it alone.

"Thank you all for showing your love and respect. Now we will send Bon's remains to rest, like so many before him." Edora opened the lid of the pot and swirled her fingers in the air above it. The ash rose from the pot into the air, a thin gray spiral. She stepped back out of the arch, pushed her hands apart, and the ash spread out, becoming a wall in the arch. It looked like a cloud of mist, a passageway to another part of this world. With a snap of Edora's fingers, the ashes disappeared.

Kima heard a few oohs and aahs around her. A few people in the crowd looked wide-eyed at the top of the hill, including Kima. It was her first Celebration of Soul Ascension. She wasn't sure what she had expected, but this was quite a show.

"Dear guests, you are now welcome to step through the arch, one by one, and bid farewell to Bon. Afterwards, we will have a proper celebration at the bottom of the Hill of Rebirth, in the Hall of the Descendants. Food and drink will be provided." Edora stepped back to the side of the arch and led the crowd to form a line and pass through.

After a long while, it was Kima's turn to step through the arch. She looked at it with a mixture of curiosity and fear. It was a little intimidating. *What will happen when I go through? Will I see Bon for the last time? Will I feel his presence, or is he long gone and this is just a little show for the crowd?*

"There's nothing to fear. It's just an arch, a symbol of a door to the next life," Edora said with a gentle smile.

Kima didn't know what to say. The only thing that came out of her mouth was a whispered "Okay..." and she stepped through.

Nothing happened, of course. Kima looked back and wondered what Edora was doing in this ritual. Just a strange act, a show to please the crowd, to give them something to remember.

Kima found a seat in the back of the hall, away from the stage and the loud, upbeat music.

What am I going to do now? The shop is closed until they find a new owner. She could make another bird and sell it. Maybe that would give her enough coin until she figured out what to do next, or until the shop opened again.

A dwarf woman sat down across from her and banged her cup on the table. Her brown hair was pulled back into a tight bun. "You Kima?" the woman said in a raspy voice.

"Yes, I'm Kima, and you?" She looked around the room for an excuse to go somewhere else. She wasn't in the mood for company right now. All she wanted was a quiet corner to hide in and drink.

"I'm Rembry, maker of the finest enchantments in Karaz. I bought the small shop that Bon Gunthard had. They told me you come with it. Is that true?" Rembry leaned on the table and offered her square hand to Kima.

Kima reached across the table and shook Rembry's hand. "I worked for Bon for the last five years. He was a great teacher and boss."

"Was he? I heard his work was a bit average. But today is not the day to talk shit about him, ha." Rembry chuckled. "We'll see what you have to offer, Kima. Then we'll decide if you're worthy to stay and work for us."

"I'm sorry, Rembry. Who is 'we?' Do you have more employees?" Kima asked.

"Nooo, it's just me, silly girl. See you tomorrow morning. We start at eight, don't be late!" Rembry got up and left.

I hate her already. How could she be so rude? It's his party today! And what is this 'we' thing? 'Don't be late'... did someone tell her about my poor time management? Did Bon know this woman?

Kima finished the rest of her drink and stood up. She should go to bed early. Hopefully Rembry was just drunk and in a bad mood. Maybe she would be nicer tomorrow. Kima let out a long sigh and left the Hall of the Descendants.

11

Avala

"What do you think she's going to do? Run back to Madin and tell them about our village? As if they'd care. They've got bigger fish to fry right now than a bunch of misfits in a swamp!" Sineth roared at Emhir, the Resistance's official cook. Emhir was a stocky man with fading gray hairline and a greasy, stained apron. His trademark mustache, however, was always immaculately groomed. And his food was delicious.

"Please, lower your voice. You forget yourself again, Sineth. There's no need for your temper. Emhir is only being cautious, and so should you. We still know little about the woman and her motives," Hartaba chimed in with an audible sigh. "Still, you are right. Madin does indeed have bigger problems right now, and I don't think she's much of a tracker anyway."

"So you're saying she's one of us now?" Quinn interjected, rising from the bench with excitement in his eyes. "I think she's great. And I really, really want to see her magic! The Air Elementals never visited us up in Shun. We only ever had trouble with the Fire Elementals of Lhudar—no offense, Sineth."

"None taken," Sineth replied.

"You do realize I'm still sitting here, right?" Avala shouted from the back of the circular hall, carved into the stone of the spire. "I've told you many times, I'm not interested in betraying you. I just want to help my friend."

They all stared at her now. *They really forgot I was here? Such a strange bunch,* Avala thought to herself.

"Well, I think you can lead her out of the village without a blindfold," Hartaba said, rising from her seat and leaning heavily on her walking stick. Her departure seemed to signal the end of the debate, for suddenly the room grew noisy with chatter and people began to get up and leave.

"Thanks for having faith in me," Avala said to Sineth as he and Quinn approached her.

"No big deal. I meant what I said—Madin has his focus elsewhere. And for the record, I do believe you, but that doesn't mean I trust you, not fully anyway," Sineth replied. "Let's leave first thing in the morning and hit the road, okay?"

"I'm ready. Quinn here has really worked wonders with me. I feel much improved." Avala smiled at the little halfling boy. She adored Quinn; he was like a little brother to her, even though she had only just met him. "I have a favor to ask of you, Sineth," she added.

He eyed her intently, as if she was going to ask him something he might not want to give.

"I... Quinn said he wasn't very good at shaving, but you are. I wanted to ask if you could shave the burned side of my head. I think it would look better if it seemed more intentional. Like a style I chose rather than scattered patches of hair." She absentmindedly brushed over the bare spots on the right side of her skull.

"Well, I mean, sure, if that's what you want."

Sineth picked up his razor and began to scrape across her soapy skin. His hands felt rough and she was a little nervous next to him. They had never been alone in her chamber before and somehow it felt more intimate than being here with Quinn. It shouldn't make a difference; he was just a man like any other.

"You have thick hair." Sineth turned her head slightly with his hand to adjust the angle for his razor.

"Is that supposed to be a compliment?"

"Just a statement. But I think it suits you—the half-shaved head, I mean. It makes you look more like a warrior than a fussy noblewoman."

"A fussy noblewoman, is that what I look like?"

"I didn't mean it like that, just in general. And your hair fits your new clothes. You're dressed like a proper tracker. It's better to wear tighter pants and sturdy leather in the wild—it won't tear as easily as the silks of Madin." He brushed over her bare head to feel for stubble. It gave her a strange tingling sensation in her neck. "I think we're done."

Avala looked into the small mirror on the wooden stool in front of her. An unknown face looked back at her. Her eyes wandered over the side of her now-bare skull, to the long black mane of hair on her left side, and over to the elaborate tattoo on her forehead. It still showed the two outward and two smaller upward swirls of the Elemental Stormguard. Like a sad reminder of the life she had left behind, it was imprinted not only on her face, but also on her soul. *A warrior? Maybe.* She had never thought of herself that way, even though she was trained in combat like the rest of her comrades.

For a moment there was silence in the room, and she realized that his hands were resting on her shoulders; he was looking at her in the mirror as well. A curiosity flickered across his forehead and made it clench in thought.

Somehow he must have come to his senses, because he pulled his hands back, began to pack the razor away, and emptied the soapy water outside, pouring it over the edge of the platform into the swamp below.

"Thank you. I mean it. I know it may not feel important, but it is to me." Avala got up to leave. "I think I needed this to accept the change. Not just in appearance, but... you know, in everything."

"I understand what you mean. You should get some sleep now. It will be a while before we have the pleasure of sleeping in a bed again." His lips curled into a soft smile as he nodded toward her small wooden bench with a layer of stuffed cloth on top.

So the next day, without a blindfold or a sack over her head, she set out to track through the swamp. Sineth led her through it, avoiding dangerous areas where he said huge scaled beasts lurked. Sleet poured down on them most of the day, becoming more bearable when they finally reached the edge of the forest. She began to admire his sense of the nature around him. He walked over the bony ground of the forest as if it were the Trade Road. Hours passed and the light began to creep low behind them by the time they reached a large clearing.

"We'll make camp here." Sineth dropped his bag onto the soft, moss-covered ground and began to set up the tent.

"We should make a fire. It's freezing cold and I'm soaked to the bone." Avala looked at the ground. "But I'm not sure if we can make a fire. It's too wet. Maybe we should move on and find a drier place, deeper in the forest?"

"It's okay, it will work. And believe me, you don't want to sleep on roots. It's nice and soft here." Sineth crouched down and drew a symbol on the ground with a stick—a triangle in the center, a hexagon around it, another hexagon around it, turned just a little, and all of it integrated into an almost perfectly drawn circle. Sineth moved his hands through the air above the symbol, tracing it with his fingers and muttering some words she did not understand. Finally, he snapped his fingers and the symbol burst into bright flame.

Avala stared at the symbol, then at Sineth. "You're a Fire Elemental. That's what Quinn mentioned yesterday, right? You were trained in Lhudar!"

"Yes, and yes. But not for long. I never graduated in the arts of elemental control," Sineth replied, curling his fingers upward as the flame grew higher. Thick, gray, billowing smoke rose from the burned, wet ground into the sky. The sharp sting of it hit her nose and her eyes began to water. Instinctively, she took a few steps back.

"Is it wise to let everyone for miles see our location?" Avala asked, looking worriedly into the forest.

"There are a lot of questions on your mind today, Avala. We should be fine. We're still far from civilization, and the fire keeps most of the creatures that wander these woods at bay," Sineth said with a wink.

Is he flirting with me? She let her eyes wander around, checking the perimeter of the clearing for any movement. Her eyes went back to Sineth, who had finished setting up the tent. He sat down in the entrance and looked into the flames. Something was so familiar about this, about him. It was a feeling deep inside her that she couldn't quite place. She studied his features—his short black wavy hair, his disturbingly intense blue eyes, the scar over his right eye. *He doesn't look familiar at all.*

"Who are you, Sineth? I mean, what did you do before you joined the Resistance?" Avala asked.

"More questions, huh? Why do you have to know everything about every little detail around you?" Sineth looked at Avala curiously. She crossed her arms defensively over her chest.

"Isn't trust a thing you need as an outcast? And doesn't trust come from knowledge, from knowing the people you travel with, from being aware of your surroundings?" Avala blurted out with more force than intended.

Sineth let out a sigh, apparently sensing her change in mood. "I'm from Enthaat. It's a small village right next to Lake Illtorm, about twenty miles north of Onja. My parents are long dead. No siblings, no wife, no children, and no close friends. I'm a bit of a loner—life is easier that way. I joined the Resistance because the Elementals killed the only person I've ever considered family." Sineth's expression changed from his usual cocky smile to a sad and melancholy look.

He was heartbroken, just like her. Alone in this world, with nothing to look forward to or to lose. They shared the same fate, but they couldn't be more different. Sineth seemed impulsive and reckless, given his outburst just yesterday. Perhaps life in the village of the Resistance had made him that way. Avala wondered what kind of person he might have been before his friend's death. What kind of person would she become after Mereth's death? She honestly could not foresee. Her old life in Madin already felt like a distant dream, like one of the memories from past lives. And somehow she felt close to Sineth, this stranger, and she just couldn't figure out why.

"Is there any way I can squeeze into the tent with you? The floor is quite wet and cold," Avala said with a shy smile. Sineth's face lit up and his usual easy grin returned.

"Sure, you're welcome to snuggle up," Sineth said.

Avala had been on Sineth's back for days, as close as one could get to another person, but this closeness felt different. The choice to be close to someone was different from the necessity of being bound to someone while being unconscious most of the time.

"I've always loved fire—the smoky smell of burning wood, the billowing clouds rising into the night sky. Staring into it as it shifts and changes with each curling flame. It consumes everything, burning its way through without hesitation until there is nothing left to burn. It can inspire both awe and fear. But it never goes unnoticed. To control it is to control yourself, your emotions, your thoughts. It takes a lot of practice," Sineth said, still staring into the flames.

"And did you manage to control it?" Avala asked. He looked so sad, as if every flame meant a broken dream. It should be a blessing to wield such power, but for him it looked like a torment.

"Not at first"—Sineth paused—"but over time. As I said, it takes a lot of practice. And there is no practice without mistakes."

Somehow she was lost for words. Maybe it was the look on his face, or the calm that came over her while she was next to him, but she just wanted to be there, in this moment, undisturbed. A strange feeling, for she had never enjoyed the company of a man the way Mereth had. Never needed the strong shoulder her friend had always talked about. Leaning on your partner, giving up all your defenses.

They stared into the flames for a long time in silence. There was only the hiss of the flames and the sound of the wind twisting the long ends of the trees, rustling and shaking them. The sky was clear now, no clouds in sight, only the towering shape of the Kuana Mountains in the distance.

After the initial awkwardness had passed, Avala enjoyed not being alone, and also being with a man without the expectant eyes of the whole city upon her. With Garon, every time they met, it was like walking towards a destined fate. Here, right next to Sineth, she could just sit and enjoy his comforting presence. Here she understood what Mereth had meant, at least a little.

"We should get some sleep now," Sineth said in a low voice.

There it was again, that feeling of familiarity. The words, the whisper, his presence beside her. Avala turned her head to him; he was only inches away. She looked into his eyes, then he leaned forward, his soft lips touching hers. His short beard brushed against her chin.

She should have been offended by his approach, but she wasn't. Instead, Avala felt a rush of excitement, a tension building inside her, and she embraced his kiss, allowing herself to feel free, to be in the moment, to let her mind be silent for a while. Avala let her hand wander to his hair, to the side of his cheek.

Then he pulled it away and looked at her, a warm smile spreading across his face. He cupped her chin in his large hand. "Should I stop?" He searched her face for an answer.

"No," she heard herself say, and he leaned into her once more. Their lips met, eager for more, and she crawled back into the tent, Sineth half on top, following her.

He grabbed the back of her head, his fingers in her long braided hair. Sineth pulled her in for another kiss, fiercer and more demanding. He drew her closer, his other hand on the back of her hip.

She pressed her body tightly against his, and Sineth chuckled a little and began to pull and tug at Avala's blouse, exposing one of her white-skinned breasts. Slowly, he kissed a line from her ear to her bare breast. He looked up at her as he began to kiss and squeeze her hardened nipple. Avala's body ached with desire, her whole body pulsating with his touch.

"Do you like that, or should I stop?" Sineth said with a broad grin.

Avala grabbed his head and pushed him back down. "Go on, please."

Sineth covered her with kisses, little licks and nibbles, undressing her even more. It was a much harder task to remove her wet leather pants, which stuck to her skin like glue. As he tugged at them and Avala leaned down to help, their heads bumped as her legs finally freed themselves from their leather prison. They looked at each other and laughed, rubbing their heads to ease the pain.

Then she watched as he slowly pulled off his clothes. He was a well-built man, every muscle defined. His skin showed a number of old scars, but this was not the time to ask about them. Her breath was visible in the air; she hadn't realized how cold it was. A small shiver ran down her naked body, but a second later he was on top of her again. His hot skin covered hers. Sineth pressed his lips hard against hers and his tongue explored her mouth. She bit his lip, just a little, to tease him.

"You're driving me crazy, Avala. I can't wait any longer," Sineth whispered under his breath against her lips.

"I never said you had to wait." She pulled her legs up and pressed his body even closer to her. He grinned at her, raising his eyebrows.

Sineth slid carefully inside. The pleasure that came over her as he began to move his body in rhythm was somehow new and unlike anything she had ever felt, but also like they had done this a thousand times before. As if they knew exactly what the other wanted.

His movement became faster, deeper. He leaned his forehead against hers. Avala let out a loud moan as he penetrated the sweet pleasure spot inside her. Sineth kissed her, smiling against her lips. Her body tensed and she grabbed his neck. In a wave of heat and desire, she fell back heavily onto the bedroll beneath her.

Sineth leaned back and looked at her, still thrusting deep into her. He groaned and grabbed and squeezed her breasts. Then his head fell back and with one last push he collapsed on top of her, his head resting on her chest.

Avala stroked his wavy hair in an all-too-familiar way.

12

Garon

"Look at you, you are even more beautiful now. Special in every way." Valeria stood beside Garon and brushed his scaled black cheek. He stared into the mirror before him. Sharp, spike-like teeth made up the lower half of the right side of Garon's face. Two horns protruded from the right side of his head, and the eye on that side was bright green. This half of his face was also covered in black cracks, as if something would break through his skin at any moment. In contrast, the left side looked grotesquely normal. Garon knew he should be frightened, or at least irritated by this change, but he felt nothing. No, not nothing; deep inside he felt whole and free. As if a weight had been lifted from his shoulders.

"Is everything all right, love?" Valeria asked, giving him a kiss on his scaled face.

"Yes, I think I'm fine, Valeria." Garon turned and looked deep into her white eyes, kissing her soft lips.

She leaned forward and embraced him. After they pulled apart, Valeria whispered into his ear, "Call me Venja, my love. That is my name here in the Dark Kingdom."

Venja, I know that name. Could it be true? I thought it was just a tale...

"You are their queen?" Garon stepped back and looked at Venja in confusion.

"Yes, I am, and I have made you my king. Frightening, beautiful, wise and powerful, equal to me." Venja stepped forward and took his hand. "Rule with me, my love. I need you for what is to come."

She is the Dark Queen, who has ruled her kingdom since the beginning of time. The darkness is her home, the beasts her servants, an army of shadows rising from the depths. Her powers are grim, but her appearance is too beautiful to resist. A poem Garon had learned at school, back at his childhood home, in Riptar. Home... he had served in Gahaal all his adult life, helping others, growing stronger and wiser. He'd wanted to be a leader, maybe even a High Monk one day. Now, every wish that little boy had had seemed silly, a waste of time and energy.

I never would have made it this far. Here I can be a leader, the leader of an entire kingdom, ruling with the most powerful and beautiful woman I've ever seen. Sure, there's Avala, but she never really wanted us to be a couple. She played with me. Venja wants me, loves me. I feel stronger, more powerful, more capable. She made me a better person.

Venja looked at him with a satisfied smile, still holding his hand. He wondered if she could read his thoughts. It didn't matter, not to him. There were no secrets he wanted to keep, not anymore.

"I'm your king, and I'll help you with everything you want. I love you, Venja, you are my queen," Garon said, the words flowing out of his mouth as if he had said them countless times before.

"Very well, I love you too, and I trust you. Let me show you your new kingdom," Venja replied.

They stepped out of the tower he had found a few days ago. At least he assumed it had been a few days—he couldn't remember exactly how long it had been. He only remembered being taken away and then finding this tower and Valeria. Being with her, loving her, transforming into something new.

Garon was standing on some kind of balcony. He remembered the all-encompassing darkness he had faced upon his arrival; now he could see as if it were bright daylight. Everything was clear. In front of him, below him, and at the sides of this gigantic cavern were buildings carved into the stone. They were adorned with intricate wooden structures—platforms, railings, windows, small huts—all connected by bridges and stairs.

"This is impressive. I didn't know what to expect, but this is beyond my wildest imagination. You created all this?" Garon asked.

"I'm glad you like it. Of course I didn't build it myself. We have very skilled craftsmen among our people. Let's go for a stroll." Venja pulled his hand and led him down a stone spiral staircase. It led to a large platform. People were laughing and shouting, and there was a fighting pit in the corner of the space. It looked like a bar; there was a counter in the back. Deep inside the cave there were tables and benches and the whole place was filled with people of all shapes and sizes—ogres, kobolds, goblins, orcs, gnomes, dwarves, and some familiar species: humans, elves, and halflings. He hadn't expected there to be people from above.

As they passed through the wild crowd, people stepped aside and bowed. A moment later there was silence. Even the ogre and orc in the pit stopped punching each other and looked at them, fresh blood dripping from their fists and faces.

"My dear people of the Kingdom of the Dark. I would like to introduce you to my partner, the king to your queen, Garon the Demon Warrior." Venja gave a small bow to Garon. The people around her did the same. Then she stepped beside him and kissed the scaled half of his face. The crowd began to murmur until Venja raised a hand.

"Please spread the word, our new king will help us conquer the world! Soon, my friends, we will rise up and take what is ours!" Venja shouted into the depths of the cave. Her voice was deep and harsh. She was smiling, her face beaming with excitement.

The people around her started stamping their feet, shouting and growling. "Ven-ja! Ven-ja! Ven-ja!" It echoed through the cave and accompanied their descent, deeper and deeper into the bottomless pit below them. Every now and then they stopped and Venja introduced him to the people in the vicinity. Everyone was respectful and honored them according to their status.

After a long time they came to a mine. A shaggy, long-haired, long-bearded dwarf with arms the size of tree trunks hammered into the stone and a fist-sized blue crystal fell to the ground. He picked it up, eyed it with delight, and began to walk away. Venja put a hand on his shoulder and stopped him.

"May I?" She reached for the crystal. The dwarf looked up in awe and dropped the stone in her hand.

"Of course, my queen." The dwarf picked up his hammer to continue his work.

They walked a little further and found a bench. Just as Garon was about to ask about it, Venja sat down and said, "This is Safral. It is the magical power source of Dohva. It is incredibly potent; you can do all kinds of magic with it."

Venja held up the stone in front of them and slowly turned it in her hand.

"What kind of magic do you mean?" Garon asked.

"Any kind. Anything you can imagine. With enough Safral, there are no limits." Venja stared at the stone and smiled, as if she had a very specific use for it in mind.

"I only know elemental magic. I've never been outside of Madin in all of my lives. What do you mean by everything?" Garon turned to her, studying her expression.

"You'll find out soon enough. Perhaps you should start testing your own abilities? You have changed, Garon, not only your appearance, but also your magic. We have a training ground a bit up and to the right. You should give it a try." Venja stood up and held out her hand.

They wandered the many paths of this underground kingdom for a while. Venja described the different sections of this beehive-like place. There were the Safral mines at the bottom, and a little higher up the first settlements of the miners. Next were the refineries and laboratories where the Safral was distilled into a liquid. As he was told, the Safral could be used for a variety of purposes, in its hard form or as a kind of potion. Further up, there were a variety of shops and taverns, and even more commonly used meeting places. At the top were the rest of the living quarters. He was surprised to learn that families lived here—somehow, he hadn't thought about these rough and tough people living an idle life here. He'd also never imagined the vastness of this place; it housed thousands upon thousands of people. Their buildings were so skillfully built into the walls of this massive cavern that he wondered how long it had taken them to construct it all, and even more, how long this hidden empire had existed underneath the outside world.

"What were your magical abilities?" Venja asked.

"I could control the wind. Also change the weather, move clouds, stop storms. I guarded the ports of Gahaal. Ensured safe landings and departures at the ports," Garon replied.

"How boring. Where is the fun in that? Besides, how do you defend yourself in a fight? Kick some dust into the air?" Venja said with a mocking grin.

"I've rarely felt the need to defend myself." He looked around; they had halted in front of some sort of training ground. It looked very different from the one back in Gahaal. That one had the benefit of fresh air and earth underfoot, which was not only good for traction, but also not as hard as barren stone when someone, often himself, hit the ground. Here there were no wooden swords or staffs to spar with, no racks of shields or anything else to indicate that this was indeed some sort of training ground. It was just a cave, but the floor was unnaturally level and clean, not a small rock or even a pebble in sight.

"Well, now you will have the need, and you can do it. Look at the target before you. Feel his pulse, his vitality. Seize it with your mind." Venja looked expectantly at Garon.

In front of him stood the towering figure of an orc, his tusked mouth clenched, as if he knew what was coming next. Garon stared into his eyes, not really knowing what to do or what to look for in them. But he could hear and feel a pulse, *dudug-dudug-dudug*.

"Good, now put your hands together, slide your right hand forward and curl your index and middle fingers and say 'Vereth-Meduc-An,'" Venja explained, seemingly satisfied with his staring into the orc's eyes.

Garon took a deep breath and began the hand movement, concentrating on the sound and rhythm of the pulse. "Vereth-Meduc-An." He saw a black, thin sliver go out of the orc's body and into his curled fingers. The orc fell face forward onto the stone floor.

The sound of clapping echoed through the cave. Venja beamed at him with pride. "Well done, my love. You did it on the first try. Perhaps we should move on to more difficult tasks."

"What exactly happened?" Garon looked down at the orc. Somehow he wasn't worried about the orc's well-being. He was just curious, which felt strange to him. Even though the orc was a terrifying figure of a man, Garon had just knocked him out and it must have hurt a lot to hit the ground like that, so why was he so unmoved by this sight?

As he stared at the figure on the ground, the orc slowly began to move again, pushing himself off the ground.

"You took some of his life and knocked him out," Venja replied.

"His life? What do you mean by that? How is that possible? What if he had died—would he have been reborn?" Garon asked.

"Of course he would. We are bound by the rules of this land. We just make sure that he would be reborn as one of us. Garon, I told you, anything is possible with Safral."

13

Kima

It had only been a few weeks since Kima had started working for Rembry, but it felt like an eternity. She really tried to motivate herself this morning, to get herself ready for the day, but the upcoming workday clouded her mind with sadness. All the time Bon had been her boss, she had loved her craft so much that she couldn't sleep some nights because she wanted to finish a new idea. Now, everything was different; she was hardly creating anything new. All she did was make mechanical golems and sometimes repair them. Kima could proudly say that she'd made half of the new members of the city's guard, but there was no joy in that.

Slowly, Kima made her way down the cobblestone street, through the crowd, checking the large clock on the side of a nearby building. She was late again, but she cared little. There was nothing to fight for, not anymore.

A few blocks away she saw the small building of Bon's Brilliant Bits, tucked between two huge stone buildings with the usual stained-glass windows. Of course, Rembry had changed the name and painted the outside of the building and changed everything about the place that had been good. So now Kima looked at the bright red building with "Rembry's Relentless Crafts" in huge gold letters filling the space between the door and the upper windows.

She's not wrong, her work is truly relentless, Kima thought as she entered the shop. The small bell rang as she walked through the door. All the shelves had been removed. The walls were lined with various types of mechanical golems, some small, some large. All of them stood on little raised platforms with metal plates engraved with their names and types of enchantments.

"We'll be right there!" Rembry yelled from the back of the room. The smell of hot metal and tobacco stung Kima's nose. She heard a clanking sound and Rembry appeared between the dark red curtains. "Oh, it's you. You're late again. If this is going to be a regular thing, you can start looking for a new job," Rembry snarled at her and went back into the crafting area of the shop.

"Actually, I'm here to quit. So you better start looking for a new employee," Kima stated as sternly as she could. She expected Rembry to be at least a little annoyed, or maybe even a little sad.

"Then get out of here, you useless little prick!" Rembry shouted from behind the curtain without even looking at her.

That was it—no goodbye, no thank you, no lecture about what Kima thought she was doing. Just like that, Rembry took all the wind out of her sails, which were not even fully raised.

A heavy burden fell from her shoulders as she walked out of the shop, slamming the door behind her in anger.

But what now? I haven't really thought about what comes next. I need a job, otherwise I'll be kicked out of my apartment soon enough. There isn't another magic shop in Jazat, but maybe in Resh? Kima thought about her parents; she could ask them for a job. They would love the idea of her working in their beloved merchant "empire". Nothing could bore her more. Maybe she could just ask them for some gold to take a trip to Resh, a vacation. Kima could avoid telling them about her lack of work, only tell them that she wanted to travel a bit.

Eagerly, with newfound joy, Kima pushed her way up the stone steps to Magisters' Square, the part of town where the rich people lived. A little further up, on top of the hill, stood the palace of the Magisters of Karaz. Kima had seen it once or twice during her childhood. Her parents bought all the goods for the palace, and sometimes, when her mother wrote down a list of things to buy for the Magisters, Kalira Saasar herself came down the stairs in the huge entrance hall and added some things to her mother's list.

While pondering her childhood upbringing, Kima reached the front gate of her parents' mansion. A guard approached the gate.

"Miss Kima, do you request an audience?" the guard asked.

"That would be great, Nhuvor." Kima looked at the tall, bulky figure of the long-horned, black-furred minotaur guard, dressed in gray and silver, with a long spear in his right hand. His polished silver septal nose ring shimmered in the midday light. Nhuvor opened the gate and escorted Kima to the front entrance of the mansion.

"Thank you, Nhuvor."

"No worries, little one." Nhuvor tousled Kima's curly auburn hair. Kima smiled at Nhuvor; at least some things didn't change. She knocked on the door with the silver dragon head in the middle. Another guard opened it—Greg, a half-orc, dressed in similar armor. The silver dragon emblem of the Magisters' Merchant adorned his breastplate. It contrasted nicely with his greenish skin tone, Kima noted.

"Hello, Miss Kima, your father is in the library. Your mother is in town right now, running some errands," Greg explained.

"Okay, I'll go see my father then. Thanks, Greg," Kima said. Greg nodded and closed the door after she entered her childhood home.

She walked down the long entrance hall to the family library, the second last door on the left. The door was open and Kima could hear her father humming inside. He seemed to be in a good mood.

"Hi, Pa, it's me, Kima," she called as she entered the room. The bright midday light gave it an orange glow. As a child, she had loved to play hide and seek here, with rows and rows of tall bookshelves to hide behind. A little deeper, behind a massive table made of some kind of red wood, sat her father.

His short, curly brown hair was neatly styled, each curl perfectly placed. He wore a leaf-green tweed vest and jacket as usual; a chain dangled from a middle button and curved around his slightly rounded belly to his right vest pocket. She knew there was a watch at the end, an intricate timepiece that showed not only the hours, but also the days, the seasons and the years. She knew that because it had been a gift from her for his birthday five years ago. It had been one of her first inventions, and it made her heart all warm and wobbly to know he had kept it in his pocket since the day she had given it to him.

"Oh, what a pleasant surprise!" Gundor jumped down from his chair, hugged Kima and kissed her on the forehead. "Would you like some tea?" Gundor led her to a sitting area next to the floor-to-ceiling stained-glass window that showed a view of the immaculately manicured courtyard with the other flying islands of Karaz and the western end of the Kuana mountain range in the background.

"Sure, and some cookies if you have them." Kima sat down in one of the leather wingback chairs. Her father grinned at her knowingly.

"Yes, of course there are cookies. What brings you here?" Gundor poured her a cup of tea.

"Can't I just come by for a little chat and some cookies?" Kima took a sip of her tea.

"You're always welcome, but I know you well enough to see that you're not just coming by for a chat today. You look worried." Her father studied her, taking in her expression and posture. "Kima, you know that we're always here for you. We know that the rebirth of Bon has been difficult for you. If there is anything we can do to help, just tell us."

"I know, Pa, it's just..." Kima struggled to find the right words. She didn't want to tell her parents that she had quit her job. "It's just not the same without Bon at work. I miss him and his inventive spirit. I thought maybe I could go on vacation and visit Resh. Get some inspiration at the magic shop over there, maybe find some things Rembry wants to add to her collection. Some new kind of golem or something." Kima tried to put on a confident smile, but her father saw right through it.

"I doubt Rembry would let you go for so long. Lady Saasar told me she has placed quite an order for new golems. I understand that this must be a lot of pressure, but we thought this was what you wanted, to create new magical things." Gundor took another cookie from the tray.

Kima couldn't take this polite talk any longer. She had to do something—break out, leave and find a way that made sense to her. "Pa, I quit my job. It's not what I wanted to do at all. I wanted to experiment, create something no one had ever seen before. To be an inventor, not a mechanic." She let out a long, deep breath. "I want to go away, see something new, get inspired, and maybe find a new job, or build something on my own, like you and Ma did." Kima stared out the window, where she could make out the shape of the flying island of Resh in the distance. Kima had never been anywhere but in Jazat, and she hadn't even been out of the city very often. *Travel. I want to travel, explore.*

"I'm not surprised you quit. Rembry is not the easiest person to work with." Gundor paused. "Your mother and I built this trading empire from the ground up, through hard work and determination. We still hope you'll want to be a part of it, perhaps even run it after our deaths, until we find our way back to it when we are reborn. If you're willing to do that, we can give you some time for your efforts. We could build you a laboratory in the backyard, next to your mother's greenhouse, and we could give you some gold to travel with, but when you come back, you will work as a merchant. What do you think?" Gundor looked at her expectantly.

What other option did she have at this point? Maybe there would be a way out in the end, a solution she couldn't quite see at the moment, but which would show up like an automaton knight in shining armor.

14

Sineth

It had been three days since they left the village, but it felt much longer. The days had been hard travel through rough terrain, accompanied by harsh, icy winds, and today it began to snow—not just a few graceful snowflakes, but heavy snow. The weather pressed against their bodies as they climbed up the mountainside, so close to the summit. Each step was a chance to slip and fall. Their vision was obscured as the force of the snow pressed into their faces, making it numb and difficult to open their eyes.

But the nights had been different. From the moment Avala had cuddled up to him in front of the tent, Sineth hadn't been able to keep his hands off her. This woman was intoxicating. He didn't know what it was about her, but Sineth felt drawn to her like a fly to a spider's web. When he wasn't with her, he thought about her, felt the need to look over his shoulder to see if she was still there or if it had all been a dream. Somehow it felt unreal, as if the events of the past two weeks had been the hallucination of a madman.

At dusk, they reached the top of the mountain, their destination. It was somewhere around here that he had stopped his search on his previous journey and rescued Avala. The steadily falling snow had turned into a real storm. Centimeter by centimeter, he pulled himself along the rocky side of the mountain. The entrance to this cave should be here somewhere. Suddenly, his hand lost its grip and he slipped and fell.

For a few moments, he thought this must be the end of his life, falling down a cliff until he hit the ground somewhere in the valley below. But instead of falling off a mountain, he fell face first onto a stone floor. Pain pulsed through his cheek and jawbone. Slowly, he pushed himself to a kneeling position. Blood dripped onto the ice- and snow-covered cave floor.

"Are you all right?" Avala asked from behind him. She brushed a hand across his back.

"I don't know. I have to see if something is broken." Sineth crawled deeper into the cave until he reached the far end.

What a great tracker I am, not even seeing the entrance to a cave. Carefully he leaned against the wall. It was pitch black. Sineth tore off a small piece of his scarf and pressed it to his nose to stop the bleeding. With his other hand, he began to draw a sigil on the ground beside him, muttering the words "Ignar-Ifner-Math" and snapping his fingers at the end. The sigil burst into bright red flames. Sineth shifted a bit to get some distance from the magical fire.

"Should I check your face? I had some medical training in Gahaal," Avala said, sitting right next to him.

Sineth drew in a sharp breath. "Man, I didn't see you there."

"Sorry, I traced my way along the side of the cave to find you in the dark." Avala looked at him worriedly, her features all soft and emotional.

Does she have feelings for me? It looks like she cares about me. Wants to care for me. Do I want to be cared for? That makes things a lot more complicated, that's for sure. I don't want to break another woman's heart. But I don't want to be separated from her either. What is this?

"Did you hear that?" She stared at the cave entrance. Sineth followed her gaze. There was nothing visible, but he had heard it, too. Like a growl or a rumble from somewhere outside. The sound cut unmistakably through the noisy storm—it must be something big. Maybe a bear, or something worse.

They waited a moment in complete silence, but nothing happened.

He turned back to Avala. "If you want, you can check my face. I think the bleeding has stopped, but my cheekbone hurts a lot."

"I'll try to be gentle." Avala began to feel slowly along his cheekbone from ear to nose, trying to see if she could feel any cracks in the bone.

"It feels like it's just bruised." Avala let go of his face. "There it is again! Even louder this time. A growl, did you hear it?" They both turned back to look at the cave entrance, half expecting to see some sort of predator approaching. But what they saw was far worse. Where they had found their way into the cave, there was now a wall of snow. They had only been in here for a few minutes, certainly not enough time to block the entire entrance with snow.

"No beast. That growl must have been a snow slide from the top of the mountain." Avala crawled forward and inspected the wall. She began to pound against it, then pushed with her shoulder. "It doesn't give at all." Avala sank back to the ground, her eyes still on the wall. "We're trapped. We can't get out."

Sineth didn't know how much time had passed since they had been trapped. The wall of snow and ice was thick enough to prevent any light from entering the cave. The pulsing pain in his cheekbone had stopped some time ago. It still felt swollen and every touch hurt like hell, but it felt much better than before. From time to time he or Avala tried to push against the icy wall, but it didn't move at all.

"How much food and water do we have left?" Avala asked.

"About three days' worth." Sineth snapped his fingers absentmindedly. Small flames flickered and disappeared. Avala looked at the flame curiously.

"Oh, I know that look by now. What question troubles you? Just ask," Sineth said, the corners of his mouth instinctively forming a broad smile, but he winced as the pain in his cheek stung.

"When did you discover your magic?" Avala asked.

"That's a long and sad story, but I guess we have nothing else to do." Sineth thought back to his childhood, the wonderful life he'd had. Loving parents, a sweet little sister. "I was a boy. My only concern was getting enough free time to finish building my tree house in the woods behind my parents' house. One day I got up from the lunch table and started to work on it, but my father stopped me and told me to help him fix the roof. Some tiles had come loose and fell down. I didn't care about some stupid roof tiles, so I started yelling at my dad and he got mad and told me that if I didn't behave, I wouldn't be allowed to go to my tree house anymore. I just remember screaming and running out with my fists clenched."

Sineth looked down at his hands. "I ran into the woods and hid for hours. I knew my father would be furious if I came back. So I waited until it was almost dark. As I got closer to our home, I smelled burned wood, and then I saw the flames, the smoke rising high into the darkening sky." He paused, swallowed, and pushed back the tears that were beginning to cloud his vision. "They all died that day. My parents, my sister, and a big part of me. I was taken to an orphanage and sent to the School of Remembrance. I began to remember bits and pieces of my past lives, and I discovered my magical abilities. When I saw the flames coming from my hands, it all made sense. My parents didn't die from lightning that hit the roof, or the oven that exploded for some strange reason. It was me. I must have ignited some flammable object in the house when I stormed out in a rage. I killed them, all of them."

Sineth's expression was blank. Such a long time had passed since then. Many human lives had begun and ended. His parents could have been born and died again, depending on which bodies they had reincarnated in.

"I only told one other person, but he is dead for good," Sineth added, grinning lopsided at Avala, trying to push away the sadness that was rising inside him. The pain of that memory always pierced his heart like a dagger. Usually, his cheerful facade came effortlessly, but with this pain, he had to squeeze it out like the juice of a lime.

Avala reached out and pulled him into a hug. "It's not your fault. You didn't mean it. They would tell you the same if you met them now."

"You don't know that, and you don't know me, not really. Not everyone is nice and reasonable. I burned them alive, that's something that is hard to forgive," Sineth said as he freed himself from her arms. He didn't want to be comforted. He deserved to feel bad about it. He wouldn't forgive himself for killing his family, not now and not in the future. In the course of his lives, this was the worst thing he had ever done. And there were so many things he regretted. So much pain he had caused. *I should have been the one to be sacrificed, not Molna. The world would be better for it.*

"Well, I told you my most painful memory, what is yours?" Sineth tried to find a way out of this emotional storm, but all he could see was his burning home, mixed with the pain of his bruised face.

"There are a few, the death of my best friend being the most recent. But I think the most painful one is from my first life. I was human, married to the love of my life, or so I thought. We were both young adults, eager to see the continent, to travel and explore. Then I got pregnant, and he had a hard time accepting that we wouldn't be able to take off and go into the wild together. A few weeks passed, and he began to come around to the idea of us becoming a family. We were happy, decorating a nursery, thinking of possible names. And then I lost the baby. I was in agony. He couldn't stand my pain and told me to move on, but I couldn't. I thought, *Will we ever have another child now that this one is lost?* He said he couldn't take the pressure and the pain anymore, so he left. He left me alone with my grief, the grief of a lost child that should have been ours." Avala looked thoughtfully into the darkness of the cave. "I have never been a mother. Over the many years and lives I've lived, I've learned to avoid it. I don't want that pain again. I don't want to be dependent on a man. Bound to someone who doesn't care." Avala looked at him, both hatred and pain reflected in her eyes. The look of a wound that would never heal.

Sineth stared into the empty space in front of him.

That's why this feels so familiar. The way I'm drawn to her, the way I feel when I'm with her. It's me—she is talking about me. I'm the man who left her. I'm her pain.

15

Avala

She poked her head in front of Sineth. He was still staring a hole in the air. Had she shared too much? Avala had thought after the story he had told her hers would be a piece of cake, but maybe she was wrong. What if he had had a similar experience and she had opened an old wound?

"Are you okay? You look a little... horrified." Avala touched the unbruised side of his face and turned his head slightly toward hers. "I'm sorry if I overshared. There's so much on my mind, sometimes it just bubbles out like an overflowing pot of milk. Or is it your own past that haunts you? I've heard of mages in Karaz who have the ability to change the minds of others. Sometimes I think about finding them and getting rid of all the pain. But it's also a part of me, and I'm not sure which part I'd be getting rid of, if that makes sense?"

Sineth shook his head slightly and looked into her eyes. She wasn't sure how to interpret his expression. "It's okay. Sorry, I..." He stopped for a second and stared at her. "The pain in my cheekbone came back and I felt this sting in my head. I should probably try to get some sleep," Sineth added, ignoring her talk about altering minds as he lay down on his bedroll.

He really is a strange guy. Sometimes I feel so close to him, like an old friend. And then, at times like this, he's a complete stranger. I think he's lying. It's definitely more than just a headache.

Avala lay down; maybe she should get some rest as well. The wall of snow would at least keep the icy wind from freezing her to a solid block during her night's rest.

Suddenly she had a thought. She got up in a sitting position. "Sineth, you should set fire to the wall! It'll melt it down and we can get out. I don't know why we didn't think of that before," Avala said, her eyes wide with excitement.

"That's a great idea. Let's try it, but we have to be careful. If the tunnel is too big, the mass on top could collapse it again," Sineth said with a crooked half smile. He didn't seem to be in pain anymore as he crawled to the entrance of the cave and began to conjure fire in his hands. As he pressed his flaming palms against the lower part of the wall, still kneeling on the ground, the ice gradually gave way.

"Do you think it will hold? I'm afraid it might crash down on us and bury us in snow," Avala said.

"Honestly, I don't know. This is the first time I've burned myself out of a snow wall. But I really hope it'll hold," Sineth replied, his voice tense.

"Let's hope then."

It took some time—they didn't know how long—but slowly the fire began to melt the icy wall of snow. Avala felt hot and dizzy from the lack of oxygen in the cave. Everything was wet and slippery. But then they heard the sound of the wind, and a moment later fresh air flowed inside. They smiled at each other, and Sineth drew his hand in one last wide arc across the ice to reveal the outside.

After digging and pushing through about four feet of slightly melted ice and snow, they were finally out, and the tunnel did not collapse. It must have been early in the morning, the hues of the past night giving way to the colorful expanse of the sky, no clouds in sight. The cold, fresh air stung her lungs. Avala stood up and took a long breath. She felt like she could sleep for a day, but she would not go back into that cave and be buried alive.

In the distance, she could make out the shapes of the Madin Islands. The large one to the left had been her home for so long. Suddenly she missed it deeply—the white stone buildings with the pretty golden roofs, the smell of freshly baked raisin bread. Avala even missed her comrades and standing around for hours at the port. Actually, she had enjoyed being a Stormguard very much. Having a purpose, helping others, controlling the elements, and simply being a part of something bigger than herself. And she missed the griffons. Nothing felt more like true freedom than flying through the sky on the back of those majestic creatures.

Behind her, Sineth emerged from the cave, carrying their bags. He offered Avala hers, and she slung it over her shoulders.

"I don't know about you, but I'm not staying in this cave another minute," Sineth said, putting on his backpack. "The weather looks good, and I think we should be close to the entrance of the Dark Kingdom." Sineth checked the surroundings and then looked up at the opposite mountaintop. "What in the elements is that?"

Avala followed Sineth's gaze.

Out of the mountaintop, where they suspected the entrance to this hidden kingdom must be, came a black cloud. Smoke-like, but thicker, it grew larger and larger. Reluctantly, she moved back into the cave, but the fear of whatever came out of that mountain was far greater than the fear of staying in the cave a little longer. Sineth seemed to have the same feeling, for he followed her, and they squeezed into the tunnel, watching the cloud expand. In just a few minutes, it had consumed almost everything around them.

Avala crept out a bit to see how far it went. Her attention was drawn back to the mountaintop when she heard loud screams—a familiar sound, squealing, screaming, growling.

There it was, only about fifty feet from them, the dragon-like beast she had seen the day of the battle in Parhat. On top of it were two shapes, a female, curvaceous, almost as dark as her surroundings, and a man, blond, with horns growing from his head. When he turned, Avala saw his face. Garon. Definitely Garon, but different, a nightmare version of him. One half of his face was normal, the other demonic, grotesque and terrifying. Both were illuminated from above, the colorful light of the elemental sphere enveloping them in an eerie glow.

What have they done to you? She wanted to call out to him, but stopped, unable to form the words. They flew off into the distance, in the direction she had seen her home moments before. Then they were gone, covered in shadows. There was only darkness beyond the mountains. A black void.

Avala felt Sineth tug on her arm. "Avala, look!" He pointed back at the mountain. They stood and stared into the darkness. Out of the mountain came many different shapes, hordes of those dragon-like creatures. Huge, lumbering hulks of men, their battle-ready armor bearing the mark of the white crown she had seen so long ago on the small creatures that had burned away. All sorts of dark folk wandered and flew, flooding the mountainside. They were so close, too close.

"We have to run," Sineth whispered to her. "Now!"

16

Garon

The wind pressed hard against his face. Icy air filled his lungs to the point where he felt like his body was about to freeze. They were flying high in the sky, dangerously close to the elemental sphere. Garon heard the rumble of thunder and the rush of water directly above him. It was a strange sight to see all the elements so intertwined. Water and Fire swirled around each other like they were performing a little dance. Lightning pulsed through them like veins, not affecting either at all.

He held on tightly to Venja, pressing his legs against the scaly skin of this dragon creature. In the distance, he could make out the shape of Gahaal in the darkness. Below them were the last lights of the Great Wasteland of Lhudar before they reached the edge of the mainland—they were close. Garon didn't know exactly what Venja's plans to invade the capital of Madin were. Probably chaos and a show of power.

"What kind of creature is this, exactly?" Garon asked, staring at the landscape below.

"It's a wyvern, a dragon-like creature, but it lacks their intellect and two arms," Venja replied, smiling at him. "We're almost there. How does it feel to return to your home?"

"Strange. I'm not sure it's my home anymore," Garon said. Buildings, parks, streets, and small shapes moving in the darkness came into view. He had been to all of these places a thousand times, and yet it felt like he was entering foreign territory. "What is your plan?"

"To liberate them, to give them a queen and a new way of life. One that doesn't exclude anyone from the use of magic and doesn't limit the endless possibilities it brings. Power and freedom for the people, who could say no to that?" Venja looked at him with an intense gaze, her smile widening into a mischievous grin.

"What if they don't want to be freed? I know some people who want to live their lives as they always have. What if they don't obey your orders?" Garon tried to find the right words, words that would neither provoke her nor ask so much that she would not answer at all.

"I will do it as I have done it for hundreds of years. They obey or they die. When they are reborn, they may choose a different path," Venja said, her sneer fading as she turned her head to look down.

They began to descend. For the people below, they must have looked like a growing shadow of doom.

As they approached the ground, Garon heard shouts and screams. People began to run from them, and when they finally landed near the Temple of Water, there was no one on the street. They climbed down from the wyvern and began walking through the city. More and more of the Dark Horde landed, and a few minutes later the place was swarming with their allies. Garon had told Venja everything he knew about the city and its defenses, about the Elemental Guard and their magical abilities and how they would use them in case of an invasion—basically, he'd told her everything he wasn't supposed to tell anyone outside the Guard.

A battle unfolded before him. Members of every Elemental Order attacked the invaders. Bolts of fire and lightning shot through the city, and the rest fought with whatever was at hand. The streets flooded with Venja's shadow soldiers, ghost-like creatures that sucked the life out of their opponents. People were hurled through the air and smashed against buildings. Many were already on the ground, unmoving, as the Dark Horde cut down their enemies with brute force. The Elementals had underestimated them, and now they were scurrying away, shot down by dark magical beams. The battle was over in a matter of minutes. This elite force that Garon had once trained with had been beaten down and forced into hiding.

A few moments later, his love, Venja, spoke to his old people, her voice echoing unnaturally loud through the city. "Dear people of Gahaal, I am Venja, Queen of the Dark, and I have come here today to offer you freedom, acceptance, no matter what race you are or what abilities you have. The choice to live your lives on your own terms, as equals. Who here would like that?"

Slowly, a few people came out of hiding and looked around the dark streets. Some lit torches and started to walk up the steps of the main road that led through the four wards of Gahaal. In the center of each ward stood a temple of one of the elements. The highest was the Air Ward, and at its apex was the Southport, which served traffic to and from Parhat.

It could work. She could win over the majority of the people.

The second he finished that thought, a woman ran out of a nearby alley, screaming bloody murder with an axe in her hand. Her voice trailed off and she fell dead to the ground. Out of the corner of his eye he saw Venja clenching her fist.

"Does anyone else feel the need to attack me? If so, please try now so we can move on," Venja said, her voice still full and loud, filling every corner of his home city. A long, silent moment passed. Tension hung heavy in the air. "No? I thought so. So these are your options: One, you could come out and try to murder me, which would result in certain death. Two, you could come out and live happily among us. Or three, you could hide in your holes until you run out of food and water and then consider options one or two. As I've said before, you have the power of choice now. It's your life, you decide what you want to do with it." After that, Venja sat down on a stone bench in front of the temple and waited.

Garon sat beside her on the bench. A thick silence surrounded them, broken only by the mournful whistle of the wind as it blew through the deserted streets of Gahaal. Scattered about were members of Venja's army, their appearance grim, their bearing resolute. Draped in dark armor emblazoned with the crest of the white crown, each wore the sinister insignia with its menacing, inwardly curving serrations. They wielded a variety of weapons, from axes and pikes to hammers. Some also carried small, curved daggers imbued with strange enchantments that could drain the life force from their enemies, much as he could now with a mere flick of his wrist.

When time passed without any sign of movement, Garon broke the silence. "What now? How long do we wait for them to come out?"

"Well, I'm not known for my patience, so now we move on to plan B. Strike one of their options," Venja said, pulling his chin toward her and kissing his lips. "Pull them out of their holes and bring them to the temple!" Venja commanded, her voice magically vibrating through the streets.

The people of Gahaal were pushed into lines, and one by one they were asked to choose an option. One line before Venja, one line before him. Garon stood there, his mind going blank. He looked at Venja.

"One or two, what will it be?" Venja asked a small boy. He couldn't have been more than four years old.

"You are very beautiful. I want to live," he begged.

"Oh, you are so sweet. Good choice, little one." Venja ruffled his hair, and off he went to the lower part of town.

Venja looked at Garon with an intense stare. Her eyes seemed to sparkle in the dark. He looked back at the line in front of him. Hundreds of people. He asked them one by one, and to his great relief, every one of them chose to live. Until a man with neatly combed short black hair stood before him, grinning. There was no sign of weariness on him, not a crease in his Stormguard robes, the silk flowing flawlessly to his ankles. Not a single thread rose from the seams that covered the hem.

"I have chosen to die for my country. Are you going to kill me now, Garon?" the man asked.

I feel I know this person. A distant memory... or a dream? Garon thought, looking at the men in front of him. They must have been comrades, but he couldn't remember much about them.

"Have you lost your mind? Is this what will happen to all of us? I mean, look at you! What have they done to you?" The man's smile had turned into a worried frown.

"Garon, my love." Venja was beside him, taking his hand and stroking the scaled side of his face. She looked deep into his eyes. "Do not listen to him. You are his king. And what do we do with disobedient subjects?" She squeezed his hand once. "We crush them."

"Come on, Garon, do it then, crush your dear friend Pentho. You have never defeated me in anything. Try it now." The man named Pentho raised his fists and took a defensive stance, ready for a fight.

Garon looked at him, his eyes starting to get wet—for no reason, it seemed. He uttered the words "Vereth-Meduc-Exeth" and hooked the index and middle fingers of both hands. With a snap, he pulled them apart and the man fell dead to the ground. A pale-skinned behemoth of an ogre came from the side, and, with a low grunt, lifted the corpse from the ground by the leg and carried it to the side.

For a moment, Garon felt a memory bubble up inside him, but then it was gone. "Next!"

Garon stood at the pier of Parhat and stared into the distance. Plumes of smoke rose into the sky over Gahaal. Parts of the city were ablaze. He could still hear their screams in his head, see them running and hiding, and the face of the man grinning at him. His hands began to shake and he felt a searing pain in his head.

What did she do? Why didn't I stop her? The questions circled in his head, over and over again. Why hadn't he done anything? This was his home, his people. Garon had become a night terror. Children fled screaming when they saw him coming. He knew he looked different, even terrifying, but had this change affected his mind as well? Maybe even his soul? Why hadn't he remembered the man and felt anything when he killed him?

Garon shook his head. He felt like he was going to be sick.

This is not what I want. None of this is what I want.

Out of the corner of his eye he saw Venja coming towards him. She hugged him from behind and kissed his neck. "My king, how do you like the look of your new kingdom? I think you did very well today. Let's go inside and celebrate our victory."

"How many died today?" Garon whispered.

"Only a few. Some tried option one, but most were wise enough to take option two and obey. After all, it was their choice. We have replaced the guards with our own, but if the people of Gahaal prove to be loyal, they can work for us as our subjects. They are part of our people now." Venja stroked his chest and belly, slowly moving her hand down. "I'm in the mood to celebrate. Don't make me wait too long."

Garon felt her hands disappear and turned around. She was gone, simply vanished from sight. Somehow he felt both drawn to seek her out and relieved that she was gone.

He closed his eyes. *Focus, Garon, focus.* Deep in his mind he searched for all the happy memories of his life. He tried to calm his breathing, to shake off the tension in his body, just as he had learned so many years ago in the School of Remembrance. *Guide your mind through meditation. Find your happy place and let the memories come to you.* But all he could see were the empty eyes of men, women, and children whose lives had been taken from them. He had done this, he had helped her do these terrible things. She had said there were only a few, but there had been piles of bodies in the end. Hundreds of people, his people, had chosen death over a life with them, a life in darkness and despair.

I don't know what she's done to me, but this is not who I am. I have to leave. Preferably without her noticing right away. But I can't wait.

Garon checked his surroundings. He saw a few griffons tied up in an open stable. Three orc guards were stationed around it.

The best thing would be to do the bold thing and just walk straight up to them. "I need to go to Gahaal. Release one of the griffons," Garon said as demandingly as he could.

The orcs looked at each other. "Yes, my king," the middle one spat out and started to untie one of the griffons.

A few moments later, Garon was in the air again, stroking the feathers of this beautiful creature. That was one of the things he had in common with Avala; they both loved to fly.

Garon wondered where this thought came from. He had not thought of Avala for a long time. It felt good, light and happy. It felt like hope.

17

Sineth

His muscles ached. His knees felt like they would snap like twigs at any second. They stumbled through the darkness as fast as they could, clinging to the edge of the mountain; a fall from this height would be fatal. It had taken them over a day to get from the valley to the mountaintop, and now they were racing back down as fast as they could. *It's a good thing I've already walked this path three times, otherwise I wouldn't know where to go in this element-forsaken darkness.*

The cliff gave way under his hand, almost toppling him over. Avala grabbed his shoulder and pulled him back. *And now I've tripped over my own words.*

"Be careful. It's no use running down if you're dead before we get to the bottom," Avala said, letting out a few heavy breaths.

"I think there's another cave here. I lost my hold on the wall." Sineth inspected the area where he had lost his grip, squinting his eyes to see what was there in the darkness. "Let's go in and pause for a moment."

"I don't think it would be wise to stop now. Besides, if I sit down, I'm not sure I'll be able to get up again. Let's just get off this mountain and hide in the forest of Ithdir," Avala replied.

"You're right, I'm just exhausted." Sineth began to inch his way forward until he found the edge of the cliff again.

The hours stretched longer and longer as they tried to re-trace the exact path they had taken before, running as fast as their feet would allow along the snow-covered path that led down the mountain. It wasn't an easy task, with darkness obscuring most of the landmarks around them and the fear of there not being solid ground under the snow.

It had taken them three days to travel from the Resistance village to the top of the mountain. Now, despite the darkness, they had managed to travel the entire distance back to the forest of Ithdir in the same time it had taken them to climb up, including crossing the Olom River and the Edge Pass Road that connected Emril in the south with Penhir in the north. On the other hand, they had been on their hands and knees for the last few miles because of the blizzard, so their accomplishment was somewhat dampened by that.

But it had taken its toll. Every part of his body was screaming, begging him to stop and rest. When they reached the forest, it felt like a sanctuary. It took them another half hour before they felt they were deep enough to avoid immediate capture. When they found a field of blueberry bushes, they lay down flat on the ground and huddled together for cover.

"What are we going to do? I don't understand what's going on. I saw Garon on that flying beast with a woman. He looked different, like..." Avala paused.

"Like what?" Sineth whispered.

"Like a demon," Avala replied, staring at the treetops above.

"There are no such things as demons, Avala. It's just a story, something adults make up to scare children and keep them from wandering into the woods or the depths of the mountains." Sineth looked at Avala, studying her expression. He couldn't see much; the strange magical darkness felt even darker than the darkest of nights.

As they lay there in silence, Sineth wondered if this could still be a good thing for the Resistance. They had wanted a change of leadership in Madin for a long time. Sineth didn't know much about Venja, but he had heard that she was a respected and fair queen.

Suddenly he heard voices, grunts and shouts. He froze under the bush. They were already here.

"Faster, you useless scum! The queen said the village of the Resistance was somewhere in the swamp," a high-pitched voice shouted.

"I'm tired. The little maggots won't flee if we take a short rest. They don't know what's coming," another squeaky voice pleaded.

"Let me through! I know the way. Venja wants to get rid of them all, every last one of the Resistance, and destroy their little village. They had their chance to join us, but they chose not to. I say we storm in and burn it all down. And we move now. Her order was to go straight from the mountain to the village," a dark, deep voice shouted from further behind. A very familiar voice…

Gorth. The orc who had visited Sineth a few weeks ago. *They want us dead?* Sineth had to do something. Warn the others, help them escape. But how? He was stuck here under a bush, and if they found him, he certainly wouldn't be able to help the Resistance. Maybe if he crawled under the bushes until he was out of sight, he could get around them. Sineth knew every inch of this forest and swamp, even in the dark, and he could take a shortcut.

"Avala, follow me," he whispered, just loud enough for her to hear.

"What? Are you crazy? They'll find us."

"I have to go and warn the others in the village. If you wish to stay, it's your choice." Sineth began to pull himself slowly through the dirt. To his surprise, Avala followed.

The grunts and shouts of the Dark Horde filled the air around them. The ground was a frozen block of ice. At least they didn't have to drag themselves through the mud; that would have been a much harder task. They slowly crawled forward. Every now and then he stopped to feel the bark of a tree, finding the mossy side of the trunk to make sure they were still going in the right direction—north. Eventually, the voices faded and it was almost quiet. He could hear the wind rushing through the trees.

"I think we're good. Let's get up and run." Sineth poked his head out of the bushes. No one was in sight. He pushed himself to a standing position and offered Avala a hand. "We must move fast now. I hope it will take them a while to find the right way through the swamp. This is our only chance to get to the village before they do."

"Then let's go."

He was impressed with her determination. She hadn't been with them very long, but it seemed she was as invested in this as he was.

Then he turned and ran as fast as he could, leaping over roots and vines. The air burned his lungs. An hour passed, then they reached the edge of the Dread Pool Marshes. He paused for a moment to check the area for the Dark Horde and crocodiles, but there was no way he could see anything at a distance in this darkness. He had to rely on his intuition and his hearing. But the only thing he could make out was his own heavy breathing and the murmur of water from the nearby Olom River. He had reached exactly the place he had hoped for. The Dark Horde must have chosen to head for the western edge of the forest, circling the Resistance village in a wide arc. Sineth decided to follow the banks of the Olom River north-east for about two miles into the swamp. This was the quickest and safest route to the village, avoiding the croc breeding grounds to the west.

Despite the lack of light, he almost flew through the swamp, making his way from one high point to the next. He had traveled this path many times and knew every puddle and every rock. Sometimes he would stop and listen to see if Avala was still there. She followed in his steps without incident. After about four miles, the rocks grew larger, forming columns that looked a bit like stalagmites, growing out of the muddy ground, their jagged outlines faintly discernible in the dark.

It's not far now, he thought, picking up the pace again. One by one, he could make out the stone spires of his home. They had finally reached the village. He could have shouted in triumph. They had been the first to arrive.

"Avala, run to every hut on the left and tell them it's a Code Croc. They'll know what to do." Sineth didn't wait for her answer; he was already on his way.

Half an hour later, the whole Resistance finally made their way into the depths of the swamp to the east. Fog was ubiquitous in this area, though they could see little of it now because of the darkness; it might help them escape. It seemed that their pursuers were unaffected by the darkness, so perhaps the fog would work in their favor and provide some cover.

Sineth led them forward. Every step had to be taken with caution in these parts, but they also had to be quick. It had taken them too long to get going. The Dark Horde would reach the village any minute. It wasn't easy to lead over two hundred people through a swamp full of monsters in the dark, or lead them anywhere at all. There were reports of creatures beyond crocodiles; some claimed to have seen serpent men at the north-west edge of the swamp.

A moment later he heard familiar screams, squeaks and low grunts behind him. Sineth picked up the pace. Then there were screams in the darkness, hisses, growls, and splashes of water. The Dark Horde had found one of the crocs. That would hopefully buy the Resistance some time.

Sineth made his way to the eastern edge of the mainland, where he'd set up markers to guide them to the bridge. He had driven a stick into the ground every thirty feet. When he'd devised this plan, he'd thought that Madin was the only problem they would have to escape from. How the tide had turned.

When he reached the edge, he looked down into the void of nothingness. At the far bottom, he could see the glittering light of the elemental sphere. For a moment, he had the strange feeling that he wanted to jump. Shaking his head to clear his mind, he concentrated and searched for the rope he'd tied around the post beside him, hidden in the murky water of the swamp. It took far longer than he remembered to pull the rope tight and secure it to the post again. As the wooden bridge was revealed from the depths below, he felt a tingling sensation at the back of his neck. He turned to see everyone staring at him.

Quinn was the first to speak. "You want us to go over that? Is it safe?"

"I've tried it before. It's safe. At least it's safer than waiting for the Dark Horde to find us." Sineth walked towards the bridge. Before he stepped on it, he turned back. "Maybe it's better if we go one at a time." He offered a confident smile, but their expressions showed their fear.

It was a brisk five-minute walk across the bridge. Sineth couldn't see the end of it, but soon he reached the tree trunks he'd tied the bridge to. As he finished crossing, he realized that Avala had followed close behind.

"You didn't wait for me to get off the bridge," Sineth observed.

"How was I to know that you had reached the other end? And if we go one at a time, we'll never make it before they reach us."

She was right. Now he regretted going first. He should have stayed behind and made sure everyone got across safely. Now all he could do was hope that they would make it in time, that the bridge would hold, and that whatever awaited them would be kinder.

18

Kima

The smell of beer-soaked wood was disgusting. Everyone in the room seemed to be drunk. In the far corner of the room, a couple, two halfling men, were talking giddily, kissing and teasing each other. *Will I ever find someone like that? Someone to be so excited about?*

Kima found an empty table near the entrance, hoping someone would come in and let in some fresh winter air. After making herself comfortable, she pulled out her newly purchased map of Dohva. Slowly, she traced the main roads with her finger. There was so much more to explore. She had only ever been to Karaz, and even there she had hardly left Jazat at all. This whole country was a mystery to her, a shiny new object to be examined from every angle.

For the first time in her life, Kima felt free. Free to do what she really wanted, without her parents in the background reminding her of her duty as their daughter to step into line when the time came to secure her empire. But that was their dream, not hers. They had always given her the subliminal feeling that it did not matter what she did with her time, with her life really, as long as she was ready to carry on their business in the end. Despite all that, she truly loved them. They had been wonderful parents, and she had received all the love and support a child could ask for. And again, they had given her money to do what she wanted to do. *Endless lives, endless money, but no meaning... and no one to share it with.*

Kima had been in Resh for a few days now. First she'd explored the city and found a cheap inn to lodge in—she wanted to make the most of the money her parents had given her—and then the darkness had struck. Every corner of Resh was filled with rumors about what it meant, where it came from, and what to do about it.

Just yesterday, she had overheard two older men at a fruit stand arguing about the end of peace between the Karaz and Madin peoples. "There will be a war, Keth, I can feel it in my bones. We have had a long ride on the side of peace, but the wind is turning. Can you smell it? Ha, can you?"

The other man had thrust his chin forward and let out a grunt of disapproval. "The only thing I can feel is the chill of winter creeping through this miserable darkness, and the only thing I can smell is your rancid farts, you old bugger. There will be no war, I'm sure of it. Who would want to fight Baldor Immos? No, no, no, it won't happen."

The other gave a grim sidelong glance at that, huffed, and raised his bony shoulders. "Ha, you feel your things, I feel mine. We'll see who's right in the end, won't we, Keth?"

War or no war, to her, it felt like her newfound freedom was being snatched away right before her eyes. She had been so close, buying this map, making plans to visit Madin. There was even a group of merchants who wanted to sell goods to Riptar, which was very rare because Madin didn't want to trade with Karaz. They'd said they would take her, but now everything had come to a standstill. *What is going on in this world? Can't a young halfling have some fun for once?*

With a squeak, the door opened and two figures entered the room. One was a tall male elf with piercing blue eyes, one of which was almost crossed by a long scar. His head was covered with a mop of wild black shaggy hair. The other was a female elf with a messy black braid that came down almost to her waist on one side; the opposite half was shaved down to her skull. But the strangest thing about her was the tattoo on her face, starting from between her eyes and covering her whole forehead. Kima had never seen anything like that before. It looked quite nice. Special. They both looked like they had been in the wild for a long time.

The woman turned and looked at her. Kima froze; she guessed she was staring at them a little too hard, something her mother had always told her to stop. *It's rude; people don't like it when you stare. It gives them the impression that something is wrong,* her ma would say, but Kima was just curious about so many things. She didn't even mean to stare; it just happened when she was deep in thought. Which actually happened a lot.

"I'm sorry. May we join you at your table?" the woman inquired.

Kima looked around the room; it was fairly empty. Why would they want to sit at her table?

"Sure, have a seat," Kima said with a hopefully neutral voice, but her face must have shown her confusion.

"We've just been on the outskirts for a long time. It would be nice if we could get a chance to talk about the recent events in the city. My name is Avala, and this is Sineth," Avala said, sitting down next to her.

She is so beautiful. Her eyes are so green, her lips are full, and she has this natural elegance about her even in those tattered, muddy clothes.

"I'm afraid I won't be much help. I've only been here a few days. I'm from Jazat." Kima paused and stared into Avala's eyes. "Oh, and my name is Kima."

Avala smiled at her, a warm and friendly half grin. "You're from the capital? We happen to be going there. Do you know where the Magisters' Palace is?"

"Why would you want to go there?" Kima asked, feeling silly because a lot of people wanted to go to the capital and she felt like she was being weird for no reason. *But why are they asking me? Do they know who I am?*

The man, Sineth, leaned into Avala. "Come on, let's go. This is a waste of time," he whispered, not very quietly.

Kima gave him a glare. *I'm sure that's what he wanted me to hear. I don't like this guy. There's just something wrong with him. On the other hand, what do they think of me? Poor halfling girl, sitting all alone, staring at the people having fun around her.*

"We wish to speak of this darkness. We know what is happening, and we seek the Magisters' help. A war is coming to Madin," Avala whispered, covering the side of her mouth with her hand.

"What? A war? With us? Why would they do that? Don't they know how powerful our leader is?" Kima whispered back—a little too loudly, it seemed, for a few heads turned and people looked at her with curiosity in their eyes. But her thoughts returned to the conversation of the elderly men at the fruit stand. *There will be a war, Keth, I can feel it in my bones.*

"I promise to explain, but time is of the essence. Could you travel with us to Jazat and show us the way to the Magisters' Palace? We are not from here, and we need guidance. We know it is a lot to ask of a total stranger in a pub, but we are desperate," Avala explained, wringing her hands on the table.

Back to Jazat. Kima's journey was over before it had begun. But if there really was a war, she wouldn't be able to explore Dohva anyway. "I can take you. My family works for the Magisters, so maybe I can get you an audience."

"Well, look at that. She's not useless after all," Sineth said with a grin.

"I am not useless, and you should stop insulting me, or you can find your way to the Magisters alone," Kima hissed, crossing her arms over her chest. *Stop it, Kima, you're acting like an upset child.*

"As you wish. When can we leave?" Sineth raised his eyebrows but still grinned.

"I don't know what time it is. This darkness is driving me crazy," Kima said.

"It should be around noon," Avala said, looking back at Sineth.

"A good guess. Does it matter?" Sineth asked.

"It does, because the airships leave at a certain time of day," Kima explained.

"Are we going by airship?" Avala's eyes shone with excitement.

"How else would we go?"

19

Garon

Even though he managed to leave, he was in a constant battle with his own mind. Several times Garon had turned around to fly back, and it had taken everything he had to resist the urge. To fight back, to regain power over his own mind. Sometimes, in the silence of the darkness, he thought he could hear her voice in the wind—moaning and hushing, not angry, but sweet and loving. Whispering words of seduction, teasing him. In a moment of weakness, he had given in just a little; he could have sworn he felt her touch on his skin. And when she left his mind, it felt like the air had been sucked out of his lungs. Like she was the essence that kept him alive. It was maddening.

During his flight, he paused every now and then, first to look at the vague outline of the Kuana Mountains, then to find the mountain pass that would lead him through them, and finally to follow the trade road to Xear. After many hours of struggle and travel through pure darkness, Garon saw small, flickering points of light on the horizon. *That must be Xear.* Garon had never been this far north before. Xear was the only Karaz outpost on the main island of Dohva. The rest belonged to Madin.

The lights grew larger and he could see the massive curtain wall surrounding Xear. It was strategically placed in a very open area, with no trees or hills nearby. From the curtain wall, one could see every bit of movement, all the way to the Kuana Mountains, to the eastern wilds behind Ustal, and to the Dread Pool Marshes in the far distance behind Fyre. He had always thought that it was a masterwork of placement. But right now, it was a problem; he had to get past Xear to reach Jazat and get help. He tugged on the griffon's leash to signal it to rise. As they flew higher, the elemental sphere came dangerously close.

With just a few powerful flaps of the griffon's majestic wings, they were almost over Xear. Garon could see the lights below; the curtain wall was well lit. Suddenly, the griffon began to squeak and turn sideways. Garon struggled to control it. *What's going on? Have they spotted us?*

Then he heard it, the sound of a release. Somewhere far below, a ballista must have hurled a great ball of fire at them. Garon tried to control the griffon, to make it fly away, but it refused his will. The next moment, pain engulfed him. Waves of red-hot flames singed his clothes and burned his flesh. But the griffon bore the full brunt of the fiery projectile. Its lower left side had been blown away, leaving only a gaping, burning hole. The griffon was dead, and they began to fall from the sky at a rapid pace. His vision was blurred by the pain pulsing through his left leg. With his new form, he could see perfectly in the dark. But he couldn't escape the darkness that came next. The last thing he felt was his body hitting something hard, but not as hard as he'd imagined a fall from that height would feel.

Slowly, he drifted through his subconscious, seeing images of his many lives merge into one: hugging his mother; holding his firstborn in another life that came before; cradling himself before the last breath of life escaped his lungs. It all formed the shape of Valeria's face, his one love, his queen he had betrayed.

Come back to me. Her voice was in his head again, whispering, soothing. *I forgive you, I love you, you are my king. You are special. You are meant for more. Come back.*

Garon had never thought his life would end like this. In fact, he had hoped it would be his last—that he would achieve enough to be chosen for the Ritual of Enlightenment. Garon's plan had been to seize this life to the fullest, give it his best, and then die for the last time.

Another sting of pain hit him, right in the face. He slowly opened his eyes, blinking in the sudden light. His hands and legs were tied to a chair. *Not again*, Garon thought.

Look what they do to you. They have to obey. They must be punished, Venja whispered in his mind.

How had he become the villain in every man's story? Garon had tried so hard to be good, to be a friend, a leader, someone to count on and look up to, to be worthy to be chosen for the ritual, to be anointed, to become one with the elements, a pure soul. But now what had become of him? A monster, a demon, the enemy?

My king, Valeria whispered.

"Wake up!" Someone slapped his face again.

"I'm alive. How am I alive?" Garon managed to mutter as he came to his senses.

"We caught you in a net, it's a defensive mechanism to catch flying enemies like you. Why were you heading for the capital? What are you?" the raspy voice demanded.

"I seek help against the endless darkness. I was captured by..." Garon tried to say her name.

Venja, the Dark Queen, Garon thought.

Valeria, your love, your queen, Valeria said.

The voices mixed in his head, hers and his. He wasn't sure which was his anymore. He couldn't get the words out. It felt as if he was blocked.

"Captured by whom?" He looked up at a square face. A dwarfish woman, dressed in silver and gray robes and thick, shiny breastplate armor. Her brown hair was braided tightly around her head.

"I was captured and tortured; she made me into this monster. I am Garon Himmon, a Stormguard from Madin. We are not your enemy. You are at war with her," Garon explained, his voice harsh and deep.

"Perhaps, but who is she? Can you tell me that?" the dwarf asked.

"I would like to, but I can't. She must have put some kind of spell on me to prevent me from doing so." Garon sighed; he should tell her about the voices, but he was afraid to say it out loud.

"A spell? Sure. You can plead your case to the Magisters of Karaz. But for now, you will remain in chains, awaiting trial in the prison of Jazat." She paused, then raised an eyebrow. "So you get what you want after all. You can ask them for help if they believe you. Show them respect; they are very wise. The Magisters will know what to make of all this." And then she left him.

20

Avala

Somehow she had expected the airship to look like, well, a normal ship, with a mast and sails and made of wood. But this ship looked like something from another world.

Throughout Resh, she had already discovered strange things she had never seen before—metal constructs of all shapes and sizes, carrying and delivering heavy goods—but this was breathtaking. The entire ship was made of shiny, polished steel, and at each end was a giant, metal-encased stone. Strange-looking iron rods protruded from the ship, forming a cross. Each of them ended in a metal ball that glowed with arcane energy. It just floated there, weightless. *How is it physically possible that a ship of this size—any size, really—made of metal can fly?* Avala thought.

A crew member lowered part of the ship's hull to reveal a railed stairway. One by one, they climbed the stairs, their tickets were checked, and they were allowed to step onto the ship's deck.

"Have you ever seen anything like this? This is incredible," Avala exclaimed to Sineth, who was right behind her.

"I have heard of the many constructions and magical things they create in Jazat, but I could never have imagined this in my wildest dreams," Sineth replied with a wicked grin. Their eyes met, and then his expression returned to neutral, as if he had stopped himself. *Something is strange about him.* She wondered what it could be.

Most of the people pushed past her to a glass dome at the back of the ship. There they went through an open door and disappeared. Only a few remained on the deck, waving and talking to the people left on the dock. Avala went to the front of the ship and tried to get a closer look at the glowing stone.

"You're looking in the wrong direction. Turn around and look at the metal rods; that's where all the magic happens when the ship embarks. Literally," Kima said with excitement in her eyes.

"Okay, thanks for the tip. Do you know how it works?" Avala asked, looking at the crackling little purple bolts of lightning that sparked from the metal orbs.

"Yes, of course I know how it works," Kima replied, looking a little dazzled.

"Sorry, I didn't mean to offend you. For me, it is just a miracle. I've never seen magic work like this before."

"It is certainly complicated, but the two most important things are the Safral Stones and the arcane air shield created by the metal orbs at the end of the staffs. It's a magnificent enchantment. If only I had been the one to create it..." Kima stared off into the distance. Her eyes darted around the construct of the rods.

Suddenly, the cross turned slightly to the side, and then the arcane field ignited in bright purple waves of sizzling energy in front of them. Now the ship was moving away from the port at a rapid pace. The trees began to sway in the wind, and the people on the dock covered their faces or turned and walked away in a hurry. The small flames in the metal street lamps flickered, struggling against the gust of wind.

"How fast does it go?" Sineth asked, leaning against the railing and looking out into the darkness.

"Very fast. Normally we'd be in Jazat in about a quarter of an hour," Kima said with a proud, cheeky smile. "But in this darkness we probably won't fly at full speed. So I guess it'll take up to half an hour or more."

Avala was really starting to like this girl; she was smart and fierce, and Kima's wild mop of curly hair reminded her a little of Mereth.

There it was, that deep-rooted sadness creeping up on her again—the image of the griffons flying away to some fateful destiny, and Leam's little arms holding her as tightly as he could. *Leam... where are Leam and Kumar in all this madness? Hopefully they've found some safe place to hide.*

"Let's go inside. It gets very cold out here, with the wind and all. Besides, there is a tavern below deck," Kima suggested, pointing to the entrance of the glass dome.

"I think I need a moment alone here, if that's okay?" Avala replied, fighting back the tears that were beginning to fill her eyes and make her voice shake.

"Sure, but don't stay too long, or you'll be an ice sculpture by the time we arrive," Kima said with a wink. Sineth hesitated for a moment and looked at Avala. She shook her head and he went inside with Kima.

All this time she hadn't really had time to grieve, to realize what she had lost. Not only Mereth, but her home, Leam and Kumar, her griffon... Her life had been pulled out from under her feet and now she was lost. What was she doing? She wasn't the type of person to fight in a war or be the hero who would rescue her friend and save the world. Who was she fooling?

One by one, the passengers went inside, leaving Avala alone. She stood there for a long time, staring at the crackling purple light that filled the darkness with a glow. It felt like a serene dream, something her mind had made up.

She brushed over the stubble on the shaved side of her head, concentrating on the texture as it prickled her fingertips. Sometimes, if she concentrated hard enough on one sensation, it calmed her mind. Like the constant flow of breathing, fiddling with a needle and thread, or even practicing magic.

"Avala, please come inside. You are shivering." Sineth touched her shoulder. She flinched under his touch. *How did he get there? I didn't see him come out. Maybe I was just lost in thought.* But she was trembling; she hadn't realized it until Sineth said it. So she let herself be pushed to the entrance of the dome, where she stood in awe. The light floated over the glass like watery purple waves. It was still cold in this chamber, but nothing compared to the icy wind outside. A woman stood at a large metal steering wheel on a circular platform surrounded by a series of raised platforms. A little to the right, a spiral staircase led down into the lower deck.

After they went down the stairs, the inside was warm and comfortable. Portholes covered both walls to their left and right. People sat at tables, talking and drinking. It looked like the inside of a large tavern.

"You can't leave me alone with that girl any longer. I think she hates me. I don't know what I've done to her," Sineth whispered to her as they came closer to their table.

Avala smiled at Sineth. "Maybe she's just not as easily enthralled as you're used to." She was grateful for his charm right now; it pushed away the dark clouds in her head.

"Maybe." Sineth's smile faded as he looked at Avala.

What is wrong with him? He's been acting so different since we stayed in that cave on the mountain. Or maybe he was strange before and this is his true self? How could she know? She had just met him.

"Before we go to rejoin Kima, can I talk to you for a moment?" Avala asked. She wanted to know what was going on.

Sineth stopped. "Sure, what is it?"

"Let's sit over there, okay?" Avala pointed to an empty table at the far end of the room.

Without a word, Sineth followed her. As soon as they were seated, Sineth asked, "What is it, then?"

Now she felt stupid, like a heartbroken maiden who wanted answers from a rake she had known for five seconds. So she just asked, "Do you think the others are okay? We left them in the middle of nowhere in a forest."

"They're used to being in the middle of nowhere. And a forest is better than a swamp. They will be fine. Is that all?" Sineth looked at her, his blue eyes piercing hers. "Not that I am eager to go back to that girl," he said, breaking eye contact. Somehow it felt like he knew what she was going to ask.

"It's just... you've been so different since we were in the cave. I didn't mean to burden you with my past life man problems. We haven't even known each other that long. I guess it was just the situation. Being imprisoned, not knowing when we might get out. But I could really use a friend right now." Avala stared at Sineth, trying to get some kind of insight. He gazed into the distance, seemingly checking out all the people in the room.

"No, it's... everything's fine. I'm just exhausted, and this darkness is really taking its toll on me. But I'm glad that my people are safe now."

"Okay, so it has nothing to do with what I told you? I'm just asking because you reacted so strongly when I told you about my past. Have you experienced anything similar?" Avala reached for his hand. He drew back and crossed his arms over his chest, as if to protect himself from her curiosity.

"I told you, it's okay. I'm fine. It was just a very uncomfortable situation. Being trapped in this cave and all." Sineth shook his head in an odd way and shrugged his shoulders.

He is obviously hiding something. But what and why? Avala thought.

"Come on, I can see that something is bothering you. Just tell me, I can handle it. But this awkwardness must end if we are to travel together any longer. I just want to know where I stand. If you don't want to be close to me anymore, that's okay too," she burst out. She could not be in this strange conversation any longer.

"Oof." Sineth let out an audible sigh and dropped his hands back into his lap, resigned. "I knew you'd bring it up eventually. I tried to act normal, but the guilt weighs heavily on me." Sineth paused. He looked like he was fighting with himself, or trying to find the right words, or just figuring out a way to escape the situation. "I'm not sure how to explain this the right way. It's just... I don't think I can be your friend, or at least I don't think you want me to be. Man, I've never been good at this, and that's kind of the point." Sineth stared at her, and she stared back, confused. *What is he talking about?*

"I guess there is no good way to say this. Avala, I'm Brimer, the one who left you."

21

Sineth

S ineth peered over his shoulder. Avala walked silently behind him. She hadn't said much since their conversation
on the ship. Her only response had been, "Okay, I understand." Then she'd just got up and gone to sit with Kima. And
he'd been left alone to think about the sum of his failures in
life.

There was nothing he could do, really. He couldn't force
Avala to forgive him, and honestly, he knew he didn't deserve
it. He tried to be a good person, but what if he was just meant

to be an asshole? It would make things a lot easier if he just gave in and stopped being nice. But somehow he couldn't do that either. There was a soft, mushy spot in him that truly cared. Cared for her still.

The whole thing was a mess. If he could, he would have just left. But he also owed the Resistance a chance to start over. And somehow he felt the need to help Madin. Even though he hated the Elementals and everything they stood for—or had stood for, he didn't know what was left of them—he still felt for the people. There were so many civilians in this battle. So many people who couldn't defend themselves or their families.

But this thing with Avala complicated things to an almost unbearable level. *Why can't I just stay away from a pretty girl? Now I've got a heartbroken ex-girlfriend on my hands. One would think that a war would be enough to deal with.* Sineth shook his head and tried to shift his focus, to concentrate on his surroundings.

The city of Jazat was mesmerizing. After the ship docked and they left the harbor, he couldn't stop looking up. The massive stone buildings were adorned with golden lines around the beautiful stained-glass windows. Each window depicted some sort of story or crest. Round devices hung from many of the buildings like signs, indicating the time of day. And then Sineth saw something so strange and wondrous that he just stopped and stared. A human-shaped metal construct was talking to a woman at a stall filled with baked goods. Talking like a normal, breathing humanoid.

"Kima, what is this?" Sineth pointed at the metal construction.

"Stop pointing, you fool. That's an automaton. It's part of the town's watch, a guard automaton."

"How is that possible? It can talk and interact," Sineth said, still staring at the thing.

"Magic. Don't you have magic on your side as well?" Kima looked at him, confused.

"There is no 'my side,' but yes, we have elemental magic—just nothing that could create something like this. This is amazing!"

"Well, if you prove that you're more than just false charms and a pretty face, I could show you how it's done. I happen to be an enchanter. Maybe this is one of my creations." Kima nodded in the direction of the thing.

If he hadn't been so fascinated by all of this, he would have rolled his eyes at her. "You can do that? That's amazing, Kima. I have a whole new respect for you," he replied with a half grin.

She just narrowed her eyes and pursed her lips. Then Kima turned and started walking again.

The beautiful, shining marble floor below him and the floating balls of light above filled the street to an almost day-like brightness. It was the first real light he had seen since they had fled the mountain.

After some time, they came to a more residential area. The streets were less crowded. Each house had a yard and an intricate metal fence around it.

"It's very nice here. What kind of people live here?" Avala asked from behind.

"Many rich people who are close to the Magisters. Council members, merchants, architects, professors, all kinds of important people," Kima answered.

"And everyone is just allowed to enter this area?" Sineth asked.

"Yes, there is no need to keep anyone back. These fences are enchanted, and they have many guards."

A few moments later, they came to a massive metal gate. Behind it, he could see a beautifully landscaped courtyard. The whole area was illuminated by a huge ball of light that dispelled the ever-present darkness. It hovered high above the Magisters' Palace.

Kima spoke to the guard at the gate and explained what they had told her just a few hours ago. The guard looked them up and down.

"You may enter, but we will keep a close eye on you all," the guard said, opening the gate. He waved to two other guards stationed a short distance away from the gate and instructed them to lead them to the audience hall of the palace.

As Sineth approached, the massive structure towered over him. It was a round main building, flanked by four towers, one at each corner. Every building was topped by a glass dome. The central dome even had another small dome on top. It was all on a scale Sineth had never seen before. The way they built houses was otherworldly, intricate, and masterful.

They passed tall conical bushes and rows of roses before reaching the front of the palace. The guard knocked on the great double door. It was silver, with a crest in the center depicting a flying dragon.

They were seated on a wooden bench in front of a raised platform. On top were two high chairs with a small table in the middle, and behind them Sineth could see a large oval table with ten chairs on each side, and one with a higher rest at each end of the table. The two guards stood a few feet to the side of them. The room was well lit and uncomfortably quiet. Sineth could hear the breathing of the people around him, as well as his own. Then he heard footsteps in the distance, echoing through the hall.

Two figures approached from the left end. One was a woman, dark-skinned, with pointed ears and long black hair partly braided into a tight knot at the back of her head. She wore a floor-length silver dress with sleeves that came down to wide, billowing ends. Her shoulders were bare, and her skin shimmered as if dusted with silver. But the other person was even more breathtaking, a male elf with very pale skin, white hip-length hair, and delicate limbs. He wore a long, tunic-like white robe over a silver-stitched vest that looked like hundreds of tiny scales.

They both sat down in the chairs on the platform. The man crossed his white-trousered legs, rested his arm on the armrest, and brushed his chin with his thin fingers.

"My dear Kima, the guards told me you brought some refugees from Madin who want to share some information with us?" The elf's piercing golden eyes peered deep into Sineth. "How rude, we have not introduced ourselves. Normally that would be a given, but you're not from here, so I guess you don't know. We are the Magisters of the Karaz Islands. I am Baldor Immos, and this is the lovely Kalira Saasar." He waved his other hand at the woman in a very elegant manner.

Kalira nodded once. "Yes, I'm also very curious what information you could have for us."

With a deep rumble, Sineth cleared his throat. "We saw darkness emerge from the mountain, followed by hordes of orcs, goblins, dwarves, kobolds and other ken from the Dark Kingdom below. They swarmed the mountain, some riding strange dragon-like creatures. We also saw the Dark Queen herself, heading for Gahaal." Sineth paused, staring into the glittering golden eyes of Baldor Immos. "We seek your help for the people of Madin."

"This all sounds very wild. But I sense no dishonesty from you. In fact, we have another Madiner here who claims to be seeking help. I think it is time to bring him to the party," Baldor said, nodding to one of the guards standing behind them.

22

Garon

It was dry and well lit for a prison. Maybe he had just been in the dark for so long that any light seemed bright at this point. Or maybe it had something to do with his newfound magical abilities; darkness didn't really bother him anymore.

There wasn't much in the cell—just a bed, a pot for his needs and a small wooden table on which they had placed a bowl with some kind of stew. Garon wasn't hungry; all he could think about was the invasion of Gahaal. The endless screams echoed in his mind, filling the silence of the prison with an eerie cacophony. Was this his doing? Had he brought this upon them? It was certain that he had taken part in it. He had helped bend them to her wishes. For the sake of the elements, he had killed people for her.

This person he had become, he didn't recognize anymore. Nothing good was left of him, just this monster lurking inside him, controlling his actions and many of his thoughts as well. Maybe he should just end it, this miserable life. He would be reborn, a new beginning.

You can't. This is your destiny, your purpose. Who are you without that power? Just a lost little boy without direction or purpose. Worthless. Venja's voice echoed through his mind.

Ever since Venja had changed him, his head had been clouded. Torn between regret and lust for power, he wanted more. Deep inside him there was a growing hunger for power, for might. With every ounce of his will he tried to suppress it, but he could feel this new magic pumping through his veins like blood. Garon could probably just break through this door and leave. Maybe if he went back now, with information about Karaz's security, she would take him back. Venja had given him a new life, love, devotion, magic beyond his wildest dreams. Empowered him to be what he truly wanted to be: a leader, a king.

No, this is bad. This is not who I am. Garon shook his head and stood up. *Focus, focus! I want to help them. Help the people of Madin. Venja is not a good person. She would kill me without hesitation if it would help her cause.*

He walked slowly towards the gates of the cell, feeling a little dizzy. The guards had told him that he would be brought before the Magisters in a few hours, but it must have been at least a day since then. He looked left and right, trying to see if he could see a guard to ask when he would be brought up.

The door at the end of the tunnel opened and three guards entered. "It's time," was all one of them said as a towering half-giant woman opened his cell. A sack was pulled over his head, and then he was led through a series of tunnels and up staircases before entering a long, echoing hall.

Suddenly a door must have opened because there was a lot of light. The sack was removed and he blinked to adjust his eyes. Normally he would have shielded them from the light, but his hands were tied tightly behind his back. A chair was pushed against his legs, and the female guard pressed his shoulders down until he was seated.

"So, who might you be? And what do you want to tell us?" said a calm, deep voice.

"And what happened to your face?" a high, crystal-clear voice added.

Garon began to look around the room. It was a massive hall. About thirty feet to his right were three people, also sitting. In front of him he could now make out two figures in high chairs. His eyes were still clouded by the light. "I am Garon Himmon of the Stormguard of Madin. I was captured by the Dark Horde, tortured and turned into a monster. The Dark..." Garon tried to tell them about Venja, but again nothing came out. "They invaded Madin. They took over all the major cities, even the capital Gahaal and our holy island Parhat. I managed to escape. They chased me, but I'm a skilled griffon rider, and I shook them off as I flew through the Kuana Mountains."

"Garon, you're alive?" One of the three to his right got up and ran toward him.

"Avala? What happened to your face and your hair?" Garon looked down into the face of the person now kneeling before him.

"Me? Look at you. What did they do to you?" Avala reached up and took the human side of his face into her hand. He flinched back from her touch, and she withdrew her hand.

"You let them take me. You did nothing to stop them. You just stood there," Garon spat out, his anger bubbling up like an overflowing well.

"I searched for you. As soon as they took you, I chased after you," Avala shot back.

"Well, it does not matter now. Maybe I was destined to be here, to become this thing." Garon looked down at his feet. Did he mean what he said? Was it his destiny to overcome his inner demons? He felt this thing inside him roaring, pressing angrily against his chest, like flames burning him from inside. There must be a way to control it, to overcome it, but he couldn't see how, and he wasn't sure he had the willpower to do it, not anymore.

"I am so sorry. I really wanted to help you, to save you," Avala burst out, tears filling her eyes. "They killed the High Monks, Garon. Those shadow creatures, they just killed them. Everyone is dying, everything is changing. There's so much pain in this world, I can't stand it anymore."

"I know that they are dead. Many people are, and more will die before it is all over," Garon said, his voice deep and hard. Were those his words or Venja's? Avala looked at him, her eyebrows knitted together, tears still running down her cheeks in streams. She looked irritated, as if she had seen or heard something she did not like.

"Look at that. If this isn't an interesting turn of events—a reunion. What were you saying about dead High Monks?" The man in the high chair got up and walked down the stairs towards them.

Avala stood up and wiped away her tears. "A few weeks ago there was an attack in Parhat. The High Monks were murdered by what I now believe to be members of Venja's Dark Horde."

The man towered over them, standing nearly seven feet tall. His hair and clothes were white, and his skin had an unnatural sheen. "Interesting. I had heard rumors of their deaths, but it seemed a bit absurd. A female demon who came in the middle of the night and killed them all in a wave of shadows? Disappeared without being seen? Sounds like a good story for a book of fiction, don't you think?" Baldor asked, his full lips curling into a mischievous smile. He stepped closer to Garon, leaning forward to examine his face. "Dark magic. You could be the demon they spoke of. Not female, but definitely a demon." He sniffed at Garon's neck, then reached forward and touched the horn protruding from his head. "I am Baldor Immos, Magister of the Karaz Islands and protector of these lands. Up there is my beloved friend Kalira Saasar, who assists me in ruling," he added as he turned and walked back up the stairs to his chair.

Garon followed his steps with his eyes, not knowing what to think of him. Somehow Baldor seemed even more dangerous than Venja.

"We don't interfere in other people's wars, but I must say, this darkness bothers me. If you know more about it, I would appreciate it if you would speak now," Kalira said, echoing throughout the hall.

Garon looked from Baldor to her and froze. This woman was the exact replica of Venja. Her face, her skin tone, her posture, her body type—the only difference was her eyes. They weren't white like Venja's, they were golden. Piercing golden eyes. And they matched perfectly with the eyes of Baldor, which he had seen up close just seconds before, an eye color he had never seen before.

"I'm sorry if this offends you, but you look exactly like Valeria—I mean Venja," Garon said, staring at her, still in shock at the sight.

"What did you just say?" Kalira's eyes widened and she leaned forward.

"You look like her. Exactly like her."

"No, the name, Valeria." She got up and walked toward him.

"I meant Venja, the Dark..." Garon couldn't bring himself to say it. Why couldn't he just say it? He'd just said her name, why couldn't he manage to say her title? It was as if he had a door in his brain that he couldn't open.

"But what was the first name? Why did you call the Dark Queen Valeria?" She stood in front of him, grabbed his chin and pulled his head up. His mind wandered to the nights they had spent together. Her touch, her kiss, her body against his. Valeria, his love. He had to go back to her, to be with her, to take care of her. She was the one he wanted, desperately, with every breath in his body. *I have to be with her, feel her... I have to go back.*

"Garon?" He could hear Avala's voice. Far away, just a whisper in the back of his head.

With all his strength he shook himself out of the trance. He looked at the two faces in front of him. Avala, his former love, with whom he'd thought he would spend this life. And Valeria, who had shown him a desire, a love and a power he had never felt before.

"Garon, I think you found my twin sister," Kalira whispered with a shy smile. Her golden eyes glowed, and Garon felt this overwhelming longing within him. Clouded memories flooded his mind again and he was lost.

23

Venja

It had been a long time since she had thought about her childhood home, and even longer since she had been there. A continent not far from here, Zamanthyr. Flying weightlessly in the sky, just like Dohva. The edge of the continent was dotted with a multitude of castles with tall, spiraling towers topped with golden horns. Each of the twenty-six castles served as an embassy for a realm in the multiverse, housing a portal to said realm. She had only seen one during her childhood, as she had not often traveled across one of the three bridges that led from Undarath across the sea to the outer land. She hadn't been allowed to see the castle up close, but she had admired its beauty from afar.

But Zamanthyr had only one city: Undarath, the place of her upbringing. It was a city larger than anything here on Dohva, over thirty miles in diameter. The streets bustled with trade and travel from every nation in the vast multiverse. Sometimes she would sneak out in the middle of the night and wander the streets, hiding if she saw anyone coming. What would her life have been like if she had been born into another family as a normal person? Venja had dreamed of finding a way to get a job as an ambassador in the Ministry of the Golden Council, but her parents had made it clear that she wasn't worthy of such an important job. Or to be around people in such high places, or even to exist at all. She hated them. Kalira had always been their pride, the golden child, perfect in every way. And her? There hadn't been a single day she could remember when they hadn't shown her how wrong she was. An abomination, a mouth they had to feed, just a waste of space in their house. A price they had had to pay to have Kalira.

Venja remembered the exact moment when she had finally decided to give them what they had always wanted—to pack her bags and go. To leave and never come back. To leave and run as far away as she could. At first she had thought she would go back, not because of her horrible parents, but because of Kalira. She had been the only person who had been kind to Venja, who had stood by her. But even Kalira did not understand how she felt in this world. Wrong, lost and alone.

Maybe one day she would be able to see Kalira and Undarath again, but not as long as the sphere remained. *On the other hand, as long as everyone is trapped in this bubble, it's easier to control them,* she thought. And it had been a long time—how long she did not know. Kalira might have died. Her parents were surely dead by now.

Venja walked toward the edge of Parhat Island, gazing into the distant dark sky where wyverns flew over Gahaal. *If only you could see me now. I am not the servant of a council. I am the queen who rules over all. But you are long dead and forgotten. May you rot in hell.*

Slowly, she turned and walked back down the hill to the entrance of the castle. Two orc guards stood by the huge stone doors. They opened them and bowed as Venja passed them.

They were her people. Underestimated abominations, just like her. And now they ruled the land. After all this time of planning and crafting and training, they were finally where they belonged. Not hidden away in some dungeon down below, but here, in plain sight, at the top.

Of course Venja had done this mostly for herself, but she was amused by the thought that the perfect, normal people had been pushed aside and had to obey the commands of what they would call monsters. Besides, her people had given her shelter, a home where she could be herself. She hadn't been pushed around or made fun of. It had been easy to be with them. Though not all of them were very intelligent, they had strong wills, and some were wiser than they looked. And, most importantly, they had made her their queen, both worshiped and feared.

Her weakness had become her strength. Her eyesight was perfect in the dark; she could see the tiniest details at a great distance, just as she had as a child, wandering under the comforting night sky.

If only she knew where Garon had gone, this victory would be perfect with him at her side. There seemed to be more of him in there than she had expected. Maybe if she tugged hard enough at the tether she had placed on him, he would come back. Just a little more of her magic, of her seduction, and he would not be able to break free again.

You mean my *magic, don't you, my darling? Remember who holds the strings of your fate, my love. Now that your little toy is gone, perhaps we should spend a night together. It's been a while.* She heard Agthod's raspy, deep voice in her head.

I think that's a wonderful idea. My life lacks a little fun these days. Everyone is so on edge, I can't take it anymore. They should all be grateful that I freed them from these terrible Elementals, Venja replied mentally.

Yes, my dear, they are an ungrateful bunch. Perhaps you should give them a little pleasure. Everyone loves pleasure. Brothels, gambling dens, fighting pits, that's what makes life fun. But come now, my dear, let us go somewhere private so that I can lure you into a wild dream, Agthod purred at the back of her head.

24

Avala

What did she do to him? Avala stood in the vast hall, her gaze fixed on Garon, who in turn was staring at Kalira.

"I think we should meet Valeria. Maybe there is still a part of my sister in her? I could try to convince her to stop this madness," Kalira offered, standing between Garon and the stairs.

Baldor leaned back in his chair, one leg resting on the other, and tapped his fingers on the arms of the chair. He seemed utterly bored, as if this were of no importance to him. "Hmm, I'm not sure there's much left of her, my dear. And if what you say is true"—Baldor gestured to Garon—"I'm more concerned about the citizens of Madin. This violence is unnecessary and will not be tolerated."

"You know I've been looking for her for a long time. I thought she was dead. At least give me a chance to talk to her," Kalira pleaded.

"We could offer her a meeting to parley. In a neutral place, of course. Did she invade Himalus?" Baldor inquired, waving his hand in Garon's direction.

"Yes, she has troops all over Madin. Stationed in every town, village and outpost," Garon replied, staring absent-mindedly at Kalira.

"Then maybe Xear, but I don't want her so close to us. Himalus is better, it's high up and can't be surrounded. I will send her a message as soon as the plan is set," Baldor added.

"Could you release him? He has given you all the information you need," Avala said, putting a hand on Garon's shoulder.

He pushed it away. "I don't need your help," Garon hissed, his eyes blazing like a pit of hot coals. A low rumbling sound came from his throat.

Baldor watched them closely. "Oh, there is some tension here. I think we can release him. Though his nature is not human, I believe his mind is still somewhat the same. We'll see what comes of it. I'm intrigued. Please, release this man from his restraints," Baldor commanded, casting a curious glance at Garon, looking him up and down like a painting.

His mind is much the same? I'm not sure. He seems very different to me, she thought.

One of the guards unlocked Garon's restraints and he began to stretch and flex his limbs.

"I think it would be best if you stayed here for now. You'll be shown to the guest quarters. You should take a bath and get some new clothes," Baldor instructed, rising from his chair and walking toward the hallway they had come from. He held out his arm, and Kalira slipped her arm through his. They began to whisper to each other as they left the room.

This looks like a place of great knowledge. Maybe I can find some information about the history of Madin, and maybe even about this disease that has taken hold in Garon, Avala thought to herself, her eyes following them.

Avala sprinted after them. "Excuse me, I'm sorry. Do you have a library here?" she asked, lowering her voice. "I want to research this mutation Garon is suffering from and see if it can be reversed."

Baldor grinned broadly. "I'm not sure he wants it reversed. I'm not even sure how long he can withstand the need to return to her. But you are welcome to immerse yourself in the study of magic. The library is in the rear right tower. I will see that you are allowed to enter." With that, he turned and left, disappearing into the main corridor that surrounded the throne room, or whatever they called it—the Magisters' Hall or something like that.

"Thank you!" Avala called after them.

"No thanks necessary," Baldor replied with a dismissive wave of his hand.

Returning to the others, Avala saw that Garon was still standing alone in the middle of the hall. Sineth and Kima were arguing again. Avala could not figure out why they didn't get along. Maybe they were both just too proud and stubborn to give in.

Slowly she walked over to Garon. He was staring off into the distance, through the leaded glass that stretched almost from the floor to the ceiling behind the high chairs. They really had spared no expense with this palace, magnificent and ornate through and through.

From this vantage point, Garon looked normal, just as he always had. A little tired and guarded, but still human. The only thing that was missing was his Stormguard tattoo on his forehead; there was nothing left of it, not even a scar. Avala took a step to stand in front of him, doing her best not to flinch at the sight of his demon-like face. Even his eye looked different on this side, as if one half of his face had been replaced by another. But even through the monstrous scales and leathery skin, Avala could still make out the proportions of the face she used to love.

"How are you now?" she asked him.

"Avala, you don't have to pretend to be worried. You weren't worried back in Gahaal; there's no need to start now. There's nothing left of what we had back then, nothing at all," Garon snapped.

"Why do you say that? I cared about you, I still do. I'm just not very good at showing it, you know that. Those great acts of romance you always talked about, that's not me, but that doesn't mean I didn't love you." Avala tried to reach out to him, to take his hand, but he pulled it away. He looked at her with a hardness she did not recognize.

"Avala, I don't want you near me. I don't want you to love me or care about me or even think about me. Just leave me alone. Whatever we had is over. We are done." Garon almost spat out the words, growling and hissing.

In that moment she saw what Baldor had meant. He was a completely different person, if he was a person at all. He was possessed, or cursed, but she would not give up hope just yet.

25

Sineth

Why am I even here? He'd wanted a revolution, and the High Monks were dead. Everything had worked out in his favor. Maybe not exactly the way he had planned, but it was a change nonetheless.

He found himself staring at Avala, who was in the middle of a heated discussion with Garon. They seemed to have been a couple, judging by the intensity of their conversation. What was that feeling inside him, this tightening when he saw Avala with Garon? Could it be jealousy? Sineth the unattached, jealous of a man with scales and a horn protruding from his skull. Jealous of a woman he'd left behind. But in spite of all reason, deep down, if he was honest with himself, he harbored strong feelings for Avala.

The way he had left her, he had been a coward, a fool to think he could run away and everything would be okay again. Deep inside, Sineth felt the images of that night come back to him. There had been so much blood. Droha had sat on the bed, sobbing, knees pulled up, her head resting on top. He'd stood next to her, feeling completely lost. The overwhelming feeling of loss had pressed on his heart. Losing someone, losing his family, he just couldn't stand it. It was the curse of his existence, losing the people he loved. It had started right then and there. His first loss, the first time he had left.

But the pain would not go away. Sineth had lost so many people in his lifetime. Though he tried to keep people at arm's length, the few he let in always seemed to perish. In subsequent lives he tried to find them, but the continent was vast and he didn't even know where to begin. And then Molna had been sacrificed, and he had shattered into a thousand pieces. His heart had filled with hate for the whole system, for the Elementals, for the world they lived in. He had to do something, change something. This endless cycle of death. Being reborn only to see his closest friends and family die before his very eyes. It was maddening.

"You're staring at her, you know that, right?" Kima interrupted him. "It's just I do it a lot myself—staring, I mean—and not all people seem to like it."

Sineth shook his head out of the trance and looked at Kima. "Sorry, my thoughts carried me away. Do you think the Magisters will help us?" Sineth asked, trying to distract himself from the two of them.

Kima studied his expression. "You like her very much, hm? I think the Magisters are interested in helping the people of Madin. Baldor Immos despises unjust behavior, especially against those who can't defend themselves. And Lady Kalira Saasar has every reason to at least talk to Venja. I mean, isn't it crazy that they're twin sisters? How is that even possible when Lady Saasar has been Magister of Karaz for what seems like forever? I mean, elves certainly live long lives, but that long?" Kima glanced at the high chairs where the Magisters had been sitting a few minutes before.

"They do, but it's all very strange. I mean, did Kalira age during that time?"

"I can't say for sure, but the paintings of her are all very similar. Baldor Immos hasn't aged or changed in any way, that's for sure. There are many myths surrounding him—where he came from, what he is, if he's even human. But the people love him; he's a good and fair leader. I, for one, believe that he was not reborn, but was the same person, living this life all these years. I've thought about this a lot since I was a child, because of our close connection through my parents and all. It's strange how everything and everyone changes and yet Baldor and Kalira remain the same," Kima mused, pausing as if some sort of internal gear was rattling in her head. "I suppose there's magic at work. I haven't thought about it for years, but now I'm curious. It's like a mystery, isn't it? I love a good mystery!" With that, Kima's excitement bubbled over, causing her to jump up and down and clap her hands together in anticipation.

"Well, then you should grab Avala and go do some research. Solving mysteries isn't really my thing. But I look forward to the answers you'll find," Sineth offered with a half smile.

"And what are you going to do? Have a man-fight with Garon to decide who gets Avala?" Kima crossed her arms over her chest. Her round face took on an almost frighteningly stern expression. How quickly her mood could change. He didn't know how to behave around her. Somehow his very presence seemed to offend her, even though he had no intention of becoming her enemy. Since his charm didn't seem to work on Kima, he decided to try a more friendly, buddylike approach.

"Why would I do that? It doesn't look like he wants to fight for her, just get her off his back." Sineth nodded in the direction of Avala and Garon, who were still arguing.

"Maybe we should intervene before he unleashes his inner demon and just kills her." Kima's head tilted to one side, her wild tangle of curls brushed over her shoulder and her brows drawn into a troubled line.

"You really like her, huh?" asked Sineth without even a hint of mockery or humor. He wondered if she liked Avala as much as he did, or just as a worried new friend. "Don't worry about her. She's a feisty woman and can fight for herself."

"Fine!" Avala shouted, her voice echoing in the great stone hall. Her face turned red as she looked at Kima. "I'm going to my room now to freshen up. Would you like to join me?"

"Sure," Kima said with an odd half smile.

As the two of them started to leave, Garon rushed past them, ignoring Sineth completely.

What's going on here? Why am I the one left behind? Maybe I should sleep in this fancy room. It's certainly more comfortable than anywhere I've slept in a long time.

In the morning I should talk to the Magisters about the Resistance. Maybe we can stay here? Quinn would love this city so much. It really is magical.

26

Kima

She had always longed to study in this library, but permission had always been denied, so the fact that Avala had been granted access bothered her a little. On the other hand, now Kima could finally explore it. It was a strange mixture of feelings, to be annoyed and excited at the same time.

But it had been a good morning, she felt well rested, and they'd had a lovely evening after going up to Avala's room. They had sat down on the floor next to the fireplace and talked about Avala's home and hers. Kima had asked Avala if she wanted to talk about Garon, but she'd just shaken her head and stared into the fire. After that they had been quiet for a while before they talked a bit more about Kima's creations. It really felt like she had made a friend.

They walked down the long corridor to a wooden double door. An older gnome was waiting for them. "Hello, my name is Trusha. I am the librarian of this esteemed place of knowledge. I ask that you be careful with the books and show some respect inside the library. If you have any questions, please feel free to ask me at any time." Trusha turned around and produced a long golden key with a chain attached to the inside of his cream-colored robe. He stood on his toes and extended his arms to reach the lock. Trusha inserted the key. With a squeak, the door opened.

As they entered, the smell of old paper and polished wood wafted into Kima's nose. Oh, how she loved that smell, almost as much as hot metal and lubricating oil.

Two chandeliers, one on each side of the door, lit up as they walked in. In front of them was a large wooden table with a blue velvet chair. Stacks of books and parchments covered most of the desk. By the time they reached the desk, more chandeliers had ignited throughout the tower, giving it a mysterious glow.

"What exactly are you looking for?" Trusha asked.

"I'm looking for information on curses, forbidden magic and demons," Avala said.

Kima expected Trusha to raise an eyebrow or be offended by the request, but he just nodded and waited, looking at her.

"I would like to research the history of Dohva." Kima didn't want to be too specific about her interest in the Magisters for fear that Trusha might reveal it to them. Yesterday, in Avala's room, they had planned what each of them would research, plotting what would be the best topics to get the information they were looking for.

"Good. For magic, especially dark magic, you should start downstairs, shelves five through ten." Trusha pointed to his right, where the stairs spiraled down. "For history books, you should go up to the third floor, shelves forty-four to fifty." He gestured all the way to the top of the tower. "There are tables and chairs on each level of the library. If you need anything, I'm here." Trusha sat down at his desk and settled into his plush chair.

Avala looked at Kima with a warm smile. "Okay, I guess I'll be down there for a while."

"I'll make sure we get all the information we need." Kima looked at Avala for a second longer than seemed normal and looked away with a shy smile.

The circular walls were lined with endless rows of shelves. Every floor looked the same, except for the last one. By the time Kima reached her destination, she was exhausted. Walking up what felt like a thousand stairs wasn't part of her daily routine, but it was certainly worth it.

The shelves surrounding her were about three times her height. Four stained-glass windows, each about ten feet high, towered above the shelves, and above them was the huge glass dome. Kima could see the bright light of the globe hanging high above the palace, and behind it glimpses of the colorful glow of the elemental sphere.

Kima scanned the shelves for labels indicating their numbers. When she found a brass-metal label at the top, the angle was too steep to read it with the bookcase towering over her. It was one of those moments when she felt like everything around her was built for taller people. She walked all the way back to the banister to catch a glimpse of the number, but now the label was too far away and the lettering too thin and intricate to make out the meaning. She pulled her little metal bird out of her sling bag. It had been hidden there for a while, since Kima had been afraid that someone might steal it during her travels.

"Lady Zua, please fly up and move from shelf to shelf so I can read the inscriptions," Kima told the bird. She placed the goggles on her eyes and adjusted the lenses until she had a clear view. She followed the path of Lady Zua's eyes, seeing through them as if she were the bird herself. *Fifty-four, fifty-three... fifty. I will start there and walk backwards,* she thought. With a practiced motion, she pushed her goggles up onto her mop of curly hair. Looking through the overwhelming amount of books in front of her, Kima pulled out a few promising-looking tomes and began to read.

After what felt like hours, Avala came up the stairs. A clock would have been useful. The whole city was full of clocks, but in the Magisters' Palace Kima hadn't seen a single one so far. It was as if time had no meaning for them.

"How are you doing up here? I couldn't find anything about Garon's curse or disease," Avala said, without needing to catch her breath after four flights of stairs. *She must be more physically active than me*, Kima pondered.

"Sorry to hear that. I couldn't find anything about the Magisters, but I did find something that will blow your mind. I don't know if it's true or just a tale, but look at this!" Kima pointed to a map in a book in front of her. "This is Dohva, but look, there are more continents, Eltreth and Zamanthyr. They are all connected by bridges. Dohva was once part of a plane of reality called 'the Equilibrium Domain,' and there are many other planes as well." Kima pulled another book from the pile in front of her. "It says here that a massive stone struck Dohva and split off parts of the mainland. 'As the newly created islands began to fall into the endless nothingness below, Magnus Athirat called upon the Elements, drawing them from the Elemental Plane and surrounding all of Dohva so that the islands would not fall.' This is insane. Can you imagine life outside of Dohva? There's a whole world out there that we know nothing about!" Kima felt a surge of excitement. *How can it be that no one knows about this? The Magisters must know. Why haven't they told anyone?*

Now she noticed Avala's expression; she was staring at the book with the map. "Are you okay?" Kima asked.

"I don't think so. If this is true, it changes everything," Avala replied.

"There's more. I found a diary of this sorcerer Magnus Athirat and another one named Nirella Khul. It was all kinds of crazy magical writings—they were trying to create new spells, powerful new enchantments. It seemed like Magnus started the journal and Nirella wrote the last few pages. She wrote about how this Magnus had managed to create a capsule around all of Dohva to keep the islands from falling. Like the shell of an egg, but made out of elemental power, if you know what I mean." She paused for a moment. Avala nodded absentmindedly, so she continued. "He had created a kind of amplifier, a link to the 'Elemental Plane.' But in order to maintain it, he sacrificed himself. And then the writing got a little weird, and Nirella wrote that he needed the most powerful source of magic to maintain the capsule: soul magic." Kima paused. Avala seemed far away. "Avala, do you think this sphere could be fueled by souls? And if so, how would you do that?"

Avala stared back at her, her gaze more focused now. "Yes, that is exactly how it works. They create a cult and then tell the people that it is an honor to be sacrificed. A salvation for them, and a service to the greater good. The Ritual of Enlightenment. Every year for centuries, ten people have been chosen. They are taken to the island of Parhat for a kind of secret ceremony, and they never come back, they are never reborn. Kima, this mountain has a tether to the sphere, and when the people are sacrificed, the tether and the whole sphere glows. It is fueled by their death, their souls. Like you said, soul magic."

27

Kalira

The last few days had been the strangest in decades. How could her sister have been so close to her all this time and yet she hadn't known? Maybe Kalira hadn't dug deep enough for the answers she was looking for? Or maybe she hadn't really wanted to know what had become of Valeria, the sister she had lost so long ago.

Kalira wanted her back. That was why she had come here in the first place—to find her and bring Valeria home. But her home was Karaz now, and her family was Baldor. So much had changed since she'd set out to find her sister.

How will Valeria react when she hears my voice? Will she recognize it?

Kalira and Baldor sat in their favorite room for their afternoon tea, which also housed a small library with a collection of their favorite books and scrolls—magical and nonmagical, the best of them all. Some time ago, a great artist from the city of Druvat had created a beautiful painting on the ceiling, depicting the cloudless sky with its colorful flares. He had even managed to indicate the various elements. Kalira enjoyed looking for the small hidden waves or flames.

"Should I do it?" Baldor's voice interrupted her thoughts. He reached out and touched her hand, stroking it gently. His calm presence had always given her a sense of peace, as if all the cards would eventually fall into place. Slowly, she turned her hand over and took Baldor's in hers. Their eyes met and he smiled at her, waiting for her response.

"No, I want to send the message. It's just hard to find the right words," Kalira explained.

She picked up a fine copper wire and began to trace a symbol in the air. The movement ended with the copper wire in front of her mouth.

"Hello, Venja, I am one of the Magisters of the Karaz Islands. We would like to parley with you in Himalus. Please name a time if possible."

For a moment, nothing happened. The silence in the room made her uneasy. She began to fiddle with the wire in her hand, pressing it against her fingers.

"What a surprise. Yes, let's meet in two days. A gathering of queens, how fun." Kalira heard Venja's voice in her head. Cold shivers ran down her spine. *It is really her, her voice.*

Baldor looked at her expectantly. "Did she answer you?"

"Yes, I think she didn't recognize my voice. After all, it's been hundreds of years since she last heard it. She sounded a bit sassy, not at all like I remembered her, but she agreed to meet us in Himalus in two days," Kalira said, staring out through the high stained-glass window into the courtyard.

"I'm glad she agreed to meet in Himalus. That's a good place to meet. It's almost exactly halfway between us. And Himalus is known for its neutrality," Baldor said, looking worried. "Are you all right, love? There's no color left in your face."

Somehow she was at a loss for words. Her head was spinning and she felt a little nauseous.

Baldor stood and leaned down to kiss her forehead. "Don't worry too much, my dear. The world has survived much worse, and you will too. I'll go and order us some tea." Then he left the room, leaving Kalira alone with her warring thoughts.

There was a hole inside her, a hole that never fully healed, no matter how many years or lifetimes she lived. She missed her sister very much. Valeria had been a part of her, her other half, and then Valeria was gone, and there was nothing that could fill that vacuum, not even Baldor.

Every time she thought about her sister, Kalira also missed Zamanthyr, her first home. Especially its diversity. The fact that one could simply mount a horse and ride from heaven to hell in a matter of days was something out of a dream. Or a nightmare, depending on which direction you rode.

Especially the city of Undarath was a rare gem in the multiverse, its sheer size awe-inspiring to those who first saw it from the distant shores. And every new traveler underestimated the time it took to cross one of the three bridges to reach the city. Once, when she was a young girl, she sat on the stone railing of the bridge all day, just to watch the stunned faces of the travelers when they finally reached the sixty-foot-high gate of the outer curtain wall of Undarath. By the time they reached the gate, it had taken them over a day to walk across the bridge. Not only was the gate huge, but each building was three or sometimes four stories high.

One man seemed rather unimpressed, and that bothered her, as she was quite proud of her wonderful hometown. So she said, "Did you know that the city is not just on top of a lake?"

"What do you mean? Of course it must be on some kind of island, silly child." The man laughed at her and looked at his traveling companions in amusement.

"But it doesn't sit on an island, sir. It *is* the island. The Aquatic live down below and have their own kingdom, still ruled by the Golden Council, of course."

He had stared at her for a moment, apparently considering the truth in her words. "That is, if true, quite interesting. Is anyone allowed to go there?"

"Yes, sir, but the Aquatic are not keen on surface people. They like to stay away."

He had just nodded in acknowledgment and salutation, wished her a good day, and walked through the open gates of her beloved city.

It truly was a marvelous land. Kalira had always wondered why it had been so hard for Valeria to fit in. Sure, she was different, but so were many others. Perhaps it had been their mother's fault. She had always mocked Valeria, made Valeria feel low and worthless. Many times Kalira had tried to change their mother's mind about Valeria, but it felt like their mother didn't even want to try to like her. They could have had a wonderful childhood, but their mother had always been there to ruin all the fun, to keep them apart, to sow suspicion and hatred. It had made her furious that Kalira had not stopped loving her sister. How could she? Their mother had never understood their bond. What wouldn't Kalira give to know the reason for their mother's disdain? But she was long dead and there was no one left to ask. Perhaps Kalira could ask Valeria now? Maybe there was a way to bring this to a happy end?

There were so many unanswered questions on her mind. So many things that plagued her. For example, why had Valeria chosen to go to Dohva? Of all the realms, she had chosen a land that had been populated by druids back then, without big cities or huge populations. It had been a land of nature and the elements. So why would she have chosen to come here? Why had she thought that they would be more accepting?

Kalira had pondered these questions for so long, ever since a woman on the streets of Undarath had mistaken her for Valeria and asked why she had returned from Dohva through the portal. It had startled her then, the thought of her sister fleeing not only from home, but from one continent to another to escape her family.

But now Kalira knew—Valeria hadn't come for the druids or the beauty of the land, or to leave their cruel mother behind. She had wanted to escape to the lands below, the endless night of the Dark Kingdom. How had this time in the dark changed her? Was her sister still inside Venja or was she lost forever?

Kalira looked out into the darkness. How had Valeria done it? To create such a darkness and to maintain it for such a long time must come at a great cost. Hopefully Kalira would get more answers soon. *Two days...*

28

Avala

The flickering firelight in the lamp was nearly extinguished. She didn't understand how this magical light source worked. There was no oil in it, nor wax or any other flammable material. It was just a small metal bead that floated inside the glass ball lamp. With increased curiosity, she watched its flame and made a mental note to ask Kima about this enchantment.

Her room was quite large, much larger than her room back at the barracks, and much more fancy than anything she had ever lived in. There was some sort of heater in the corner, radiating warmth, but there was no sign of a fire inside. The walls were covered with an elaborate wallpaper of flowers, bees and butterflies. It was like sleeping in a lush valley.

She sat on the edge of her huge bed, stroking the soft, silky texture of the blanket, and thought about her recent conversations with Garon and Sineth. In the depths of her mind, thoughts swirled incessantly. *It's all my fault. If I hadn't switched shifts with Garon, he would be fine. I would have been the one with the horns. Or would Venja have done something else to me? Maybe I could go with the Magisters? I have to see her face, hold her accountable for what she did to Garon,* Avala thought, trying to imagine Venja, but only seeing Kalira's face. And then there were the thoughts of Kima's discovery that plagued her as well. Soul magic... how is this even possible?

She pressed the palms of her hands to her head, trying to concentrate, trying to stop the thoughts, the memories, but it was no use. There was no cure for her illness, no remedy for her own personal nightmare. What she would give just to have some silence, some peace of mind, but there was no point in wishing for something that would never happen.

When the light flickered, she got up to check the lamp, but she still wasn't sure what to look for. *Maybe I should ask one of the servants to check it.*

Grabbing her new robe, she pulled it tight and headed for the door, but as she pushed the handle down, a knock interrupted her. "Who could that be? It must be almost night, not that the darkness outside ever changes," she muttered to her-self.

With a small squeak of the wood, the door opened.

"Sineth, what are you doing here?" Avala felt her heart quicken.

"I want to talk to you. Can I come in?" Sineth asked with a warm but somewhat shy smile.

"The lamp is about to go out. I was on my way to get someone to fix it. I don't know how these things operate. Some kind of enchantment, I guess," Avala replied, trying not to look too deeply into his eyes.

"I can fix it. I mean, I can't fix the enchantment, but I can make light," Sineth said, snapping his fingers to summon a small flame on his index finger.

There was a long pause as they stood there, the door be-tween them, the small flame illuminating their faces.

"Sure. Let's talk then." Avala stepped aside and let Sineth pass.

She did not know how she felt about this. Her head was so full of drama, all she wanted was some rest, but she had the feeling that more drama was about to come her way.

He walked over to the light and flicked the flame in the glass ball of the lamp. Next to it was a round table of dark wood with two chairs. Sineth sat down and Avala did the same. The silence in the room was painful, and Avala stared at the darkness outside the window.

"I want to apologize. I'm not very good at explaining how I feel. But I am truly sorry for leaving you back then. It changed me deeply. I don't know what my life would have been like if I had stayed and helped you through that terrible time. I didn't know how to deal with all the grief, the pain, and seeing you struggle with it. It was just too much for me. So I left," Sineth confessed, his gaze intense. "I came back for you after two weeks, but you were gone."

Tears welled up in Avala's eyes and she sobbed a little. Sineth reached across the table and brushed away her tears, holding her face in his hand.

"I traveled to Himalus and joined the Earthbinders. I served as a nun for the rest of my first life. It helped me find peace and purpose," Avala said between tears.

"I never expected this. You, a faithful nun in the Earthbinder Monastery?" Sineth gave her a curious look.

There was a long, silent pause. Avala did not really know what to say or do. Her head was still flooded with thoughts. Even more so now, after everything she had just been told. It was hard for her to be in the moment and not drift far away on a wave of memories and images from the past.

"Avala, I want to try to make up for what I've done. And maybe we could try again," Sineth said, his voice low, just a little more than a whisper.

"What?" Avala couldn't figure out if this was coming from the voices in her head or if he'd actually said it.

"I want to be your partner. For this life and the ones to come," Sineth continued, staring at her, obviously waiting for her answer, but she didn't know what to say. After a while Sineth spoke again. "You know, I never had a relationship after us. Of course I had a lot of loose connections, but no one could hold up to what we had, so it never became something more serious. I understand that this could be overwhelming, so maybe I should just go and let you think about it."

With a careful movement, Sineth stood up and walked to the door, perhaps not wanting to disturb her in her pondering.

But what if it works? What if this is our last chance to try? Nobody knows how this war will end. Maybe I should be a little more open, even reckless. And Garon made it abundantly clear that whatever we had is over. I was never really invested in the relationship with him. Loose connections... So I might as well.

Avala rushed to the door as Sineth was about to close it and wrapped her arms around him. She kissed Sineth—a long, passionate, emotion-loaded kiss. The kind of kiss you know has meaning and will be remembered forever.

29

Kima

The next morning, they were all back in the main hall. Today it felt as if this vast hall was closing in on them with every word that echoed through it.

"What do you mean you knew? Why didn't you tell anyone?" Kima's voice rose to a high pitch.

"It's not that simple. What exactly were we supposed to tell the people? At the time, everyone was grateful that the islands hadn't fallen. The great city of Gahaal stood for well over a thousand years before Dohva was struck and partially destroyed. Everyone wanted to rebuild. And a few centuries passed with the excitement of a new way of life. Being isolated wasn't all bad. We were protected from the influences of the other realms. Not all of them are good. Some seek power over others more than anything else," Baldor said in a calm and rational manner. His demeanor only fueled Kima's anger, tempting her to run up the stairs and shake him.

"But what about the sacrifices? The people couldn't have been grateful for that, too?" Kima retorted, her frustration obvious. *This is still the Magister of Karaz. Get a grip,* she scolded herself.

"In the beginning, there were many who chose to sacrifice themselves for the good of the people. Some were sick with an incurable disease, others were simply old and tired of life. But after they discovered that when you die, you are reborn and can start a new life with new opportunities, the number of volunteers dwindled. But the sacrifices had to be made for the sphere to remain. In addition, the druids of Madin, once dedicated to the forces of nature, became obsessed with the new powers the sphere had given them. They created a cult, banned all other magic, like powers that had been given by deities or learned magic. For many years the druids manipulated the people, putting lies in their heads and crowning themselves as their new leaders. The High Monks became sorcerers, servants to the elemental sphere and its power. Then I decided to extract myself from their madness and took the northern, as yet uninhabited, islands as my own and created this sheltered haven for all who chose to join us, and many did. With the help of my dear Kalira, of course."

He paused and took a heavy breath. "Well, after that, the newly installed leaders simply chose who would die in the name of honor. But the people had already lived more than one life, more than any mortal being in the depths of the multiverse is allowed. They should all be grateful for what they have been given here. It is, after all, a miracle. To defy death for so long is something others would easily kill for," Baldor said, with a cynical smile.

"And you were there?" Avala inquired.

"Yes, I've been here for a long time. You know, Kima and Avala, I don't appreciate your tone. You pick into pockets of history and politics you know nothing about and blame us for their outcome. It was not as if we sat here and did nothing. We went to great lengths to find a way to make the islands fly on their own, independent of the function of the elemental sphere. That is why I dedicated this place, Jazat, to knowledge and magic of all kinds. Over the years it grew, and more towns and villages were created, all of which are now known as the Karaz Islands," Baldor explained, a hint of self-satisfaction coloring his words despite the gravity of their situation.

"But why didn't you help the people of Madin? Stop the Elementals, free us?" Avala pressed, her eyebrows furrowed in frustration.

"As I said, it's not that simple. What was I supposed to do? As long as we were dependent on the sacrifices, the Elementals did what needed to be done," Baldor repeated, his tone unwavering.

Kima could hear Avala gritting her teeth, her stare angry. Kima reached up and touched Avala's forearm.

"I'm sorry this is not the answer you want to hear, but it is what it is. I think you should also be grateful for the many lives you have been granted. And that's enough story time for today. I have a meeting to prepare for," Baldor declared as he got up and left the room before they could ask any more questions.

"What are we going to do?" Kima asked, her voice filled with uncertainty.

"We go back to the library and find a way to destroy the orb, the amplifier that Nirella wrote about in the journal," Avala said through clenched teeth.

"But if we do that, the islands could fall. There are a lot of lives at stake," Kima observed, watching Avala's expression with a hint of concern.

"Then we will find a way to prevent that," Avala assured her and started to leave.

Kima stood there for a moment, letting all the information sink in. *Why is Avala so insistent on tearing down the sphere? There won't be any more rebirths after that. And if we don't find a way to make the islands fly, more people will die than in many years of sacrifice. If Baldor spent a thousand years looking for a solution to this problem and couldn't find one, why should we succeed?*

And yet Baldor didn't say he hadn't.

30

Venja

Slowly, the jagged outline of the Kuana Mountains broke through the darkness. A gust of wind hit Venja's face, and snow fell in thick, fluffy flakes, creating a magical atmosphere.

"Barach-Daracc!" With a hard push and these words, she urged the wyvern to fly lower and lower. There, deep within the mountains, nestled among the jagged peaks, was Himalus, the City of Waterfalls. It was an ancient place, far older than any of the other cities and villages here in Dohva, perhaps even older than Undarath.

Many spires of different sizes, topped with round tops, were built on the stone. The different parts of this vast city were all connected by bridges to cross the waterfalls that forced their way down the mountainside. Everything was covered in vines and other vegetation that took advantage of the stone structures. Near the upper part of the city was a flat area where the water slowed down into a pool and then ran down with speed to the next flat area to pool again. She had almost forgotten how beautiful this place was, with the fresh air and the constant gurgle of the streams.

It had been the first place she had come to in Dohva. She had bribed a monk in Undarath to let her through the portal in their temple to Simbradil—Mother Nature—and that had brought her here.

Himalus also had many temples and a monastery dedicated to Simbradil, but I'm sure that has changed since then. Maybe I'll rebuild it for her. I've always liked the idea of a goddess of nature. The reign of the goddess and the queen, she pondered.

A few minutes later, the wyvern hit the ground in the upper part of the city. Next to the monastery and its many temples, there was an open space. It gave way to a huge round platform, crowned with an intricate mosaic depicting vines and waves intertwined, an homage to the symbiosis of water, earth and all growing things. The entrance to what was once the temple of Simbradil—Mother of Nature—was guarded by two of Venja's subjects, grave-faced dwarves with spears and shields showing her white crown. She knew them well enough to know that there was a joy in them that was not apparent at first glance. But it was a good thing that the ordinary people feared them; it had made Madin's invasion much easier. Fear is a powerful motivator for obedience. And it seemed that Venja's forces had done a good job of besieging this city without her.

They bowed and let her in. This was now a common room for shared meals and lively conversation. Inside the round spire was a pool of clear water, with an island in the middle that could be reached by a massive stone bridge. On the island was a round table with eight chairs. She remembered from her first visit that there had been an altar and a stone figure of Simbradil instead of this seating arrangement. Everything else had remained the same—the columns surrounding the pool, the vines wrapping around it. It seemed that the Elementals had kept it in good shape.

Venja made her way to the table. No light had been lit inside. It was just the way she liked it, dark. She sat down in the chair facing the entrance, folded her hands in her lap and listened to the darkness outside. It shouldn't be long before they arrived.

After a while, Venja began to play with her necklace. She ran her finger over the twisted metal that held the stone in place. It had been around her neck for so long, a constant reminder of the new life she had begun here. Finding it deep in the tunnels of the Dark Kingdom had truly changed her destiny.

There had been a woman in Undarath who had seen her during one of her nighttime excursions. She had taken pity on Valeria, hiding in the dark, and told her about this famous Dark Kingdom. With the woman's help, Valeria had managed to create a somewhat vague map to the entrance of said kingdom.

With the map in her hand, Valeria had wandered through the mountain passages, looked into every cave, and searched behind every patch of vegetation that grew along the mountainside. She had only searched at night; her eyes were so sensitive to the light that she could hardly see. As a result, it had taken her nearly two weeks to find the entrance. It had been such a relief to finally be in the dark. Sure, it lacked the beauty of the world above, but it gave her a freedom she had never known before.

Searching for a good place to make a home, she had found a tower that overlooked a massive drop that went on for hundreds of feet. The tower was old and broken in places, but it was something she could work with. And it wasn't empty. There was furniture, old cloth, books, chests, and all sorts of strange decorations, all covered in a thick layer of dust. *Who used to live here?* she wondered, but decided to make this tower her home regardless.

Then Valeria had to find a way to get food and water down there, so she had gone deeper into the mountain to find a source of fresh water or signs of civilization. And she had found both, and much more. She had come upon an ancient crypt of sorts, with a stone altar depicting a tall, muscular humanoid. The statue was made of what must have been polished obsidian, now covered in dust and pebbles and chipped in places. His eyes were made of shiny green stones. He also had fangs, pointed ears, six slender fingers on each hand, and six small horns. A fiend, clearly, but a handsome one.

Valeria began to examine it more closely, tracing her fingers over the smooth stone. In his left hand, which he held behind his back, was a necklace. Platinum chains held a palm-sized white stone. Carefully she tried to remove it from the stone hand.

I see you found my gift, a pleased male voice said in the back of her head. *It comes with great power. A treat, truly.*

"Who is this? And how are you talking in my head?" Valeria asked aloud.

No need to talk, my dear. I can hear your thoughts. I'm Agthod, the most powerful demon prince, and of course the most intelligent and handsome. Some call me the Prince of Pleasure or the Shadow King. I can grant you many gifts if you decide to be my companion, my partner in mischief, my princess, it crooned in her head.

And what would I gain from such an alliance? I have heard of the persuasions of your kind. There is always a catch, she thought.

Oh, you want to negotiate? I respect that. The necklace you are trying to free grants the bearer endless life, great magical powers, and the confidence to be a true leader. What more could you ask for, my dear?

I want to be loved, adored, and feared. I want to feel beautiful and strong. Can you give me that? Valeria didn't know if she would have had the courage to say these things out loud, but the thoughts came to her naturally.

Of course I can, my dear. I can also give you a great deal of pleasure if you let me. You look like you could use some fun. Agthod's voice was as smooth as the stone hand she still held, tempting and erotic.

I could use some fun and some help. What do you want in return?

Only your loyalty. Be my disciple, my acolyte in this realm. Spread the word of my power flowing through you. Be my princess, or even a queen if you wish. He let out a chuckle that filled her entire mind.

Tempting. What would I have to do to gain access to this power?

I'm glad you asked. Just say the word 'Agna'rathar' and the necklace will be released, and so will I. His voice sounded low and enticing at the end.

That's it?

That's it.

There was a pause. Valeria stared at the necklace. *What do I have to lose?* she thought. "Agna'rathar!" Her voice echoed off the cave walls around her.

Then she heard a crack, then another. Valeria stepped back until she hit the wall behind her. She watched as the statue slowly began to shift and move, coming to life. The green stones became real glowing green eyes, the fangs changed from black stone to yellow teeth, and a mane of black hair grew out of the stone, partially hiding its horns.

There stood Agthod, stretching his magnificent demon body, wearing nothing but a pair of billowing black satin pants.

"Thank you, love. Here is your reward." Agthod approached her and held the necklace in front of her face. "It will look beautiful on you, my princess."

The white crystal stone was embedded in a spiral of polished shimmering silver with two chains attached to each side. Valeria reached out to take it from him, touching his hand briefly. A shiver ran down her spine, a tickling sensation, and then a warm, welcome feeling of lust, something she hadn't really felt before. She looked from his hand to his face.

He was smiling, a wide, joyful smile. "I didn't even ask your name, my love. What should I call you?"

"I am Valeria."

"Oh, that's not a name for a demon princess, is it? Too soft, too playful. You need something strong. How about Venja? It reminds me of vengeance." He stopped and looked at her. Then he reached out and touched her face with his other six-fingered hand. "My beautiful Venja. Come now, try it on."

Carefully she pulled it from his hand and put it around her neck. All four chains came together in the back. The moment she closed it and the stone touched her skin, the crystal began to glow red, but after a few seconds, the glow faded and the crystal returned to its almost translucent white color.

"Ah, can you feel it, my love? The connection, the power? You have much to learn now. But first, let us have some fun,"

Agthod said softly, almost a whisper against her cheek. He was very tall, about nine feet. He towered over her and with a firm grip he lifted her off the ground and placed her on his hips. Instinctively, she wrapped her feet around him. Heat radiated between them and she could feel him harden beneath her.

Oh, my princess, I have waited so long. Now you are mine, was the last thing she heard in the back of her head, before he kissed her, not soft, but wild and demanding. A low growl came from his mouth. She should be afraid—after all, he was a demon, a beast—but his lips and his hot body pressed against hers were all she could think about. His wicked hands touched her in places no one had ever touched her before. He showered her with the gifts of pleasure, desire and being desired.

And why should she have been afraid of him? Agthod had embraced her and shown her what she was capable of. He had turned her into Venja—strong, powerful, beautiful—and no one dared to say anything else.

31

Garon

The sky hung gray over the windswept steppe, a desolate landscape that echoed with muffled screams, fading into the background like a haunting refrain.

Garon began to run, his pace quickening with each step, but the surroundings remained unchanged. It was as if he were trapped in an endless expanse of nothingness with no way out. Questions swirled in his mind, each more urgent than the last. *How did I get here? What is this place?*

Another scream pierced the air, louder this time, causing Garon to turn, his gaze sweeping the horizon in search of its source. But with each turn, the landscape remained eerily uniform, leaving him disoriented and adrift in the gray expanse.

Sitting on the barren ground, Garon struggled to remember how he had gotten here, but his memories remained elusive. As he looked down at his feet, a surge of confusion ran through him. He was clad in spiked black leather boots, his hands and arms encased in intricate black plates of armor. Horns protruded from his head, and jagged teeth filled his wide mouth. Panic threatened to engulf him as he struggled with the incongruity of his appearance.

Suddenly, the sound of rushing water reached his ears, mingling with muffled screams in a cacophonous symphony. Garon raced toward the sound, a flicker of hope igniting within him. After what seemed an eternity, he stumbled upon a broad river, its waters shimmering beneath the gray sky. But when he bent to drink, he recoiled in disgust—the water tasted of salt, leaving his mouth parched and his senses reeling.

Choosing to follow the riverbank, Garon soon encountered a forest shrouded in thick mist, its gnarled trees devoid of foliage save for long, sinuous branches that twisted and curled. Despite the eerie atmosphere and the unsettling hiss that emanated from the shadows, he pressed on, determined to escape the oppressive gloom.

Emerging from the forest, Garon was confronted by a massive city surrounded by towering stone walls. The sight of it stirred a sense of foreboding within him, but he pressed on, his curiosity overcoming his trepidation.

Within the city's labyrinthine streets, Garon encountered a multitude of creatures—demons and otherworldly beings, each more bizarre than the last. Shackled figures trudged alongside their captors, while others cast indifferent glances in his direction, their eyes betraying recognition of his demonic form.

Navigating the fog-shrouded streets, Garon eventually arrived at a palace made up of countless ivory towers clustered around a central river. Feeling an inexplicable pull toward the imposing structure, he passed through its gates unhindered, the absence of guards already unnerving.

Inside, the corridors were lined with mirrors, reflecting a kaleidoscope of demonic visages as Garon wandered aimlessly in search of guidance. It was not until he entered a wide obsidian chamber that he encountered another presence—a figure seated on a throne, its form obscured by darkness.

"I'm glad you made it. I know the journey through my land is not an easy one." More movement came from the throne, and then two green eyes pierced the darkness as if lit from behind. The creature approached him, taking his chin in his hand. "Venja told me that you are a pretty one, clever as well, and quite talented in the field of magic. Should I be jealous?" he said in a dark, rolling voice, almost a whisper. He was very close, his face only inches from Garon's.

"Who are you?" Garon managed to ask back.

"Oh, how rude of me. I'm Agthod, the demon prince of this land. I am Venja's partner, her source of power, if you will. Not like a god, but more like a very persuasive leader." Agthod let go of his chin and walked around him, inspecting him from all sides. "She told me about you. I'm quite proud of her. The way she managed to capture and seduce you... Venja is a capable student."

"Why am I here? What do you want from me?"

"Don't be like that, Garon. Show some respect. Others are tortured and killed for less. You are here because I wanted to see you. I reached into your mind and nestled deep within. I see through all your thoughts, hopes and dreams. You aspire to be a great leader. You care about honor and respect. I can give you that and a great deal of power as well, if you help my lovely princess rule her land—and keep her bed warm at night when I'm not there to do it myself." Agthod's eyes lit up even more, and Garon could see his wide, fanged grin.

"Why don't you help her and join her in bed all the time? It seems to me that you are very fond of her, and not lacking in magical abilities either," Garon hissed back.

"How rude you are, Garon. I guess manners can't be forced on anyone." Agthod paused and stepped in front of him again, bending down. His face was so close that their lips almost touched. "I can't reach my dear Venja, at least not physically at the moment. There is some kind of barrier. That's why you will do the job for me. It's either that or end-less suffering, pain and loneliness for the rest of your useless life," Agthod murmured against his lips. Garon could feel his warm breath against his face and his lips tingled from the vibration of his words. "I understand the attraction. You are much like me. She made herself a little copy of me. How sweet. I guess she missed her prince."

Garon didn't know what to say. He just stared into Agthod's glowing eyes, trying not to move or show any sign of fear. He knew that this would not end well for him either way. He also felt this strong pull inside of him, this feeling that he should just let go and surrender to whatever they had planned for him. There was no way back. No scenario where he could just be himself again, normal and free. It was probably less painful to be that way and let his old self go. Get rid of all the moral conflicts in his head. *Just give in...*

Yes, just give in. Give yourself to me. To our cause, to Venja, Agthod murmured in his mind, almost like a cat's purr.

And then Garon just let go. His memories faded. Familiar faces went blank. Garon saw only Agthod, smiling, pleased. Agthod stroked his cheek, kissed his lips. Garon closed his eyes and let it happen. He heard the snapping of fingers, and when he opened his eyes again, he was in another black room, but this one had a round bed in the middle, covered with black satin sheets. There was no source of light in this room, but the darkness didn't bother him at all.

Agthod led him to the bed. "Have you ever been with a man? No, I didn't think so. I think you will enjoy the experience very much. Just let go. Maybe we could get together sometime, the three of us."

Strangely, Garon felt desire building inside him. Garon would never have thought to feel that way about a man, but this was no ordinary being. There was something about Agthod, the way he spoke and moved. The way Agthod touched him was mesmerizing, enticing.

Garon felt his arms around him, his lips all over his body. He looked down and there was no armor on him. It was just gone. He was lying naked, with Agthod's equally naked body on top of him. His heart was racing, but not from fear. He gave himself to Agthod and it was the best feeling he had ever had—free, strong, full of energy and life. Their lips met. Their bodies intertwined. And he could feel Agthod's cock pressed against his body.

Succumbing to Agthod's influence, Garon surrendered to a torrent of desire and submission, his senses overwhelmed by the allure of the demonic prince. As their encounter escalated into a feverish embrace, Garon found himself consumed by a tumult of conflicting emotions, his identity and control slipping away in the throes of passion.

But as the echoes of their encounter faded, Garon was jolted back to reality by a distant voice calling his name. Disoriented and disheveled, he struggled to reconcile the vividness of his experience with the barrenness of his surroundings.

Was this all just a dream? Garon wondered, his mind reeling from the intensity of his encounter with Agthod. Though the memory lingered, he struggled with the dissonance between fantasy and reality, unsure where one ended and the other began. His skin was hot, even burning, the sheets wet with his sweat and the results of this vivid dream.

As the voice persisted, Garon tried to compose himself, the remnants of his desire still lingering like wisps of smoke.

"Not now," he replied, his voice tinged with uncertainty. But even as he dismissed the intruding voice, he couldn't shake the lingering sensation of Agthod's presence, a haunting reminder of the darkness that had enveloped him.

Well, this was fun. We should do it again, soon, he heard Agthod's pleased voice in his head.

32

Kalira

A cold breeze brushed over Kalira's arms, giving her goose bumps. She glanced out of the window of the entrance hall of the palace, past the terrace district, toward the harbor. The skyship had been prepared and armed for whatever challenges might await them in Himalus. A mixture of stress, fear and anticipation filled her mind and made her shiver. What would her sister be like? A stranger? Or perhaps her sister was still inside Venja somewhere, buried beneath layers of hardness and drive. Despite the difficulties they had faced, Kalira had always tried to be a good friend to Valeria, to be there for her, no matter what their mother had tried to do to prevent it. Kalira loved her with every fiber of her being. There was no other way. Valeria was her other half. It was a bond that could never be broken.

A sound interrupted her daydream, growing louder and more insistent: knock, knock... knock, knock. "Kalira, are you ready? It's time." Baldor's familiar voice echoed through the closed door. Without another word, the door opened and Baldor stood in the doorway. He was the nicest person she knew, despite his occasional fierceness and harshness. To her, he had always been a true friend, loyal in every way.

With a careful movement, he crossed the room and sat down on the windowsill, staring into the distance with her. "What are you thinking about? Maybe I can help?"

"I was just thinking about Valeria. About what a nice child she was. We were very close back in Undarath. At least I thought we were."

"I know. You've told me so much about it over the past few hundred years, I feel like I was a part of it myself." Baldor paused and let out a sigh. "Kalira, please prepare yourself for the possibility that she isn't the person you want her to be. It may very well be that Venja is past any kind of familiarity you once shared. It was a long time ago, and whatever power she has gained is consuming her completely." His eyebrows furrowed and he looked very sad—a rare sight.

"I know. But I can't help but dream a little. I thought she was dead, that she had died after a normal elven lifespan, but now there's a flicker of hope, and I can't help but wonder what she might be like."

"Terrifying, powerful, beautiful, determined to rule the world?" Baldor said with a wink. Kalira gave him a weak half smile. He was just trying to lighten the mood.

They made their way through the terrace, past the opulent white stone buildings with their high metal fences, toward the harbor. From this vantage point, one could normally see all the way to Xear and the massive mountain range of Kuana. But the darkness and a heavy fog obscured even the nearest building. It worried her, this darkness, and what evil it might hold.

The air was crisp and the wind made the airship move slightly as Kalira walked up the stairs onto the ship. It was painted white, with golden waves just below the railing. The bright color pierced even the dreadful gray tones that colored their surroundings. It was a slim, fast ship with two huge Safral stones embedded in the bow and stern. It had always reminded her of a river galley, perhaps because of its elegant, elongated shape. The only ships Dohva had were small fishing boats on Lake Methar. Kalira missed seeing the ships sail into the sunset outside of Undarath—the glistening light on the ocean waves. *Will I ever see that again?*

Inside the captain's quarters, she sat down with Baldor to discuss their approach to the meeting. Baldor placed a circle of clay dust around them and whispered an incantation. She knew the phrase and what it meant—he had done it many times before. Baldor had sealed them in, making sure no one could overhear their conversation. After a few moments, he sat down in an ornate wooden chair and ate one of the grapes from the small round table between their chairs.

"So, sisterhood aside, we must be extremely careful. My love, you know we should not be in such a dangerous situation together," Baldor said, staring at her.

"You could have let me go alone," Kalira replied with a smile.

"You know very well that was not an option. Venja just needs to say the right words and you'll be utterly convinced that she is still your sweet twin sister."

"I'm not that naive, Baldor."

"Not naive, but a little too hopeful?"

"Perhaps, but I know what's at stake. Not just for all of Dohva, but for us as well."

"If she tries anything foolish, you must promise me that you will run to the airship and leave. I can handle her on my own, but if you are there, we will both be in critical danger."

"I know. I promise I won't hesitate to escape." Kalira smiled.

"Don't joke, Kalira. Not now. If she kills you, I'll fall too, and then everyone is lost," he said, looking out the side window. "We are so close to getting enough Safral to make all the Madin Islands fly on their own, if only they would let us help them... We could be part of the world again, Kalira. I long for change."

After a long, silent pause, Kalira asked, "What do you think of our new group of misfits? They seem very driven, passionate."

"Perhaps a little too driven for my taste. I don't appreciate people yelling at me." Baldor pressed his lips together.

"Well, they did bring back a lot of good information. Maybe they are just rough diamonds, ready to be shaped. With a little help, they could shine." Kalira let out a small chuckle.

"And I should be the one to shape them? I don't think so. Kima, perhaps. I've always been quite fond of her—she is very talented and eager to learn. But let's focus on the task at hand, my dear."

"I can try to reason with Val... with Venja. Try to appeal to her humanity. Maybe even align with her against the Madin government. We've never been fans of the monks anyway," Kalira suggested.

"Good. We can offer her peace in her quest to rule Madin if she ends the darkness and the bloodshed of innocent people."

"Sounds reasonable. We just need her to be reasonable too."

33

Sineth

Every footstep echoed through the sparsely furnished marble hall. A large, floating orb of light hung from the ceiling, dividing the room into light and dark. In the shadows behind one of the tall pillars sat Garon, his head resting on his knees.

"There you are. I've been looking for you everywhere," Sineth said, approaching Garon.

"Why did you search for me?" Garon asked with a sinister tone in his voice.

"I want to talk to you," Sineth said, sitting down on the ground in the light a few feet from Garon. "Why are you sitting in the shadows? This is the best 'daylight' we can get right now."

"Monsters don't sit in the light of day," Garon whispered against his knees.

"I don't believe you're a monster. It's your actions that might make you one," Sineth said, maybe thinking more of himself than of Garon. A sadness filled his mind as he remembered the flames that had consumed his home, the inevitability of their all-consuming heat, lingering in the darkness like an old friend.

"And who said my actions were not monstrous?" Garon looked up and met Sineth's eyes.

"I guess I don't know you, but I don't care anyway." Sineth returned the hardness of his tone. "I wanted to talk to you about Avala."

"There's nothing to talk about," Garon said, leaning his head back against the pillar and staring at the ceiling.

"You were very close. Avala told me you wanted to marry her. So it's not nothing."

"And what a foolish ambition it seems now, but what does it matter?" Garon gritted his teeth.

"She did not return your... serious affections?" Sineth wondered if it had been for her as it had been for him. Never again had he been with a woman he had loved, adored even, with every fiber of his being. Every relationship had taken a

turn for him as soon as it got too close, too attached, too...
serious.

He paused to take a closer look at Garon's expression.
From this perspective, Sineth could only see the demon-like
side of Garon's face, covered with scales and jagged teeth,
and the large horn protruding from his skull. It was hard not
to recoil from the sight. It seemed as if Garon was somewhere else, his eyes flickering left and right, but not reacting
to Sineth's question or even his presence.

After another minute of awkward silence, Sineth decided
to just get it over with and ask what he'd intended on. Just
to be polite and do things right for once. Avala had made it
clear that even though there was nothing left between her
and Garon, Sineth should try to clear the way, so to speak.
But it seemed like a terrible idea now that Sineth looked at
the grim figure in front of him. He stood up, just to be ready
in case this thing inside Garon wanted to take a bite out of
him.

"Okay, so you would be okay with me and her getting
close? You know, like a couple?" Sineth swore he saw Garon's
demonic face flinch.

"I don't care. I have all the affection and passion I need."

*What or who does he mean? Venja? I thought he hated her and
left her because she turned him into that thing?*

Before he could stop himself, Sineth asked, "Have you met
someone new? Are you and Kima getting along so well?" It
was more of a joke than anything else, but he was curious
about this strange man.

With unnatural speed, Garon shot to his feet. His chin was lowered, his head tilted to one side. He began to walk slowly towards Sineth.

Sineth instinctively backed away until he hit the cold stone surface of a pillar. He tried to maneuver around it to get some distance between himself and the beast. "Garon, what is going on? Talk to me!"

"I meant Venja, Queen of Darkness, lover of mine, follower of the great Agthod and the Order of Chaos," Garon said right in front of him, his demonic hand wrapped around Sineth's throat. Sineth just stood there, frozen, panicking.

Garon squeezed hard and Sineth felt the air escape under his grip. He felt hypnotized, at a loss for words and willpower.

Floating through an endless array of memories, he could hear the distinct, low, barking rumble of Molna's laugh mixed with the happy chirping of birds and the rustle of the wind through the trees of a dense forest. He could not tell which one it was, but he loved them all, Ithdir, Nyate, the once-close Emril and Enthaat. Each forest gave him shelter and peace when he needed it. A friend that was eternal, never withered, never died.

Then, like a soft illusion, he saw Avala enter the room from the library corridor. Sineth could hear muffled shouts and screams, and he felt himself surfacing back to reality.

Coming to his senses, feeling the urge to protect Avala from whatever madness had overtaken Garon, he seized that moment of clarity and punched Garon in the face with as much force as he had left in him. Garon stumbled backwards. Guards came from every corridor, shouting orders. Garon straightened and shot a beam of black energy at him. Quickly, Sineth tried to get out of the way, but the beam split into four, hitting him right in the chest.

Blackness filled his vision, the birds stopped chirping, and there was the fire again, lingering in the darkness, burning its way through his beloved trees to the tiny house he had once called home.

34

Kima

It had been another grueling day in the library. Her initial excitement had worn off after spending day after day in the gloom of the towering bookshelves. Now it felt more like a necessary chore than a wish that had finally been fulfilled. Kima's eyes began to burn and tear from hours of poring over scrolls and books. The unnatural light of the floating orbs in the library gave her a pounding headache. How she missed the natural rhythm of daylight, the soothing cycle of day and night. As for time... *What time is it exactly?* She couldn't tell.

Slowly, she lowered herself into the uncomfortable wooden chair. A myriad of materials and objects lay scattered before her: glass, metal, stone, parchment, tools, and vials filled with all manner of liquids.

Despite her exhaustion, she found herself smiling, even grinning. *I did it. I actually did it. I created the device, enchanted it, all by myself.* Granted, she had done numerous enchantments and even major projects on her own before, but this felt different. She looked down at the object in her hands—a four-sided metal plate, each side rounded inward, with an arcane rune etched deep into the metal.

Excitement surged through Kima as she picked up the gems from the table in front of her—one for each element: Air, Earth, Fire, and Water—and placed them on the pointed corners. Each of them had been marked with a unique draconic rune that corresponded to its respective element. She had pored over a book on runes and ancient writings related to the power of nature to make sure she got the glyphs right.

Somehow I made it happen. I created something that could do the job, that could destroy the orb. It felt exhilarating. Normally, she would have shared this accomplishment with Bon, and he would have been excited with her. This kind of joint happiness over an accomplishment had forged a strong bond between them, a deep connection on another level. It made her wonder if she would ever experience such a bond again—creating and building something together, living through the lows of failure and the highs of success.

Kima turned the object in her hand, examining it. It was aesthetically pleasing, resembling a king's amulet. The enchantment process required her to speak the command word, toss the object into the orb, and activate the gems to dispel the magic of each element. This should sever the elemental flow from the orb. Once done, the gems would shatter into dust, activating the plate. It would create an anti-magic shield within the orb, preventing the elemental flow from reconnecting. Without its amplifier, the elemental flow should cease and return to its point of origin. *Easy... then we should have about thirty minutes or so before the island falls into whatever depths lie beneath it. I should tell Avala.*

It took some time to find Avala; she was on the top floor of the library, surrounded by an equally large pile of books and scrolls, just as Kima had been moments before. Avala was asleep, her arms resting on a pile of books. *No wonder she is exhausted, with Garon thrown back in prison. At least Sineth wasn't badly hurt.* Kima looked at her beautiful features, her elegant jawline and perfectly shaped eyebrows, the curve of her lips. She looked away, suddenly feeling quite ashamed to stare at Avala like that. But Kima's eyes kept coming back to her.

For a while, Kima considered waking her, but decided against it and instead sat down beside her, leaned against the leg of a large mahogany table, and allowed herself to close her eyes.

The islands will fall, all of them. Even Karaz. Why would Baldor allow us to build some kind of bomb that would kill his people and his kingdom, everything he and Kalira have worked so hard for? No, he must have found some other magical means to keep his homeland from falling, or he would never support our efforts. But what about Madin and all its people and cities? Avala told me stories about Gahaal. It sounds like a wonderful place, and it would be gone too.

We have to think this through. I was so excited to finally create something new and unique again that I didn't think about what it might mean. Even if there was a way to keep the islands from falling altogether, not everyone might be happy about the change. My parents, for example. Their plan for me to run their business until they came back with a whole new life ahead of them would be ruined. But that would also mean that they no longer need me as their heir. I would be free of my promise to help them.

No more rebirths, but also no more sacrifices. Which way is better? I need to talk to them, to the Magisters, but also to Avala, who is so eager to get it over with. Yes, we'll talk... She felt herself drifting off into a series of confused thoughts, her eyes moving under her lids to see faraway places with bright white buildings and golden, onion-domed roofs.

"You did it!" a voice called out beside her. "Does it work?"

Slowly, Kima opened her eyes to see Avala kneeling beside her, her eyes filled with joy.

"I think it did," Kima replied, looking down at the small device in her halfling hand. It felt like she was holding the fate of the world in her palm, a foreboding of doom.

35

Venja

S till distracted by her thoughts about Agthod and their first meeting, Venja was jolted back to reality. There was a loud noise coming from somewhere outside the old temple of Simbradil, so she got up and went to the entrance of the cave.

She didn't know what she'd been expecting, but certainly not this. What kind of magic was this? Venja had seen many ships in Undarath, but none that could fly and none that looked like this.

The ship docked at the edge of the bridge, right next to the small square where she had landed. It was large enough to easily hold a hundred people, and it needed the entire length of the bridge to accommodate its size. With the vine-covered stone buildings on one side and the jagged outline of the rocks on the other, the ship had also blocked the way to the mountain path leading down to Lake Methar. *Clever. Perhaps they have not heard of our flying beast friends.* She chuckled.

The crew was busy securing the ship to the bridge with ropes. Part of the railing was pushed outward, revealing a set of stairs that conveniently ended at the top of the bridge. A waterfall rushed fiercely around the stone pillars, dropping just before it could hit the ship. *Whoever docked it really knew what they were doing,* she thought.

A beautiful white-haired elf walked down the steps of the airship, his posture impeccable, his head held high. *He is not afraid,* Venja said to herself, and then a wave of nausea hit her hard. She saw herself leaving the ship. Blinking and rubbing her eyes, she tried to focus on the person who was walking down those stairs, but it was still her. *This cannot be... Is that really my sister? But she must have been in Dohva since the island was isolated. How? How could she still be alive after more than a thousand years?* Venja had found a way to still be here; maybe Kalira had found a way as well. It felt strange to stare at herself walking towards her. Could she really do what she had planned? Kill the image of herself, her sister? They came closer and Venja watched her twin closely, following her every step.

"Greetings, Dark Queen! My name is Baldor Immos, and this is Kalira Saasar, but you might have already figured out as much." Baldor halted about ten feet from her. Kalira was standing next to him, smiling her unbearably ingratiating smile. *It's her, it's definitely my sister. This might complicate things a lot.*

Venja led them across the square, the roots of the nearby trees digging into the stone mosaic floor, making it bumpy and uneven. Imperfect, altered by the forces of nature. She loved it and stepped carefully around each root. They walked on in silence through the huge arched entrance of this old temple and crossed the small pool with the slender bridge. Venja sat down on the same stool as before, facing the arch to watch the comings and goings from the temple. The strange elf named Baldor and her adorable sister sat down on the other side of the round table.

There was even more silence as they waited patiently for the food to be served and the wine to be poured. Now it was time to talk about war.

"This is a new era, an era of darkness, an era of outcasts rising from the shadows. The druids had their time to rule; now it is time for a new leader. Not a corrupt panel of fanatics, but a queen, dark, wise, and more powerful than any of the druids have ever been. It is the rule of men that is bringing this land down. They don't understand the needs of the little people. I will give power not only to elves, but to humans, halflings, dwarves, orcs, and goblins alike. They all deserve the power to choose their own destiny," Venja said, staring into the eyes of Baldor, who seemed rather unmoved by her speech.

"How exactly do you help the people of this land by condemning them to a life in darkness and killing those who do not obey your will?" Baldor replied, swirling the glass of wine in his hand.

"They have a choice. To accept my leadership, or to be executed for the benefit of the greater good. And even if they are killed, they come back anyway. Born into a new life, with new choices to make. Hopefully the right ones." A hint of a crooked smile crept across her face.

"And what role do we play in your scheme?" Kalira asked, her features soft and worried, a look Venja had seen many times in her childhood. A look often worse than pity, a sad concern. As if Venja were a lost cause and all her plans were doomed to fail.

"You could simply accept me as the supreme queen of Dohva and resign as the Magisters of Karaz."

The second she finished her sentence, Baldor burst out laughing, loud and echoing through the huge stone dome they were in. "That's why we're here, why you accepted the invitation to parley, is it? You want us to resign? Why would we do such a thing? It's ridiculous. We have ruled Karaz for a very long time, my dear, and we have no intention of stepping down any time soon."

"How is it that you have managed to rule for so long? Even for an elf, that is an astonishingly long life." Venja looked at them. They didn't look to be more than three hundred years old at the most.

"Well, my dear, we all have our secrets, don't we?" Baldor looked at her with the same curiosity with which she looked at them.

"So how do we go forward from here? I'm going to rule over Dohva, all of Dohva. If you don't swear allegiance to me now, I will bring the war to you, and your people will have the same choice as the people of Madin. It is as simple as that." She studied their expressions carefully. Her sister looked sad, a hint of pain showing across her worried brow. But Baldor looked at her with a cold stare, his nostrils dilating every time he exhaled.

"I will say this only once, Venja. If you dare to hurt my people, I'll end you and your wretched band of followers before you even think of setting foot in my throne room. Do you understand?" His voice had changed, no longer smooth and confident like before, but cold as death.

She rose and called to her shadow friends, incorporeal shapes of herself, spread around the room. Death was on her side, darkness was on her side, and she felt the power of Agthod pulsing through her with savage intent. There was a strong force of her kin stationed throughout Himalus. With her mind alone she could reach out to her soldiers and they would come to her side. What could Baldor and Kalira possibly have to stand against her?

Kalira and her rude companion also rose and started to leave the island, crossing the bridge, turning their backs on her as if they had nothing to fear. *I'll show them fear.* Venja started to conjure, but stopped halfway when she saw a blur around Baldor, a change in his features. The two began to run. Venja dropped the spell and rushed after them, sending her shadow army in front of them. They reached Kalira and began to drain her life force. A steady stream of glowing white energy poured from her chest into the form of a non-being that looked strangely like Kalira herself. There was a part of Venja that ached at the sight. Was it because Kalira looked like her? Or did Venja really feel sad at killing a person she hadn't seen in a thousand years?

Suddenly she heard a loud cracking sound, and then Baldor's legs grew longer, scaled, with long, pointed claws. His body shifted and grew, higher and higher, a long tail protruding from his back, and then wings appeared. In front of her was no longer Baldor, but a huge silver dragon, pushing its way out of the tower's entrance. She was unsure of what she had just witnessed.

A moment later Venja came to her senses and ran after them. "Stop them, shoot them down!" she shouted to her guards, but they were already at work. To her dismay, their arrows found no weak spot in the shimmering silver dragon hide.

Kalira was nowhere in sight. The dragon lifted into the fresh air, flapping its wings, flying higher and higher toward the mountain peaks. Just when she thought it was going to fly away, it turned and charged down with enormous speed. Before they could even think of running, an icy blast hit them. They all fell to the ground, paralyzed by the cold. Venja fell as well, unable to move. Every fiber of her being fought against the cold, but she was helpless.

How could she have been so arrogant to think that the leaders of a country would just walk up to her without anyone or anything to protect them? *How could I have been so stupid to think that they would join my cause? How could I have thought that Kalira would be on my side, fighting with me?* was the last thing she thought before another blast hit her and she drifted into the sweet arms of death.

36

Garon

Garoooon, Garon, wake up! I have a task for you! a familiar voice called from the back of his mind. *It is rather urgent, hurry!* The voice was harsh and angry, and with a sudden surge of fear, Garon was forced to open his eyes. He was unsure of his surroundings or what had happened. Sluggishly, he shoved his aching body to rise, only to find himself facing metal bars. He was in prison again.

Go on, no time for your hesitation, Agthod said in his head, urging him forward. Garon pushed against the gate and it sprang open.

Strange, didn't they lock me up? Garon thought to himself.

No, you mortal, foolish boy. I opened it for you. Now move! You must run to the courtyard. I command you to run up and touch the necklace around Venja's neck. Go! Agthod ordered him, and Garon felt a sting in his chest. Somehow he felt pain—her pain—piercing coldly into his flesh. He could feel her pulse, her blood coursing through her body. The connection to her felt weak, almost broken. Garon felt a glimmer of hope creep into his mind, but he did not dare to ponder about what this could mean, not with Agthod listening to every word that crossed his mind.

She's here in Jazat? How? Why? Is Venja invading the Karaz Islands?

Yes, she's here and I command you to go, now! Agthod growled. Feeling hope drift away from him like a leaf in the wind, Garon began to run.

With every step upwards, he felt his sore muscles ache, and that strange piercing sensation inside him spread like a rapidly growing disease. Sweat poured down his face, not only from physical exhaustion, but also from fear. Fear of him, Agthod. The demon's power over him, making him drain himself in whatever way Agthod felt necessary. Suddenly Garon felt very aware of the fact that he had lost all self-control, and what that might entail.

There were no guards around, and he wondered where they had all gone. Every corridor and stairway he passed was empty. When he reached the top, he found out why. As he pushed open the heavy metal gates of the subterranean prison, he saw wyverns swarming in the sky, attacking the city; war was here. The darkness was filled with screams and shouts as he made his way through the streets. Somehow he knew where to go, even though he had never left the palace or the prison to wander the city of Jazat. The string inside him was pulling him like a leash. It was all so familiar, reminding him of the attack in Madin, the night he had escaped from Venja. But now he could do nothing but seek her out. He felt her presence somewhere above. Garon looked at the sky again.

A massive beast, triple the size of a wyvern, flashed across the sky like a bolt of lightning. Silvery-white scales covered its entire body, glistening in the light of the orb that hung above the Magisters' Palace. It had four legs with evil-looking claws on the ends, and claws on each of the pointed ends of its wings. As it spun in the sky, he could see a multitude of horns curling over its skull and evolving into ridges on its back, all the way down to its snake-like tail. He had never seen one, nor had he believed such a thing existed, but from its appearance and everything he had learned from old fairy-tale books, this had to be a dragon. A massive silver dragon. It turned in the sky again, headed right in his direction, the sound of its enormous wings cutting through the screams of its targets.

Its breath, freezing the air around it, hit the wyverns and their riders with crystallized shards of ice that burst into them like shrapnel. One by one, they were swatted from the sky like flies. Garon ducked behind a stone alcove near the entrance to the courtyard, hiding from the sight of this monstrosity.

Where did it come from? There are no records of dragons in Dohva. Garon watched as the dragon swooped down and dropped something near the palace entrance, then flapped its giant wings and pushed itself higher into the air. As soon as the dragon was out of sight, Garon ran towards the palace.

There on the ground lay Venja, her hair frozen, dead.

He looked down at her cold, marble-like face, traced his fingers across her lips, and down the side of her jawline.

Suddenly, the palace doors flew open. Without realizing what he was doing, Garon touched the necklace that adorned Venja's chest. The jewel glowed and he felt the air leave his lungs. Garon slid to the ground next to Venja, his eyes wandering to the entrance. There, in the doorway, stood Avala, with Sineth and Kima behind them. He glanced at Venja next to him.

As she took her first breath, he slipped into the darkness.

37

Avala

G aron!" Avala shouted as she saw him fall to the ground. She started to run towards him, but at the same moment the other figure rose from the ground and ran away at a rapid speed. *Venja,* she realized as the echo of Kalira shot into the darkness.

Before the horrid woman could reach the outer gates of the palace grounds, a wyvern hauled her into the dark sky. Hundreds of enemies were above them and on foot outside the palace grounds, but one by one, each monstrous creature retreated. Like the answer to an unheard signal, Venja's foot soldiers were scooped up by her flying beasts.

Avala kneeled down beside Garon and placed her hand on his chest, then checked his pulse at the veins in his neck. Nothing. She pulled her hand back and stared at him. He looked peaceful and like himself again. All the scales and hide-like skin were gone, as well as the horn sticking out of his skull, the fangs in his mouth. His beautiful face was so innocent, so honest. Avala stroked his wavy blond hair, touched his full lips with her thumb, and cradled his head in her hands. Then she began to cry. She held his dead body in her arms. "No, no!" she screamed into the darkness. But the sky was empty. The enemy was gone. No one to scream at, no one to blame.

"Avala, let's get him inside," Sineth said from behind her. He helped her to her feet and picked up Garon's body. She didn't know how to feel about the sight of one man she loved carrying the lifeless body of the other man she had loved. On the other hand, she didn't know what to feel at all. Sadness that she had lost a dear friend, relief that his torment was over, that he was free of the disease that had plagued him. But most of all she felt anger—no, that wasn't enough. She felt furious rage at this woman who had caused nothing but pain in her life. Venja.

"I don't understand. What happened to him? Was he poisoned or did his condition kill him?" Kima asked, leaning forward to inspect Garon's body. They were in one of the smaller living rooms of the palace. Garon lay on a large, low table surrounded by leather armchairs. The crackling fire illuminated him from behind. It was a grotesque sight.

"No, I don't think so. There would have been some kind of foam around or in his mouth if he had been poisoned. His condition, perhaps. It certainly has gotten worse in the last few days," Sineth replied, rubbing his chest where the black rays of Garon's strange magic had hit him. He sat down on the other side of the table and examined Garon's mouth, eyes, ears and hands.

"Please stop looking at him like a crime scene. I think it had something to do with Venja's necklace. It glowed just before Garon fell to the ground, and then Venja took off," Avala explained, pacing around the room. She was restless, her thoughts bouncing around, considering every possibility. "Maybe she wasn't happy with her creation, so she took back whatever it was that possessed Garon, and that's what killed him?"

"Could be, or she uses her necklace as a magical focus and killed him with a spell," Kima said, crossing her arms and staring into the fire.

"What is a magical focus?" Avala asked. Sometimes Kima seemed to forget that she and Sineth didn't know as much about this kind of magic as she did.

"It is a kind of object that enhances the abilities of a mage. Like channeling energy. I hope that makes sense?" Kima shrugged, as if she didn't really know how to describe it better. So Avala just accepted it, even though it was still not clear to her how this could have helped Venja.

The door burst open, and a disheveled-looking Baldor stormed into the room, followed by a weary-looking Kalira. "Where is it?" Baldor yelled, and his eyes glowed unnaturally. This was a version of the Magister she had not seen before. He had always been intimidating, an aura of dominance that allowed no argument. But this was monstrous, untamed, raw rage.

"Where is what?" Sineth asked, casting a confused glance at Baldor.

"Venja's body! She was killed in Himalus, and I dropped her in the courtyard. But the body is gone. Who in the nine hells is that?" Baldor pointed at Garon, his voice still raised in rage.

"This is Garon. You know him—you threw him in prison. And what do you mean, you dropped her body in the courtyard? From an airship? How could she survive that?" Kima asked, looking as puzzled as Sineth.

"She ran off and was picked up by a wyvern. Garon died by her hand before she fled," Avala said through clenched teeth.

"How? I killed her. I froze her and held her body in my claws for hours. There is no way she could have killed Garon or just run away," Baldor said, rubbing his face in frustration.

"The necklace. It had a strange gem in it, and it started glowing just before Garon died and Venja got up. What if Venja's life was saved by taking Garon's away?" Kima said, seemingly more to herself than to them.

38

Kima

"Wait, what? What kind of strange magic freezes someone to death?" Kima looked across the living room at Baldor, scanning him up and down. He was pacing in front of the floor-length window like a restless beast. Was the leader of her people also a druid? Did he use the same magical practices he had condemned for so long?

"I think the more important thing is that Venja probably stole Garon's life force and flew off to plot her next terrible plan. Probably to destroy us all," Avala said, sitting in the chair next to Garon, her focus still on his lifeless body. "We must strike first. Destroy the damn necklace and kill her for good."

"Don't you forget one little thing, Avala. No one can die for good in Dohva. We are all bound to this land, doomed to live on forever." Baldor sat down in one of the armchairs, rested his elbows on the side of the chair and folded his hands in front of his face.

"What would you have done with her body then?" Avala asked, her patience wearing thin under the pressure of their doomed situation.

"I wanted to shield the body so that her soul could not venture elsewhere. A small version of the elemental sphere that surrounds Dohva."

"But how did you kill her?" Kima wanted to know what was going on and she would not let this go. She needed answers and this time she would get them.

"Well, I guess this is as good a time as any to tell you. My dear Kalira and I have a few secrets. The first is that I'm not an elf. I am a silver dragon, born in Eltreth, long before Dohva was isolated."

"You're a dragon, a real dragon?" Kima couldn't believe what she had just heard. How could that be? She had read about dragons, more fairy tales than facts. But no one in Dohva actually believed in their existence.

Baldor smiled, his eyes glittering, and extended his arm. Slowly it grew larger, long claws protruding from his fingers and shiny silver scales covering every inch of his arm. "I can't change all the way here. It would ruin the room. I could fit into the main hall if you want a full display."

"That's awesome!" Kima couldn't be more excited. She wanted to touch the scales, study their matter and magic. This was the very thing that brought her such a rush—seeing something so rare, so fascinating, she could instantly get lost in her thoughts. How could she create something like dragon scales? Was there a way to create an entire mechanical dragon?

"And what about Kalira? Is she also a dragon, or how did she not age for over a thousand years? Even for an elf, that is a very long lifespan." Sineth inspected Baldor's arm from a distance. He did not seem very impressed by Baldor's new appearance. How could you not be impressed by a real dragon?

"I wanted to keep Kalira with me, so we found a spell that could bind the life of one to the life of another. It was a complicated and somewhat dangerous ritual, but it worked. Kalira's life is bound to mine. If I die, she dies, and vice versa," Baldor explained with an unusual softness in his eyes. He looked at Kalira, who was sitting on a bench in the corner of the room. "You are very quiet, my dear, are you all right?" Kalira did not answer.

Kima looked at the faces of this strange group of people. They all had some kind of magical abilities, or in her case knew how to bend it to her will, but what exactly could Kalira do? "So does Kalira have magical powers of her own?" Kima asked, her curious mind getting the better of her.

Baldor exchanged a look with Kalira, then said, "She is a powerful sorceress. Her magic comes from the bond we share."

"You know, this is all very interesting, but what about Venja? Every minute that we waste chatting is a minute that she gains to recover and make a plan, probably one involving revenge and death. Baldor, do you think you can do it again, kill her?" Avala asked, her voice clouded with suppressed tears. Sineth took a step toward her and placed a hand on her shoulder.

"Well, the advantage of surprise is gone now. She knows what to expect. But I think we haven't seen what each of us is capable of yet. So I can't say for sure, but I still think whatever power she's gained is no match for me." Baldor's face curled into a confident smirk.

Silence again, just the crackling of the wood burning in the hearth and Baldor's finger tapping on the arm of his chair, a somewhat unnerving sound that made her mind twitch a little every time. They all seemed to be contemplating their next steps, and Kima could feel the tension in the room growing by the second. "Oh!" she exclaimed in sudden enlightenment. "I didn't tell you what I found out about the orb! There has been so much going on, I completely forgot. I figured out how it works. The orb binds the magic of the Elemental Plane to the sphere. If that connection is broken or destroyed, the sphere will fall. So I created an object that has to be thrown into the orb. It dispels the elemental magic and cuts it off for a few moments. The plate then creates an anti-magic field so that the elemental flow can't connect to the orb again." Kima looked excitedly at Avala, who gave her a weak smile in return.

"Kima, my dear, I always knew there was something special about you. This changes things. All we have to do is fly to Parhat, throw your invention into the orb, kill Venja, and this odyssey will be over." Baldor's eyes flashed with a wild gleam. Kima wondered that she had never seen it before. How could she have missed the way his magic surrounded his entire body, making him glow and look so unnatural? She was trained to see magical things, to create and dismantle them, so how could she not have seen this?

"How often do you turn into a dragon? It's still a mystery to me how you managed to keep it a secret all this time." She looked at him with a sudden curiosity, like a new project she was trying to figure out.

"Hm, that is indeed a wise question. I haven't changed in a long time. As you said, it is hard to conceal it from the servants and visitors of this palace. It also makes me a bit... uneasy, bad-tempered even. I guess it comes with the dragon form. It's also why I quite enjoy being in this elven body, it's just... more balanced, I guess." Baldor gave her a warm smile, a somewhat reassuring smile, a smile she had been given before, by Bon.

Bon. Her dear beloved Bon. The thought of him always made her heart ache and jump at the same time, made her think of the happy memories that were imprinted in her mind like a spell on parchment. Suddenly, her mind took a leap, as if two ends of a wire were suddenly connected, and she had a strange thought. *What will happen to the magical abilities of those who draw their power from the elements? If the source of power is gone, will their magic fade as well? Or is it possible to connect with the elements of the Elemental Plane?* She didn't know how such magic worked, but there was a slight possibility that they might end more than just the sphere and the cycle of rebirths.

39

Sineth

The room they were in felt like a bubbling cauldron at this point, each of them huddled in a corner, seemingly unsure of what to do or say next. There was no air in here; Sineth felt a sudden need to be outside, to clear his head and feel the comforting presence of nature around him. *Nothing to be done now,* he thought. But there was no way he could just get up and leave, not with Avala still in that state of tense agony.

He sat down on the arm of her chair and rubbed her back while she leaned with her arms on her knees, staring into the fireplace. Kima sat across from them, her eyes darting back and forth as if she were cooking something up in her mind. Still motionless and silent, Kalira sat at the far end of the room, and Baldor, sitting next to Avala, watched her carefully. Sineth did not understand the bond they shared—a friendship perhaps? They did not seem like lovers to him, but maybe the look of it would change over the span of such a long time. He wouldn't know, but he understood the bond of siblinghood and the pain of losing one. This made him wonder about Kalira's allegiance. Would she remain loyal to Baldor, or would she choose her sister instead?

As for Baldor and his very simple plan to just go after Venja, Sineth felt it had a few holes in it. Destroying the orb was definitely what he wanted as well, destroying the very energy that fueled the Elementals and their madness. And he was almost as furious at that damned witch as Avala was. But Sineth had the feeling that they hadn't really thought this through.

Finally he broke the silence: "I think it is still a very dangerous endeavor. We have to make sure that Venja is not killed before the connection to the orb or whatever is severed. I don't want this woman to be reborn and hunt us down when she starts to remember things, assuming we are still alive after this coup. Then there is the matter of getting to the island unseen and back to the mainland of the continent before the island falls into whatever awaits us outside of the sphere."

"These are not impossible tasks," Baldor said. "We wait for the deathblow until the sphere is gone. That should be a very obvious sign. I could fly to Parhat in my dragon form and take you all on my back or in my claws. We must be sure to fly underneath Dohva so that none of her spies will see us. Then we will land behind the mountain. I think I remember there being a second entrance they carved into the mountain to create a passageway to the orb chamber. What's actually a problem is that this woman has other means of staying in this life than just being part of this miserable cycle of endless lifetimes."

"What do you know about the misery of this cycle? You have lived only this one life. A very long one, but the same. You know nothing of the feeling you have when you begin to remember all the crap from your past lives. When you start to feel the guilt and shame for everything you have done before your new life has even begun," Sineth spat. He despised Baldor. The arrogance of this creature made him so angry that he wanted to kick Baldor's pretty teeth in.

"Stop this nonsense. This is not the time to talk about any of your life experiences," Avala countered. "We've already talked about that, and we got distracted by the fact that you are a damn dragon. It's Venja's necklace that brings her back. We don't know what it does, but it glowed the second she woke up and Garon died. So it must have something to do with that."

"Remember what we found in the library? The sphere around Dohva is powered by some kind of soul magic. What if this necklace does something similar? Like... if the bearer is dead and the necklace has access to that kind of magic, it gives that energy back to the bearer, resurrecting them in some way?" Kima looked intently into Avala's eyes, as if she were explaining it just to her.

"Yes, that might have been it. But do you think it can be destroyed?" Avala asked, locking eyes with Kima. It seemed like they had formed some kind of connection, as well, during the time they had spent together. As if there was some meaning between the lines that Sineth did not get.

"Maybe... with enough force. The way you described it, it's some kind of crystal. Depending on its material, it could be very hard to crush."

"And how do we do that—the crushing, I mean? It's still around her neck. So we definitely have to kill her first, otherwise there's no way we could get close enough to snatch it away. We don't even know for sure where she is..." Sineth said, still irritated by the intimate nature of the women's conversation.

They talked about it for a long time, arguing back and forth about all the possibilities. Baldor was certain that Venja would flee to Parhat, for it was the furthest away and a well-guarded castle, difficult to ambush. Built around and into the mountain, it was like an impenetrable fortress. This brought up the issue of how to get inside said fortress, but Avala was sure she could find her way in, as she had been a guard there many times and knew the surroundings quite well.

It was also clear that they had to break the sphere and kill Venja at the same time. When the sphere ended, they would not have much time to kill Venja, destroy the necklace, and get off the island safely. If they killed Venja first, there would still be a chance for her to be reborn before the sphere was destroyed.

Then came the moment he had been waiting for. What about Kalira? "I'm sorry to point this out, but I don't trust Kalira to be on our side of the plan. She should not be with us when we try to kill her sister." Sineth shrugged matter-of-factly. He stared at the hunched figure in the corner. Kalira did not react at all. He had thought that this would start a debate. On the other hand, her sister had just tried to kill her and her best friend and then killed Garon. Maybe Kalira knew that this was the best way, the only way.

"So we'll divide into two groups, one to destroy the orb and the other to kill Venja and destroy the necklace," Kima suggested, her eyes fixed on Baldor's scaled arm again—Baldor had obviously forgotten that it was still altered in this way. Somehow Kima always looked like she was creating a new metal toy in her head.

"Kalira and Kima will go for the orb. Sineth, Avala and I will go after Venja. It pains me to part with you, my love, but Sineth is right, you don't look like you're up for another encounter with your sister." Baldor stood up and walked toward Kalira. He placed his elven hand on her shoulder and transformed his other arm back before placing his hand on the side of her face. He whispered something that Sineth could not understand.

"There's something else that bothers me. What about the people on the islands? We cannot warn them, and it will be too late for most of them to escape before the islands fall. That was why this Magnus created the sphere in the first place, to protect them from the certain death of whatever lies below. If we go on with our plan, we will doom them all," Kima pointed out, and it looked like it had taken her some courage to speak up.

"Oh, I've been thinking about that for a long time, my dear. The way Garon talked about it, it sounded like there were not many Madiners left on the islands. Their will was strong and they did not want to follow this new heretic queen. Nevertheless, you are right, we will condemn the rest of them to death for what will hopefully be a greater good. There is no other way. We cannot risk warning them, or our chance of a surprise attack will crumble to nothing," Baldor explained, standing next to Kalira, his face blank as he stared into a distant corner of the room.

"What about the specifics? We know exactly how we'll destroy the orb, or at least Kima knows what she's doing. What's our plan for killing Venja? What are her tactics, her weaknesses and such? Is there any way we can prepare our-selves?" Sineth felt a sudden weariness, the hecticness of the last few weeks piling up inside him. Not only physically, but also emotionally. All the stress and tense anticipation of what might come next tore at his core, leaving him like an empty shell. He just wanted to know what would happen for once. He needed a solid plan; his nerves would thank him for it. Still, he had the feeling that whatever they planned now would never reflect the true outcome.

"I would like to give you a plan, if I had one. The only sure thing we can play on is her arrogance. She feels superior to us, as if there is no one who can stand up to her. What a foolish thought…" Baldor looked at Kalira, as if considering his next words. "We need to make sure she has no time to start conjuring. If you two manage to overwhelm her and give her no time to react, I can do the rest."

Sineth's eyes wandered down to the beautiful, fair-haired, boyish-looking Garon lying dead on the coffee table in front of him. Sineth wondered if they would survive this mad mission or if they would all end up like Garon. It was the definition of high risk, high reward. If they failed, their heads would probably end up on pikes. But if they succeeded and escaped, a new era awaited them. Would it be better than the one they'd had before? Sineth didn't know.

40

Kalira

It took them an hour to prepare after the others had finished their discussions and formed a plan. They packed only the most necessary basics: food, water, some tools in case they needed to gain entry somewhere, and of course the object Kima had created to destroy the orb.

Somehow Kalira felt empty, lost and sorrowful. She had finally found her sister after all these years of fruitless searching, after accepting that she might never find her and might have to live the rest of her life without her. Now she knew

Valeria was alive, but she couldn't shake the image of Valeria raising her hands and summoning those shadow creatures, the spark in her eyes as she hurled them at her. Then seeing her die from the back of Baldor, Valeria frightened and paralyzed by the power she had not seen coming. But then to learn that Valeria had come back from the dead, and now Kalira would be part of this mission to kill her again... It felt impossible.

Baldor had been right when he said that she could not face her sister again. If she had to see the monster that had become Venja one more time, it would surely break her forever. What had corrupted Valeria to become so cruel? Kalira wondered. She had been an innocent child, full of joy and love, often misunderstood by others just because she was different. Kalira had loved her sister more than anyone. But her love had never been enough for Valeria.

They set the plan in motion, huddling together in the center of Baldor's large, scale-covered back. Sineth suggested tying a rope around Baldor's neck to give them a better hold in case he needed to make some kind of midair maneuver. Then Kalira had the idea of casting a spell on them that would make them invisible for a while, so that no one would see them descend.

With a few strong beats of his gigantic wings, they were up in the dark sky, flying toward Jazat's port and then dropping down underneath Dohva. Kalira couldn't see much in the darkness, but what she could make out was an alien sight: the rough, rocky underbelly of a lush green land illuminated by the colorful display of light from the elemental sphere. It felt like they were in a different realm of existence. The sight of it made her feel like an intruder in a sacred place, like interrupting a ritual in a temple. Perhaps the others felt the same way, for they spoke in hushed voices, though no one could hear them down here.

After about six hours of them desperately trying not to fall asleep or slide down the shimmering silver hide, Baldor gave her a little nod over his shoulder and she recast the spell for their flight up.

They reached the island unnoticed. Baldor landed as close to the mountain as possible, and they all climbed down and sat on the ground.

"I need some rest. We can't go in like this. Venja will kill us in an instant," Sineth whispered as he lay flat on the ground. "You know what would have been a better idea? We should have tied ourselves to the back with the rope, not just held on to it. That would have been much more comfortable."

They all smiled at each other. Kima even let out a little chuckle. Whatever came next, they had made it here, and they all seemed to be glad for it.

"Okay, let's get some rest. After that, we'll find a way to get to the castle without being noticed and wait until we have eyes on Venja. I can communicate with Kalira, so I'll let her know when it's time to throw the thing into the orb," Baldor told them, his voice changing midsentence as he returned to his elven form. To Kalira, this was a normal sight, but the others still watched him with wide eyes and expressions of wonder.

At least they are not afraid. They trust us.

After a short rest, they separated, and Kalira and Kima made their way to the area Baldor had pointed out as having a secret back entrance to the orb chamber. They began to search the wall carefully, but there was no door or obvious entrance. What they found was a part of the wall filled with rocks. *Maybe the cave collapsed over the years? Or maybe the elementals thought this second entrance was a risk to their secret efforts inside?* For the moment, it didn't matter. The only thing that mattered was that they now had to dig their way in, pushing aside a huge amount of rock.

"I think this is the entrance Baldor meant? The rest of the wall is solid," Kalira pointed out, starting to remove some of the smaller stones at the top. "We just need to get a hole big enough at the top to get inside."

"I just hope the island tilts the other way so the rocks don't fall in and block the way when it's time to get out, or worse, hit us while we're running. We have to move quickly once the plate is inside the orb. There's not much time before this island falls like a ripe apple from the tree," Kima replied, helping her push the stones away. "You don't have a spell for that, by any chance?"

"I'm afraid I haven't."

It felt like they were working impossibly slowly before they finally managed to climb inside. There was no light; it was pitch black. Kima pulled out a small glass ball the size of her palm and whispered "Agnar-Limar" into it. It began to glow and float in front of Kima's chest.

"I could have just cast a light spell, but this is a beautiful creation. You have so much talent, Kima. When all this is over, you should consider becoming a professor of enchantment. Teaching can be very fulfilling," Kalira suggested.

"Thank you. It would be nice to share my thoughts again. My mentor passed away a few months ago. He taught me everything he knew about magic and enchantment. I miss him very much." Kima stopped and looked at her, tears filling her eyes.

"Oh, I understand that pain very well, Kima." Kalira smiled at Kima and gave her arm a small squeeze. It was so strange; pain had a way of sneaking up on you at the most impossible moments, just when you least expected it.

Ahead of them was a long, winding tunnel with no end in sight. Carefully, they made their way deeper into it. Kalira had expected it to be trapped or barricaded in some way, hidden behind a magically protected door or bars of some kind. But so far, there had been no sign of additional protection. *Maybe it was the arrogance of the Elementals, thinking that no one would dare enter this island, let alone this cave, without their permission... without them knowing.*

After a while, they could see a multicolored glow in the distance, reflecting off the walls of this tunnel. Kima, in front of her, let out a reverent sigh as she moved around the last corner of the tunnel. There in front of them was the orb: a glowing ball of elemental power that filled the room almost from floor to ceiling, about forty feet at its thickest point. It looked like a smaller echo of the sphere that surrounded Dohva, only now they were looking at it as a whole, not from within. The elements intermingled in a magical dance, ever moving, flickering and hungry, ready to devour anything that dared come near.

On top of it, the ever-flowing stream of energy nourished it like an umbilical cord to a baby. Kalira didn't know what she had expected, but the sight left them both in awe. The air seemed to vibrate with the power of the orb. It was impressive and very intimidating. Even Baldor had been denied access to the orb chamber by the Elementals. They knew he was not fond of them and their ways; perhaps they had feared he would do something to stop them, to end their magic. *Like he's doing now,* she thought. So all the information he could offer was told through others and the diary he had acquired so many lifetimes ago.

Seeing the orb now, she could sense the power that emanated from the strange magical monstrosity. It looked like it had a mind of its own, like a living organism. It twisted and turned within its confines, ready to burst out at any moment.

41

Avala

Avala, you know this place best. Please, take the lead from here," Baldor ordered her—he was generally not much of an asker. But Avala was glad for the distraction from her dark thoughts.

"Of course. It should only take about half an hour from here. We should speak only when necessary, and as quietly as possible. There might be guards on this side of the castle as well as on the towers." Avala pushed to the front. Somehow she felt like she was just reacting to what might come next, unable to see the scope of it all. Maybe she was just deflecting all the consequences her actions might have. But she couldn't allow herself to drift into that part of her mind for fear of what she might find there.

It had been two days since Garon had died, and most of her thoughts had revolved around seeing his pale body on that table, his face looking relaxed, at peace. Maybe this had had to happen; maybe this was the best thing that could have happened to him. What would he have become if he had lived on? A monster, a demon? It had been clear that it would only get worse. The way Garon had attacked Sineth... there had been nothing left of him. The Garon she had known would never have attacked someone like that. He hadn't just wanted to hurt Sineth; he had tried to kill Sineth with magic she had never seen before.

They walked in silence along a small river, knowing it would lead them directly to the castle. With growing tension, she watched the mountainside and then caught a glimpse of the massive tower rising out of the rock. They were close now, very close. Avala could hear the roar of the waterfall cascading from the tower. It was a surreal sight, this great construct of a tower built around the force of nature, emphasizing its power and beauty. She had always enjoyed working on this island. It had been the most peaceful place to escape the hustle and bustle of the city. But now that memory was clouded by the images of the wyverns and orcs who had attacked them—a vision of death and disaster. And, of course, Garon being dragged through the air and taken from her.

That had been her point of no return, the moment when everything fell apart. Avala had thought it had been long before, when her dearest friend Mereth had been sentenced to death by the Elementals, but no, that had been the moment when her life had changed forever—her mad chase to retrieve Garon, then escaping the forces sent to capture her, and then meeting Sineth, a soul she had feared and sought to meet for so long.

"We need to climb up this side of the tower and try to get to the terrace above the waterfall. From there, we could easily sneak in and make our way through the castle to find Venja," Avala whispered to the others.

"Okay, and how are we going to find Venja in this castle? There must be a lot of rooms to search. Besides, I'm sure this castle isn't empty, so we'll have to make sure no one sees us." Sineth looked nervous, something she hadn't seen very often.

"With the ego she has, she'll probably sit where the Elementals have ruled for so long. Steeped in her triumph, you might say. We could start there?" Baldor suggested with a face that looked like he had eaten a sour plum. She would love to know what went through a dragon's mind all day long.

"Okay, I know the way to the council hall. I guess we just have to be careful and stealthy, and we need a little luck," Avala replied, unsure if she believed the words herself. Baldor and Sineth certainly did not look convinced.

"Let's get on with it, then. There is no time to waste," Baldor urged, shooing them like chickens back to the barn.

It was hard to climb an almost straight wall without moving a single stone. She thought about every step and every rock she grabbed to hold on to, but they managed to reach the terrace without drawing attention. She glanced around the corner to see if there were any guards posted outside the entrance, but there were none. The strange feeling of walking into a trap crept up her spine and made her shiver. What if this was exactly what Venja had wanted, for them to expose themselves like this? On the other hand, they had the dragon, and he had defeated her before. But she had the advantage if this was indeed a trap, and they would lose the element of surprise.

"What are you waiting for? Are there guards?" Baldor whispered from behind.

"No guards," Avala replied, and began to hoist herself over the low wall that surrounded the room. The others followed, and they made their way to the elaborate double doors that led inside. Avala carefully pulled the bronze handle of the door and peered inside. Her eyes had adjusted somewhat to the omnipresent darkness, but the inside was a pitch-black gulf. She closed the door and looked back at the others. "Baldor, can you see in the dark? Because I cannot see at all. There is no light inside. Not a single candle lit, nothing."

"What are you thinking, Avala? I can see you're worried. What is it?" Sineth asked.

"I just think she might be expecting us to come to her."

"So? Even if she does, she might not see everything we have planned. The most important thing is that Kalira and Kima can do their part. I can handle Venja," Baldor said, stepping to the door. He opened it and stared in. For a moment, Avala thought he might not see anything, but he waved her inside. "Hold on to me, I'll guide you. Avala, tell me where to go."

She took Baldor's hand, cold to the touch and strangely soft, like a child's skin. It contrasted with the hand she took from Sineth, the familiar calluses of hard work. Somehow it calmed her nerves to hold hands with these two very different men.

It was quiet inside, no footsteps, no voices except for their movements and breathing. What could she do without being able to see? It was so strange; usually the darkness didn't bother her that much. She could at least make out the general shapes of things and maneuver around if she was careful. But this felt different—a darkness her eyes could not penetrate.

They moved at a slow pace, but made steady progress. Finally, they made their way down a winding staircase that would lead them directly into the council hall. Avala felt her heart race in her chest. *I won't be afraid; I'll let my rage be the fuel to set her body on fire. I will wield the storm, and I will bring the thunder.*

Baldor was the first to step out into the hall. For a split second, a flickering green light shot through the darkness, with the sizzling sound of a missile being fired from somewhere inside. Baldor's body collapsed to the ground. Then a huge wall of fire appeared directly in front of Baldor. Behind her stood Sineth, hands raised, pushing the flames higher and higher to shield their unconscious ally. With the light of the flames filling the room, she could make out a sea of dark figures, not humanoid, but translucent, hovering away from the flames. And in the far corner of the room stood Venja, arms raised, a mad smile on her beautiful face. *She knew, she knew we were coming, and we walked right into her trap.*

Avala felt her body grow cold, sweat wetting her brow. She shook her head, trying to concentrate, and bent down to Baldor, checking his pulse; he was breathing, he was fine. With only a little force, she slapped his cheek. *You can't be defeated so easily, you're a dragon, for the elements' sake!*

"Wake up! Please wake up!" Avala began to shake his shoulders.

With a sudden "huuuhhh," Baldor inhaled heavily and jumped to his feet. In a flash, he transformed into the gigantic, monstrous creature he truly was. His silver scales glowed in the flickering light, and he walked right through Sineth's conjured wall of fire.

Avala closed her eyes for a second, inhaled and let the elemental power vibrate through her body. When she opened them again, she pointed at Venja, exhaled, channeling all her anger and rage, and watched as a storm emerged from the ceiling, growing larger and larger, with Venja at its center. Things began to fly, and the air howled with the storm. Venja covered her face and Avala threw a bolt of lightning at her, hitting her right in the chest. *I'm going to make you suffer for what you did to Garon!* she thought as Venja leaned forward, clutching her fists. At first it looked like she was in pain, reaching for her chest, but then the light went out and Avala knew it was a new trick from the demon woman. Avala spun around to look for the other two, but the darkness prevented her from seeing anything.

"Sineth! Baldor!" she shouted into the darkness. No answer. Avala tried hard to concentrate on the storm, on the place where she knew Venja had stood a second ago. She needed light to see what was going on, and she needed to know that her companions were safe. But a cold sensation flooded her mind, and then a piercing pain—the pain of everything she had lost, of every cut and broken bone she had had in her many lifetimes. An overwhelming amount of grief flooded her mind like a tidal wave, and she felt her body hit the ground. She was lost, lost in her pain, unable to move or react to what was happening around her. *What am I doing here? Why should a little wind stop such dark forces? How could I even try to defeat someone like Venja?*

Someone yanked her from the ground, forcing her back to reality. "Avala, come with me!" Sineth shouted over the roar of Baldor's beating wings. Baldor shot a cone of icy breath from his massive mouth. Venja looked desperate, and it seemed as if the tide had turned. The shadow soldiers were gone, and Sineth had a ball of crackling fire in his palm, which grew and flickered until he hurled it at Venja. It met the breath of ice, a wondrous fusion of the elements. Wondrous and hopefully deadly. Sineth instantly created another fire in his palm, creating light for both of them.

In the dim, wavering flame, Avala could see Venja, charred and angry. *We can win this!* Avala's hopes were on the rise again until Baldor dropped to the ground with a thud. *What happened?* She had watched Venja closely and she hadn't done anything. But there was no time to think. Venja came back to her feet and began to create a new madness for them.

Avala shot a bolt of lightning at Venja, missing her by a foot. It hit the wall behind her and part of it came loose. Venja stopped casting and started to run, but she wasn't fast enough. A huge chunk of stone fell on top of her and smaller ones followed burying her under a pile of rubble. This was their chance to get close to her. Avala glanced at Sineth; he had the same thought and they both ran toward her.

"Let's see how you get along without this," Avala hissed in Venja's face as she ripped the necklace from her. She could see that Venja was on the verge of death, slipping in and out of consciousness. Could Avala be so cruel as to give her the final blow? Could she really kill someone in cold blood? No time to think. The necklace hit the ground and she forced crackling energy out of her hand. With a crack, the lightning struck the gem, shattering it into a thousand pieces.

A growl came from Baldor. She hadn't noticed that he was back on his feet. Now his massive maw turned into a grin and his chest began to glow blue from within. Avala and Sineth rushed back to see Baldor unleash his ice breath on Venja one last time.

42

Kima

"It's time, let's go," Kalira said, eagerly looking back to the tunnel they had come from. "I really hope we're fast enough to get out of here. I can cast a spell to make us fly, but we have to get out of the mountain first."

Kima nodded and set down her small brown leather backpack. Looking around the naturally shaped cave, she wondered if it had been here before the orb and had just been given a new purpose. The walls and floor were black and covered with some kind of dust. At the top of the ceiling was a hole, completely filled with the colorful elemental stream that fed the orb and then flowed back through the hole. It was fascinating. *Magnus Athirat was a genius, not only to create something like that, but to do it under the pressure of a dire situation. Truly inspiring.*

Carefully, she pulled out the device she had created in the library of the Jazat Magisters' Palace. It was wrapped in a thick linen cloth to prevent it from breaking during their dragon ride to Parhat. Kima folded the layers away to reveal her creation. The four-sided metal plate shimmered in the serene light of the flickering lightning and fire of the orb, like they were somehow connected already.

"I hope this works." She handed it to Kalira. "Please, be careful. Are you sure you want to do this? I really don't know what will happen if you throw it in."

"It's okay. We'll be fine. Let's just get this over with," Kalira reassured her and began to practice her aim with the device. With her eyes fixed on the center of the orb, she held it in her right hand and drew it back and forth. On the fourth try, she nodded to Kima.

"Fatharal!" Kima shouted towards the device, and Kalira let go of it and it flew inside, nestled in the middle of it. *Perfect!* But the moment Kima had thought of the word, she regretted it.

Kalira flew backward and fell hard to the ground, pushed away as if struck by lightning. A beam of the orb's energy burst away—a lilac and orange tangle of magical force had struck her in the chest and recoiled back as fast as it had come. Kima ran over and checked her pulse, feeling the slow, steady beating of her heart at her wrist. *She's alive.* Steam lingered over the burned part of Kalira's chest and right shoulder where the elements had burned away her shirt. Kima fumbled in her coat pockets and found a small vial of ever-moving red liquid. She pulled off the small cork at the top and opened Kalira's mouth, placed the bottle to her lips and let the liquid flow in.

It felt like ages of waiting, but it must have been just a second until Kalira inhaled sharply. "Haaahh! What happened? Did it work?" Kalira asked, out of breath.

The sound of small cracks, like a roaring fire, came from inside the orb. Kima's eyes widened as the stones of her creation shattered one by one. They both stared at it as the engraved seal began to glow with a searing light and a translucent shield emerged, spreading across the galvanized iron ring on the ground. Suddenly, the elemental flow stopped, and she knew what would happen next.

The anti-magic field is activated.

The island will begin to fall...

"Run!" Kima yelled at Kalira and ran into the tunnel as fast as she could.

They stumbled through the darkness. Kalira had created light on the ring on her hand so they could at least see where they were going. Kalira stumbled from side to side, and Kima wasn't at all sure if Kalira was all right. On the other hand, Kima herself was reeling around like a drunken sailor. At some point, Kima even hit the wall as the tunnel took a hard turn. Her shoulder burned and the pain pulsed through her body. But it didn't matter; they just had to get out of here. She felt the floor begin to tilt sideways, then forward, and they lost their footing, sliding down the tunnel at a rapid pace. Huge boulders hurtled down the tunnel, missing them by inches.

"Kalira, the thing with the flying. I guess now would be a good time to do it!" Kima exclaimed. She saw an endless black void coming towards them at a rapid pace. At first, it was like a dark spot, but it grew fast, and Kima had the distinct feeling that they were about to drop into the darkest and deepest lake she had ever seen.

"Good point!" Kalira said from behind, along with some other words Kima did not understand. And a moment later, Kima felt her body get weightless in the air.

"Perfect timing," Kima replied as she drifted out of the tunnel and into the black, lightless sea.

"We should find the others," Kalira said, panting for breath. "Give me your hand."

Kima couldn't figure out how to move; she just doggy-paddled in the air and nothing happened.

Kalira looked at her with a weak smile. "You have to think about where you want to go and your mind will carry you there."

Kima tried to concentrate on Kalira, on her hand, and suddenly she pushed herself towards her. *Oh, how I love magic!* "This is amazing!" Kima giggled a little and took Kalira's hand. It was cold and clammy, and Kima had the unsettling feeling again that Kalira had been hurt worse than it had seemed back in the cave. But there was nothing she could do for Kalira now. She had no more potions, and they were floating in midair over a dark void.

She turned around. They were a little lower than the edge of the mainland. It was as if she was in an ocean of dark water and the mainland was a distant shore. Below her, she could make out the rapidly shrinking form of the island as it fell into the lightless abyss below. But not only Parhat fell—the largest island of Madin fell, and with it the ancient city of Gahaal, and the smaller one to the south as well. Kima wondered if they had done the right thing, but now was not the time to discuss ethics. They scanned the darkness below for the others, hoping they had made it out in time.

"There!" Kima had spotted a little winged creature appearing underneath the falling island of Parhat. It grew in size as it came closer to them. "They made it!" She looked towards Kalira, who had tears in her eyes.

"I knew they would," Kalira said with a weak smile, both happy and sorrowful at the same time. Of course, it meant she had lost her sister.

43

Baldor

For the first time in a thousand years, he saw the clear, dark blue sky—not the colorful flicker of the sphere of energy. The air was fresh and cold. *This is the scent of a new age,* he thought. *And, oh, how long I have waited for it to come.*

Everything had worked out fine in the end. All his allies were alive, most importantly Kalira. Together they had accomplished the impossible—killing the mad Dark Queen, destroying her necklace, the orb, and freeing his beloved Dohva from its imprisonment. *It's not good for humanoids to live so long,* he reflected. *They tend to get foolish ideas and think they are gods themselves. Except dear Kalira, of course, but she's a wise soul. There aren't many of them among the humanoids.*

"We should go back and save the citizens of Gahaal! And the city of Huhl is only a few miles away on another island. There are a thousand people living there!" Avala shouted from his back. "Please, we have to help them!"

"We talked about this. There weren't many of them left," Baldor growled through clenched teeth. "Only orcs and other creatures of the dark. We wouldn't be fast enough to help any of them. And some might be able to help themselves. Fly to the mainland." He looked back at the now-vanished islands of Madin. "I must tend to my wounds and Kalira's. I can feel her pain—she is badly wounded."

"Look! The enemies are fleeing back towards the Kuana Mountains!" Kima shouted from his back.

Baldor looked down and saw them scurrying back like ants retreating to their anthill. He wondered how long it would take them to plan another invasion; they would certainly not stop. *Their greed and lust for power are too strong to keep them bound to their realm beneath the mountain for long. But without their queen and her magic, it's going to be hard for them to stand against the outside world. Especially now that the sphere is gone.*

Vaguely, he could hear his passengers murmuring behind him about recent events, but Baldor had little interest in their conversation. He longed to return home, to see his palace illuminated by the rising light of day, to feel its warmth on his scaled body as he rested in the glass dome.

As they emerged on the other side of Kuana's mountain range, his passengers fell silent.

"Wait, what? Why did Karaz not fall down?" Sineth asked from behind his neck.

"You really thought I would have agreed to this mad plan if my people had been in danger? Certainly not." Baldor let out a satisfied chuckle.

"We haven't talked about that, have we?" Kima asked. "Karaz has found the source—the core material of Dohva, the reason why our continent floats in the air. It's called Safral, a sort of gemstone. We use it to craft our airships and to stabilize the islands in case the elemental sphere doesn't work anymore. Correct, Baldor?"

He hummed for a moment, feeling the tension fading. The sight of his home filled him with pride. "Yes, that is correct, Kima."

"And why didn't you help Madin do the same?" Avala asked from behind, her voice high and shaky.

He could understand her sadness and frustration. He had felt the same way for hundreds of years, and more than once he had thought of taking matters into his own hands. But it was difficult to place the stones inside the islands, and without the help of the inhabitants, it was an almost impossible task. If he had overturned the rule of the Elementals, their many followers would have revolted and no one would have been willing to help him.

"It was simple, they were arrogant. They relied solely on the sphere and its elemental power. They would not consider any other solution. I tried to persuade them, but they saw it as blasphemy against their ways." Baldor felt anger rise within him. *Oh, how I hated their ignorance.* "But it's over now. They're gone, and with them all that they have built in the last thousand years."

Baldor found himself pacing the room again. They had been back at the Magisters' Palace for a few hours, his people demanding their presence, seeking answers to the recent chaos. But he couldn't think of such things right now. Kalira lay in her bed, pale, her heartbeat slow and irregular. He had tried everything—every spell he knew, every bit of knowledge he had gathered about healing herbs and potions. Nothing worked. *How could that be?* he wondered. *I accomplished everything. The Safral worked. I saved my people only to die at the peak of my triumph?*

His knees weakening, he sank into an armchair beside Kalira's bed and reached out to take her hand. He'd known this would be the most likely outcome when he'd decided to link their lives—Kalira was the weaker target of the two. But they had managed to protect themselves so well that the possibility of death had become a distant shadow in the back of their minds. He also knew he had to retreat to his room or find a large open space that would accommodate his normal form. His heart was heavy with grief, and he was overwhelmed by the thought that it was all coming to an end. Slowly, he ran his hands through the air, perhaps for the last time. "Infantar," he whispered, casting invisibility on both of them. He picked Kalira up, carried her out through the back entrance into the courtyard, laid her on his lap and kissed her forehead.

"My dear Kalira, I've failed you," he lamented. "I should have taken more care, kept you safe in my sight. Maybe this is destined for us. An empty victory. One we will not be able to enjoy."

Weakly, Kalira fluttered her eyelashes. "Don't be sorry," she whispered, her voice barely audible. "You've granted me a longer, greater life than I could have ever imagined to live, full of wonder, beauty, and love. Rest with me now. I can feel the light coming towards my soul, claiming it and guiding it to its final destination. Maybe we'll find each other again on the other side."

The last thing Baldor felt was his body enlarging, reshaping, and the tingling sensation of the invisibility spell ending. At last, his people would see his true form.

44

Avala

Something inside her felt strange, out of place, and she couldn't figure out what it was. Not quite pain or sadness, it felt deeper, gnawing at her core. Perhaps it was guilt, or some other unpleasant emotion that might come with destroying parts of her own home. Or maybe it was just another haunting memory that forced its way to the surface.

As soon as they reached land, Avala had insisted on boarding an airship and flying back to Madin. She had to see what was left of her home, her people. Unable to stay in this unfamiliar place any longer, she longed for the simplicity of her life back home, without all the inventions and technology here. What had happened to Kumar and Leam? She didn't even know if they were still alive, and if they were dead, it was her fault. Avala had understood the consequences of going after Venja, of destroying the orb, but she hadn't fully considered the aftermath. The last few days had been a whirlwind of chaotic plans and decisions, and she felt adrift in the middle of it all. She was immensely grateful to have Sineth and Kima by her side. They had been her anchors, her steadfast support while everything around her seemed to crumble and dissolve. They were her only remaining friends.

The ship ascended into the unfamiliar sky as dawn broke, shrouding everything in a mystical mist that made it seem as if they were sailing through an ethereal milky liquid rather than the air. The distant mountain peaks were the only indication that they were airborne. It felt surreal to think that everything had changed on the other side of those mountains. But wasn't change what she had wanted most? To alter the way the Elementals had ruled their lives, to disrupt the monotony of her daily routine, to resist the pressures of the world around her trying to mold her into something she wasn't. *So why does it all feel so wrong now?*

Her mother and dearest friend Mereth had once said to her, "Sometimes you have to break something apart so it can be put back together again." Avala couldn't remember the context, probably referring to her loom rather than the world falling apart. She had treasured that old loom. But could she do the same for Dohva? Would they be able to mend it, make it better than it was before?

"Avala, could you summon some wind and blow away the fog so we can see what's going on down there?" Kima asked, touching her arm.

"Sure," Avala replied with a gentle smile. She truly adored this woman—her ready wit and her adorable quirkiness. But most of all, the joy Kima held within her was like a light breaking through the darkness of Avala's thoughts, bringing her often back to reality as she drifted away.

Avala raised her hands, channeling the energy within her body, but nothing happened. Every inch of her felt empty. There was no magic left in her. She felt that strange feeling again, like a wound that needed scratching, but she couldn't reach it. "I can't do it. I... there's nothing left. There's just nothing left... What have I done? I've destroyed Madin, and now I've probably stripped most of my people of their magic."

"What are you talking about?" Kima asked, her expression filled with worry.

"I can't use magic anymore. It must have been connected to the elemental sphere. And if I can't use magic, then everyone else who got their power from the elements can't access it either." Avala sank heavily to the deck of the ship. She saw Sineth approaching.

"Hey, what's going on?" Sineth asked, looking between her and Kima.

"We've lost our magical abilities. Try it," Avala said from the ground. Sineth snapped his fingers, expecting a small flame to appear on them as usual, but nothing happened. There was a moment of stunned silence as the three of them stared at Sineth's fingers, almost expecting a miracle.

"Well, that is unfortunate," Sineth said, his voice subdued. "I have to admit, I'm not entirely sad about it. It felt like a curse to me. It caused the death of my parents, led to the loss of my best friend, and resulted in my long exile. So you could say it's for the better, considering what good it's done me. Still, it feels a little odd, like something is missing. It's going to take some getting used to, and I should definitely practice making a fire with flint again." Sineth let out a confused chuckle and stared at his finger.

"Yes... I have to tell you, I wondered if this would happen, but I wasn't sure if I should tell you about it. I thought maybe the elemental magic was just drawn from farther away, the Elemental Plane Magnus had written about." Kima paused and crouched down in front of her. "I'm so sorry I didn't tell you this was a possibility. Everything happened so fast, and to be honest, it slipped my mind while we were preparing for our flight to Parhat. But there are other kinds of magic you could learn—magic you choose to have, not one that's forced upon you. Magic that can create things and bring them to life," Kima pleaded, a flicker of enthusiasm spreading across her face. "Perhaps I should open a school in Madin to teach different forms of magic, magic that could help rebuild Madin."

"You're both right, and I'm not angry because you didn't tell us; it wouldn't have stopped us carrying out our plan. I just feel responsible for the mess we're in, for the lives we've lost, for the destruction of Madin."

"Don't be ridiculous. We saved them from Venja. What kind of life would they have had if she had become their queen?" Kima reasoned, squeezing Avala's hand in hers. "Avala, look at me. You are not to blame. We did what we thought was best, the only thing we could do to help Dohva. And look around you. It's the dawn of a new day, and all we can do is embrace the change we have initiated."

45

Sineth

He let his gaze sweep over the fog-shrouded horizon and further up into the sky above. It looked strange, an expanse of lightless pit. It would take some getting used to; the colors of the sky had been the only thing he had liked about the sphere. Now there was nothing left of it, perhaps a reflection of what awaited them on the other side of the mountains.

Sineth looked to the railing where his newfound friends stood. They had all been unusually quiet during their journey.

Sineth couldn't tell what was on Avala's and Kima's minds, but his own thoughts were troubled—about their future, about Madin, and about what lay ahead for him. There was an overwhelming sense of aimlessness. He had dedicated his life to freeing Madin from the Elementals and their tyranny, and he had succeeded. *But what now? Should I just build a house, sit in a rocking chair on its porch, and puff on my pipe until I die?* He could not imagine being idle; even without magic, he needed to find a purpose. For now, he could help with the rebuilding. Perhaps he could offer guidance to those who sought it, help them make sense of their situation. He had been a leader before; perhaps he could lead again, if they would accept him. With Avala at his side, they could lead together and bring the peace their people deserved. Kima could serve as their advisor and establish the school she had mentioned.

But what if the people refused their help? It was quite possible that people would blame them for the disaster, since there was no one else to blame. Venja was dead, and they had left so quickly, they didn't know if Kalira had recovered. Also, the Magisters were far away in their own part of the country, leaving only the three of them as witnesses. And why should anyone trust their testimony? They had no credibility. A girl from a foreign land with unconventional ideas about magic, an alleged traitor accused of elemental murder, and an outcast who had challenged their political order. *Maybe we should turn back. There's a chance they'll just execute us on sight.*

And what of the rebellion? Would they be allowed to settle in Karaz and start a new chapter? He hadn't thought about them for a while. Maybe he should have gone back to them to tell them what had happened. *I miss them, Quinn and Hartaba, even thick-headed Una. We should go back and think about what we can do.* He had let Avala carry him away, not thinking about what he wanted at this point. It was clear to him now that he saw a future with Avala, a new beginning of sorts, but he wasn't sure if her vision of that future was the same.

Sineth gazed into the distance as daylight slowly dispersed the fog. There was something out there, the crooked outline of a massive form. And a little further north, almost out of the reach of the light, was another shape. At first, he couldn't make sense of what he saw in the distance, but as the light grew brighter, he had a clearer view of what lay before him. Two landmasses hovered in the distance. The northern shape had a massive mountain jutting out of the land, so high that it disappeared halfway into the sky, only visible now and then when the clouds dissipated. The other island was almost completely covered by the glistening, reflective surface of water, making it look like a flat mirror. Endless clouds moved above and below, and there was only a thin rim of land around it, giving the impression of a frame.

He was in awe of this beauty, unable to convey what it could mean to them. Swallowing hard, he found his voice. "Hey, look over there." He pointed at the shapes. The women followed the motion of his hand with their eyes, and Kima's eyes widened.

"No way! That must be the land Kalira mentioned, where she and Venja came from. It's so beautiful it seems unreal... Oh, I'd love to go there. Can you imagine? A whole different country, culture, and magic. How thrilling!" Kima clapped her hands together, bouncing like an excited child in front of her birthday presents.

Avala stood at the railing, staring absentmindedly toward the new land. "I just want to go home and have peace, if only for a moment." She rubbed three fingers over her close-cropped hair, as she had done so many times since he had shaved her head. It felt like years ago now, but he could still remember the electrifying sensation of her soft skin. He should have known then that something was different. But he had put all the memories of his past lives into a metaphorical box and sealed it with a wall of repression. Well, until Avala had begun to tear down said wall brick by brick.

Sineth stepped behind her and rested a hand on her shoulder, not knowing if she wanted him to hold her or not. So much had happened, he could feel her tension, her sadness, and he felt it as well. It made him wonder if this feeling would bring them together or tear them apart again. With no words of true comfort in his mind, he simply said, "Me too. But I'm not sure where home is anymore. At least not for me. And I'm even less sure that this country is capable of peace, given its track record of corrupt leaders and landscape-altering disasters."

She took his hand and pulled his arms around her, leaning her head against his chest. "Well, we'll see soon enough."

"How about a group hug? It's not every day you survive a... I don't know what exactly. A night like this?" Kima stretched out her arms and they all began to laugh. Their voices echoed over the deck of the ship as he and Avala leaned down to hug Kima.

"You're a strange little woman, but I like you a lot," Sineth said as he let go of her.

Epilogue

It was a crisp and clear autumn day, some fifteen years since what was now called "the Falling," the doomsday when the islands were lost to the dark void below. The cottage was at the edge of the small town of Emril, near the forest, and it was inhabited by a modest family of three who were known as respectable and kind. But their quiet life had been disturbed by an incident that could not be ignored or covered up for much longer.

"Look at him, he's just a boy." Jula nodded toward the window where her young son was playing with a ball. His face was tense as he kicked the ball hard against the barn wall across the yard. A bang echoed from the wooden wall towards the house and the edge of the forest behind the barn. Eram's heart skipped a beat as he looked towards the forest path that led to the house. For a second, he thought someone was approaching their humble home, but it was only a frightened deer that scampered back into the safety of the forest.

"Yes, he is, but we can't ignore what Izzmir did, Jula," Eram replied, lowering his voice to a whisper. "He killed that girl. Without a knife or any other weapon. There was no blood, but she just dropped dead in the barn. How could he do that? She was twice his age."

"I know. I know. We have to tell someone before they find out she's missing," Jula said with a sad sigh, avoiding eye contact.

"No! You will not take the blame for him. I know you love him very much, but there's something wrong with him, and they have to find out what it is, or he'll kill someone else. I'm sure of it. He's not even sad or scared. This isn't normal behavior for a thirteen-year-old; he should be shocked, devastated by what has happened." Eram waved his hands in frustration. He understood that this was a serious decision for his wife, but he couldn't think of any other way to handle the situation.

"You're right, something is wrong, and we need to find out what it is. I won't take the blame for it. I promise." There was sorrow and pain in Jula's eyes, and tears began to fill them as she leaned against his shoulder and wept. He could tell that she had meant what she had said, but there was still a flicker of doubt in his mind as to whether she would be strong enough to make the right choice when it came down to it.

"I love him too. Izzmir isn't my son by blood, but he feels like mine all the same. I only want the best for him. Maybe there's a cure for whatever possessed him, and he'll be fine," Eram said softly against Jula's hair. And he really hoped there was, because otherwise Izzmir would end up in Dustfort and probably never see anything but the Edge and the Wasteland again.

In the courtyard, the young teenager stopped kicking his ball and looked at his weeping mother. He had a wild mop of raven hair, and his eyes glowed with an ominous green light.

Pain flickered across his face as he kicked his ball once more and it exploded into black smoke. Then he ran, fleeing deep into the forest behind Emril, as fast and as far as he could. There was no good outcome for him; either his mother would take the blame for his mistake, or he himself would face some terrible consequence. He had no real idea what that might entail, but surely the Lawmaster would not go easy on a murderer.

Izzmir's eyes began to water as he stumbled over roots and thickets, half-blinded by tears. *I didn't mean to do it. I wanted to stop. I wanted to walk away and leave her alone, but he wouldn't let me. He wanted to do it, not me. But I couldn't stop him.*

Don't be silly, you wanted it too. She taunted you. Always a harsh word on her lips and a raised hand when you did not do exactly what she wanted. We can't be treated like that, can we? the tempting voice in his mind assured him, and he felt the tears stop and his mind harden against this terrible woman.

Acknowledgments

I would like to thank my lovely mother Anita and my wonderful husband Ben, who have always had my back since I started this wild ride. Without their support and help this wouldn't have been possible, and I am so grateful to have them.

Another thank you goes out to Sebastian and Eva, who took the time to read a fairly early draft and gave me great feedback and guidance on where to go from there.

I also want to thank my publicist Hannah, who helped me navigate the wilderness of publishing, and my editor Eleanor, who did an amazing job of polishing this story to its finest.

And finally, I want to thank my dear friend Rebekka, who was kind enough to be my beta reader and work with me throughout the book. Her feedback was invaluable in shaping this story into what it is now, and I am eternally grateful for her help.

About the Author

Born in 1992, Sophie Haeder lives in the picturesque countryside of Bavaria, Germany, where she embraces her nerdy nature alongside her roles as a wife and a mother of a little girl.

With a lifelong passion for fantasy, encompassing everything from fairies to witches to trolls, she has found solace in imaginative play since childhood. Serving as a gamemaster for her Dungeons & Dragons group brings her immense joy.

This love of storytelling eventually led her to writing, a natural progression from her professional career as a content marketing manager.

She loves fantasy and art, and her writing combines all of her interests into one. That's why she did all the artwork for this book herself, including the cover, the map, and every other illustration in this book.

9 783911 451017